SUMMER PLANS

and other disasters

Happy
Reading!

Karin
Berg

ENDORSEMENTS

I thoroughly enjoyed the time spent with Callie and Ryan in this story. I was swept away to the dunes of Lake Michigan, felt the sand between my toes, and laughed at the antics of an accident-prone young woman desperate to plan out her life. The heart-warming relationships between siblings and best friends make this a real page-turner. A wonderful debut novel that I expect will be followed by many more.

—**Pegg Thomas** Author of *The Great Lakes Lighthouse Brides Collection, The Backcountry Brides Collection, A Bouquet of Brides Collection,* and *The Pony Express Romance Collection*

Move over Cedar Cove and make room for Traverse City, Michigan. With an engaging style and characters that light up the page, Karin Beery's debut romance, *Summer Plans and Other Disasters*, will charm readers in this picturesque and historic town set "up north" among some sweeping Lake Michigan vistas. Through the heroine's tangle of mishaps and missteps, we are gently reminded of the quagmires that happen when we forget that, despite all our planning, it is the Lord who establishes our steps. There's a lot of fun and romance in this sweet story that entertains like a delightful Hallmark movie, but a lot to be mindful of in our own Christian walks too.

—**Naomi Musch**, author

Karin Berry's debut novel, *Summer Plans and Other Disasters,* is a triumph! Engaging characters, witty dialogue, and a few mishaps and misunderstandings on the way to love will keep you turning the pages on this charming read—perfect for any time of the year!

—**Dori Harrell**, author, *A Christmas Hallelujah*

Karin Beery's charming tale of thwarted plans and misplaced love will have readers turning pages as fast as Callie creates another catastrophe. Her summer plans to restart a relationship with an old flame go awry, but will her new plans involve love? Readers will laugh and cry with Callie as she navigates her feelings, her spills and stumbles, and her future. Don't miss *Summer Plans & Other Disasters.*

—**Ann Byle**, *author of Christian Publishing 101: Advice and Inspiration for Christian Writers*

SUMMER PLANS

and other disasters

Karin Beery

ELK LAKE PUBLISHING, INC.
Plymouth, Massachusetts

Cover and Interior Design: Derinda Babcock

Editor(s): Cristel Phelps, Deb Haggerty

Author Represented by WordWise Media

PUBLISHED BY: Elk Lake Publishing, Inc., 35 Dogwood Dr., Plymouth, MA 02360, 2018

Library Cataloging Data

Names: Beery, Karin (Karin Beery)

Summer Plans and other disasters / Karin Beery

246 p. 23cm × 15cm (9in × 6 in.)

Description: Elementary school music teacher Callie Stevens thinks she's finally figured out God's plan for her life—she even made a list to keep her on track.

Identifiers: ISBN-13: 978-1-948888-24-0 (trade) | 978-1-948888-25-7 (POD) | 978-1-948888-26-4 (e-book.)

Key Words: romance, contemporary, choices, lighthouse, lost love, beach read, women's fiction

LCCN: 2018951166 Fiction

DEDICATION

To Yooper Stewart, my favorite person in the whole, wide world.

ACKNOWLEDGMENTS

I started my writing journey in 2007. Since then, there have been so many people who have supported, encouraged, and helped me, I couldn't possibly fit all of their names on one page. There are a few people, though, whom I have to point out.

First, my agent and his wife, Steve and Ruth Hutson at Word Wise Media. Steve, you could have (and probably should have) given up on me a long time ago. Thanks for ignoring common sense. And Ruth, thanks for your patience in helping me appreciate a novel's setting. I see it now.

Deb Haggerty at Elk Lake Publishing Inc. You have literally made my dream come true. Thank you.

Cristel Phelps, my editor and (now) friend. After working as an editor for a publisher, I found being on the receiving end terrifying! But your encouragement and kindness made editing an enjoyable experience. I hope one day my authors remember working with me as fondly as I'll remember working with you.

To Pegg Thomas. You have opened so many doors for me in this crazy profession. I honestly don't know how to adequately thank you for your faith and support.

To everyone at American Christian Fiction Writers, American Christian Writers, and the Christian Editor Network. You've helped this extrovert survive and thrive in an isolating profession. I couldn't have done this without you.

To Trixie Belden, Nancy Drew, Jessica and Elizabeth Wakefield, Kristy Thomas, Claudia Kishi, Mary Anne Spier, and Stacey McGill. You entertained me for hours as a child. My love of novels started with you. Thanks for sharing your adventures with me.

To my family. You're so weird. I love that you're mine. Thanks for always supporting me.

To my husband. I can't believe you put up with me. You have done nothing but encourage and support me through this journey. You even learned to unload the dishwasher for me. That's love. I love you.

When God called me on this journey eleven years ago, I had stars in my eyes. If I had known how long and difficult the road would be, I don't think I would have started. I'm so glad He didn't tell me. The experience has been more about getting to know God and letting Him refine me than it has been about getting a book published. I'm not the same person today that I was in 2007, and for that I'm grateful. This book actually being published is an added bonus.

CHAPTER I

"Need a hand, sweetheart?"

Callie peeked over the top of her sunglasses. A slick-haired young man in a lime green polo shirt stood bent over, grinning at her through her open car window. She flashed him her best Julia Roberts smile as she inwardly groaned, then flicked her left wrist, popping the car door open and into his forehead.

"Sorry." She slid out of her car. "My older brother will be here any minute now. He can get some ice for that. Would you like to stick around? I think he went hunting. I could introduce you after he skins something."

The tall, tanned pretty boy shook his head and walked toward a group waiting nearby. Callie rolled her eyes.

"Nice technique." A familiar baritone voice rumbled.

She smiled.

"Lying's a sin."

Callie spun around. "Didn't you go hunting?"

Her brother stood twenty feet away with his arms crossed, but he chuckled. "I don't hunt."

"Are you sure?"

"I'm glad you're here."

So was she. Callie launched herself at Jack, aiming for the waist.

He laughed as he moved, and she shot past him, but he grabbed her belt and pulled her back, wrapping his arms around her and squeezing until she giggled. "You never would have survived on the football field. You telegraph."

She squeezed him back. "It's so good to see you."

"It's good to see you too. I hope you're ready to get dirty this summer." He dropped Callie back onto the gravel driveway and marched toward her car. "I've got less than an hour before I need to do rounds, so let's get your stuff in the house."

As she followed him toward the Cavalier, Callie inspected her brother. His once neatly-trimmed brown hair, now sun-kissed, hung in shaggy waves. His shoulders seemed bigger. Obviously, his job as a park superintendent kept him in shape and also kept him tan.

He was lucky to be naturally handsome. The filthy boots, ripped shorts, faded t-shirt, and baseball cap did nothing to improve his appearance. Apparently, he was still relying solely on his God-given assets.

He popped the trunk, but Callie wasn't interested in unpacking yet. One thing after another caught her eye. To her left, a pebble-covered parking lot surrounded by lush, freshly-trimmed grass that still scented the air. Tourists wandered through the field and parking lot, some stopping at a picnic table to eat.

In front of her, she noticed that Jack had replaced the rotting log fence with hundreds of feet of white picket planks surrounding the lighthouse, garage, and nearly an acre of private lawn space, including his fire pit and chairs, a rope hammock strung between two giant oak trees, and their own picnic and grill area. Even from yards away, Callie recognized the angles and craftwork of the picnic table as her brother's work. Obviously, he was still building furniture.

Off to her right past the garage, and hidden among the leafy green trees, families talked and laughed as they hiked through the trails that filled the park. Eventually, they would come out on the far side of the lighthouse to the same place the picnicking tourists were migrating. Callie's toes curled as they anticipated a dip in the cool Lake Michigan water.

"Help me out, Cal."

Jack's voice dragged her back from the shore. She met him at her car and pulled a box from the trunk. They paraded across the driveway, through the open gate and across the yard. As the manicured lawn tickled Callie's exposed toes, a gentle puff of air tousled her bangs. It whispered in her ears, promising a summer in the sun, a summer to start over. The quiet promise grew louder until she recognized the voice—the rhythm, the tone, the timbre. The beach.

Jack led Callie into the shadow of her home for the summer. Decades of history creaked beneath their feet as they stepped onto the faded deck of the Old Mission lighthouse.

She smiled as a long-forgotten peace settled over her. "I can't believe I'm here."

"Can't believe good, or can't believe bad?" He propped open the screen door.

"I'm still deciding, but mostly good I think."

She followed Jack into the lighthouse. He walked right in, but she couldn't help stopping to admire everything she loved about early twentieth-century construction. The outdated but solid oak cupboards in a cozy kitchen that opened into the quaint, window-lined dining room with its corner booth seating and well-used table top.

Turning right and moving up three stairs, she froze. Gone were the ripped couch cushions and laminated build-them-yourself bookshelves. The wood-burning stove still greeted her at the top of the stairs, but everything else had grown up. The new brown sofa and recliner appeared to be on steroids, but they weren't what captured her attention. She couldn't resist the magnetic pull of the built-in entertainment center. Blond wood intricately crafted and carved with a rustic but delicate ivy inlay.

Through the open archway in the adjoining room, she spotted a matching desk and bookcases. What had once been a bachelor's sitting room, complete with a splintering Papasan chair and two cracking bean bag chairs, appeared to be Jack's new office.

Jack walked up to Callie and grabbed the box from her arms.

She ran a now-empty hand over the carved ivy leaves trailing along the side of the desk. "You made this, didn't you?"

He cringed. "It's one of my early pieces. It's rough."

"It's beautiful. I didn't think you were ever going to get rid of that old furniture."

"You harassed me about it every time you visited. After five years, I figured you might have a point, so I decided to go back to these pieces and see if I could make them work."

"When did you have time to make it?"

"I have to do something during the winter."

"I thought you tinkered with your truck."

"I don't tinker." He carried her box to the nearest bedroom, the one connected to the living room.

"I don't want that room." He ignored her and nudged the door open with his foot, then disappeared. He reappeared without her boxes. Callie popped her hands onto her hips. "I don't want to stay in that room. It's like a powder blue bomb exploded in there, and the wallpaper is awful."

"Sorry." Jack walked past her and out the front door.

Callie hustled after him, but the heel of her sandal snagged the carpet and she tumbled down the steps into the dining room. Her elbow smacked the thinly-carpeted cement floor. Pain shot up her arm and shoulder. Grabbing her elbow, she rolled onto her stomach to muffle the moans.

Two feet appeared out of the corner of her eye. "What are you doing?"

"Testing my balance." Callie hissed the words through clenched teeth as she willed the throbbing to stop.

"Well, get up and help me." Jack tapped her foot with his heavy work boots as he walked by. Callie pushed herself up with her good arm. She couldn't let Jack think she couldn't handle a little pain.

She grimaced, but not because of her elbow. "Why can't I have your old office? You obviously aren't using it. Can't I turn it into another bedroom?"

"It's already a bedroom. Ryan's staying there."

Callie blinked. "Ryan Martin?"

"Yep."

Tall, handsome, off-limits best friend to the big brother? Her heart dipped. Fabulous. "Why?"

"His roommate decided to get married. Ryan had to move out." Jack walked past her and out the front door. Never mind that he'd just altered Callie's entire summer plan. She followed him outside. If she was going to share a bathroom with Ryan for three months, then she needed to know how everyone felt about the arrangement.

"Does he know that I'm staying all summer?"

Jack opened a car door and pulled out two suitcases. "Yep."

"And he's okay with that? You're okay with that?" Callie stepped right up to Jack. At almost six feet tall, she still looked up to her brother.

"He's not sharing a house with you. He's living with me."

"Whatever. We'll be in the same house."

Jack looked at her like she'd sprouted horns. "You've lived in the same house before. It's no big deal." He moved around her and back toward the deck.

Callie's heart skipped. "He went on vacation with us and spent the night. This is different." Jack ignored her as he banged the black luggage into everything on his way inside. He clearly didn't care about the living arrangements. Well, if Jack didn't mind, and Ryan didn't mind, maybe she was overacting.

Or not.

Callie slumped against her car. Ryan Martin. The schoolgirl crush that wouldn't fade. He'd known her since she was ten, and she'd been invisible to him for just as long. Not that she could blame him. She'd been an obnoxious, weird-looking, awkward girl until five years ago.

Femininity hadn't hit her until her junior year in college. Make-up, clothes, hair—they suddenly made sense after her roommate explained their subtleties and benefits. Callie had never realized how blue her eyes could look or how the right shirt could flatter her curves instead of amplifying them. People didn't ignore her anymore. Now they talked to her, and the more people she met, the stronger her confidence. She finally understood how to capitalize on her features and femininity, but Ryan had missed all of that.

Not that he would have cared. Ryan didn't judge people based on their looks. He'd dated a few women over the years. They'd all been attractive in their own way, but they were also intelligent, kind, godly women.

Callie sighed. Jack was right. Ryan used to spend the night when they were kids. It wouldn't be much different now. How much she dressed up or how nice she looked wouldn't matter. Ryan had always treated her the same way. She would always be Jack's little sister. Six stupid years between them and she would forever wear the "little" label.

She could handle the situation. She had to. She hadn't left her life in Alma so she could hang out with her brother and daydream about his best friend. That was a dead end, and she knew it. She was in Traverse City for Kyle. Only Kyle.

Kyle Berg. Blood rushed to Callie's cheeks. Her heart stopped skipping—it thundered.

"Squirt!"

Callie cringed. "Do *not* call me that."

Jack laughed. He was already back in the driveway walking toward her. "It got your attention."

"So does saying my name."

"I said your name. Three times."

Her eyebrows popped up. "You did?"

"I did." He stopped in front of her, his face crinkled in amusement. "I've got to go. Someone called in a complaint from Haserot Park. I shouldn't be gone long."

"Don't worry. I can get the rest."

"Is all of this yours? You're only here for three months." Jack frowned as he looked at the remaining boxes.

Callie hauled a bag out of the back seat. "My landlord knows someone who might need a place this summer, so I agreed to sublet the apartment until August. I didn't want to leave any personal items behind."

Jack shook his head as he walked to his truck. "All I needed was a yes, Cal." He climbed into the cab of his shiny green, extended cab, heavy duty pick-up. "I have my phone if you need anything."

As he drove away, the weight of her situation pressed on Callie. She'd left her home and summer job to follow what she hoped were God's plans for her summer. Having a room with Jack had worked out easily enough, but not everything was coming together like she'd hoped. Conditions weren't perfect, and there were a lot of variables. Scenarios played through her mind, pushing up her blood pressure. What if this had all been a mistake? What if, what if, what if—she couldn't let them suck her in. Only one thing could help her refocus.

Callie tossed the bag back into her car and slammed the door. Spinning around, she jogged past the garage, through the yard to the north line of the white picket fence. She planted her feet and pulled in a deep breath. Spread out wide before her, the beach began to soothe her soul.

The horizon rippled toward her, washing wave after wave against the rocky shore. Near the lighthouse, children and adults climbed on and around large rocks that broke through the water's surface. Further out, a few adventurous teens waded in to their ankles. Knees. Thighs. Beyond them, two jet skis bounced by, spraying their wake as the whine of their motors reached Callie's ears. And in the distance, past the surf and motors and chaos, a bulging white triangle pulled a barely-visible boat across the water, gliding near the horizon.

Few people understood the breadth, width, or depth of the Grand Traverse bays, much less the expanse of the horizon. With Lake Michigan feeding into the bays, Callie would have to climb to the lantern room of the lighthouse to see past the sailboat, but even that height couldn't show her the full measure of the water. The higher she climbed, the further back the horizon would move. As a child, she'd dreamed of being tall enough to finally see the other side of "her" lake. Not until Jack first invited her to the lighthouse six years ago did she finally realize the truth—sometimes God's beauty was too much for a person to take in all at once.

"Excuse me, where's the lighthouse?"

Callie turned to see the pretty boy who'd met her at her car. Behind him, a group of friends had their phones out as they snapped photos. She tried not to roll her eyes as she pointed to the square white building beside her. "This is the lighthouse."

Slick looked at the building. His face crumpled. "That's it?"

She'd heard Jack field similar questions dozens of times. This summer it would be her turn. Callie smiled as she leaned against the fence. "It's surprising, I know. Most people expect a tall, cylindrical building with red and white stripes, but lighthouses were usually built with whatever materials the builders had nearby." She motioned at the forest around them. "With all this wood available and the rocky shoreline, it made sense for them to build the lighthouse like this."

A tall, curvy redhead stepped beside Slick. "Does the light still work?"

Callie shook her head. "There's a buoy in the water now, but if you're willing to get your feet wet, you can stand out in the water far enough to get a picture with the lantern tower in it."

Red smiled as she slid her sunglasses onto her nose. "Thanks." She slid her arm around Slick's. "Let's go."

They walked away, their steps falling into time with the cadence of the waves. She'd love to go spend the day on the beach, but she had work to do. The faster she unpacked, the sooner she could meet up with Kyle. Of course, that depended on whether or not she could get a hold of him, since he hadn't yet returned her call ... s. It didn't matter, though. It was still in her best interest to unpack fast. If she couldn't get ahold of Kyle, then she could go to the beach.

Callie shuffled to the lighthouse and back inside. She'd just stepped into the awful blue guest room when the phone in her pocket chirped. She pulled out the cell and held her breath. Her heart dropped, but she smiled as she answered. "Hi, Mae." Callie slouched against the wall.

"That doesn't sound good," said her best friend. "What's going on? Did you make it to Jack's?"

"I'm here. I was just hoping you were Kyle."

"He still hasn't called?"

"Nope." Four messages with no responses. The reality of that started to sink in. What if he didn't want to talk to her? What if he refused to see her? What if he was seeing someone else? It had been years. Anything was possible. She'd been trying to ignore those possibilities, but they always popped back into her head. When Callie thought about Kyle with someone else, her throat constricted. She forced the air in and out of her lungs.

"You're wheezing," said Mae. "Stop it. You're already considering the worst-case scenario, aren't you?"

"I can't help it. What if I'm right?"

Something crashed. "Ruby!" Mae sighed. "Cal, I need to run. The girls are repotting my house plants. Keep praying about this and stop worrying."

Callie didn't have time to respond before the phone disconnected. Mae was right. Callie had a plan. She just needed to give the strategy time to work. Until then, she needed to relax and wait for her chance to talk with Kyle, assuming he wanted to talk with her. Three years had passed since she'd broken up with him. He might still be upset. Or dating that imaginary leggy redhead. Or maybe he was engaged to her.

Callie hiccupped, and a tear dripped from her chin. When had she started crying? What if there really was a redhead? Did Kyle love her? Were they serious? Every horrible possibility raced through her mind until Callie leaned against the ugly bedroom wall and sobbed.

"Oh, Squirt." A warm hand slipped behind her shoulder and pulled her away from the wall and into a broad chest. One arm held her close while the other hand smoothed the hair across her shoulders.

Callie tried to calm down. She gulped for a breath of fresh air but inhaled spicy pine with a hint of Tide. Her spine stiffened. Jack smelled like sweat and sawdust.

Ryan.

CHAPTER 2

"Rough day?" Ryan asked, enjoying the silky feel of Callie's hair beneath his fingers. Had it always been so soft?

"I'm so sorry." She pushed out of his arms, drying her face with her hands. Her cheeks were still red, and her eyes were still puffy, and when she hiccupped, he smiled.

"Want to talk about it?"

Callie shook her head. "It was a long drive up here, and I'm tired. I'm getting upset about nothing."

Ryan stepped into the living room and grabbed two tissues from the end table. He offered them to Callie, and she snatched them away without looking at him. "Your plan's not working?"

Her eyes widened, and she looked him in the eyes for the first time. "How do you know about my plan?"

"You always have a plan. And I've only ever seen you cry when they fall apart."

Callie pushed out her chin. Ryan tried not to smile. Her dark blue eyes contrasted the soft pink of her lips and cheeks. He tried not to think about those. Not yet anyway. She licked her lips. They were moving. She was saying something.

"What?" He shook his head, refocusing on her eyes.

"I said there's nothing wrong with my plans. I have a ninety-five percent success rate."

"You've kept track?"

Callie mumbled something, stepping around him as she marched through the living room. "I don't want to be rude, but I have to finish unpacking my car."

She walked away without looking back, so Ryan followed. She looked different. She'd gained weight. He'd never tell her that, even though he approved. He'd always appreciated a woman who looked less like a stick and more like a woman. Callie had always been the squirt. She didn't look like the squirt anymore.

Her clothes were different too. She wore those short pants that just covered her knees and a pretty blue shirt that almost matched her eyes.

Much more grown up than the shorts and t-shirt she usually wore. Even the way she walked was different. She looked older, like a real teacher, not just Jack's sister. Ryan had noticed two Christmases ago when she visited and over the past couple of fourth of Julys. Every time he saw her, thinking of her as Jack's little sister got harder.

She tripped in the grass but caught her balance and kept going. Ryan grinned. New clothes, same Callie.

"I hope you don't mind that I took Jack's office," he said.

Callie jumped in the air before spinning around to face him. She pressed a hand to her chest, sucking in air. "Don't sneak up on me."

"Sorry. I wasn't trying to." He walked by her while she collected herself. He had just reached her car when he heard the pebbles crunching behind him. "What do you want me to take first?"

"There's not much left. Jack took a couple of loads before he had to leave, and I can grab the rest. I mean, I did pack it all by myself—"

She was still yammering when Ryan reached around her into the trunk and pulled out the last box, dislodging it from the tight corner.

"Oh, well. Okay, then. Thanks."

"It's the least I can do. You're stuck in the blue room."

Callie narrowed her eyes, but the corner of her mouth twitched. "Yeah. Thanks for that."

"You're welcome." Ryan handed the box to Callie before closing the trunk and pulling the last two bags from the back seat. She stood there watching him, so he pushed her toward the house with one of the bags.

"Right. Moving." She headed back toward the lighthouse.

Once again, Ryan watched her walk. It might be time to have a talk with Jack. Until he did, he needed to keep his mind on other things. "Why'd you decide to come to Traverse City for the summer?"

"I have a plan." She looked over her shoulder with a grin on her face.

"What kind of plan?"

Callie kept walking. Maybe she hadn't heard him. Ryan was just about to repeat himself when she stopped beside the deck and turned to face him. "I'm going to take Kyle back."

Ryan's feet refused to keep moving. He stood in the driveway and watched Callie for any sign of teasing. "Kyle Berg?"

"He's the only Kyle I've ever dated."

"Right. Sorry." Ryan urged his legs to walk. They grudgingly agreed. He focused on the ground as he walked past Callie and up the stairs. "Why the change of mind?"

Callie sighed. "It's a long story. I'm just glad I finally figured out what I need to do."

Ryan looked down at Callie. She seemed even smaller and more innocent as she stood on the lawn staring up at him. "And you need Kyle?" He regretted the words the second they left his mouth. He didn't want to know the answer. "I'm sorry. That's none of my business."

"No, it's not, but I don't mind talking with you about it. You're a good friend."

Ryan's heart clenched. "Anything for you, Squirt."

He thought he saw Callie flinch, but then she smiled. "I'll tell you all about it after I unpack."

Ryan whistled in the kitchen. Callie shoved her last box under the built-in desk as dishes clanked together and cupboard doors banged. She rubbed her hands over her face while her heart slammed against her chest.

Ryan had cooked at Jack's house before. She'd been alone with Ryan before. This whole situation had happened a dozen times before. Why was her heart acting weird *this* time?

She didn't have time to figure it out. From somewhere near the bed, a muffled version of "Walk the Line" interrupted the silence. Jack's ring tone. She shifted her bags and clothes as she searched for the phone. The song kept playing. As the verse neared the end, she groaned and pushed all of her bags off the bed. A pillow fell over in the mayhem, and she spotted the phone. Callie answered as Johnny Cash admitted he was a fool.

"Jack, where are you? Will you be home soon? Ryan's here. He helped me move, and now he's cooking dinner—"

"Stop!"

Callie clamped her jaw shut. Her heart still thumped.

"This is going to take longer than I thought, and I'm going to need your help."

"But I just got here. My stuff is still packed."

"I know, but you wanted to be my assistant."

There was a knock at the door. Callie looked up. Ryan stood in the doorway with an apron around his waist and a smile on his face. Her heart fluttered. Stupid cardiac abnormality.

"Are you sticking around to help with dinner?" His eyes twinkled.

Stupid schoolgirl crush.

"Jack's on the phone. He needs my help. I've got to go."

"No problem. You guys can eat when you get back." Ryan winked before he walked away.

Callie released a breath that she didn't know she'd been holding. "Where should I meet you?"

"I've got to get some tools. I'll pick you up in five. We're going to patch the outhouse roof."

Callie's stomach retched. She rolled down the window to breathe some fresh air. Instead, the wind whipped through the cab, stirring up the stench. As the smell intensified, she realized it was coming from her. She leaned toward the fresh air, practically hanging out the window. "That was disgusting."

Jack chuckled. "I can't believe you slipped in dog poop." He pulled into the driveway and parked next to her compact car.

Callie looked at him. His skin glistened with sweat. Soggy curls hung out from under his ball cap. His dirty clothes were still dirty. He looked like a hardworking man. She looked at herself in the side mirror and sighed. She looked like a hardworking man too.

An angry tree branch had yanked half of the hair out of her ponytail when she helped Jack replace some missing shingles. The rest of her head featured twigs, leaves, and dirt, as well as a scratch on the skin above her right eye where the tree had continued to attack her. It stung as the sweat rolled down her face. There was blood on her t-shirt, a snag in her shorts, and Fido's little present on her shoes, socks, and—she suspected—the back of her shorts. "How did you escape unscathed while I look like this?"

"I don't know, but you look awful."

"Thanks. I smell even better."

"Maybe it'll work better if I have you mow lawns." He jumped out of the truck. She followed. They trudged toward the house together.

"I'll pass. I mowed plenty in high school."

"Too bad you're not the boss."

"You'd really make me mow lawns?"

"Yes. It'll build character."

Callie rolled her eyes. If she wasn't so worried about her job, she'd quit on the spot, but she needed this. Plus, he was giving her free lodging and the occasional meal. She couldn't afford to pay rent if she wasn't working. Besides, this job was part of her plan. She needed to stick with the plan.

The dirty pair stepped into the kitchen and Callie sighed. Ryan stood at the sink and smiled.

Definitely not part of the plan.

CHAPTER 3

BANG! Callie jumped, her heart thundering as she sat up and tried to figure out where she was. Her eyes slowly adjusted. Thumps, scratching, and bumps filled the air as she focused in the darkness. She finally spotted the glaring red numbers of her alarm clock—5:15 a.m.

Callie groaned. She'd only been asleep for two hours, since a young couple of lovers had decided to express their feelings for each other on the beach near her window. She rubbed her hands across her face and neck as she tried to push away the exhaustion, not to mention the memories of the couple. That wouldn't have been so bad if the group of drunk college kids hadn't woken her up two hours previously with their whooping and singing.

How did Jack function like this?

Another crash startled her. She listened for Jack's footsteps. He must have heard the banging. A breeze danced into the room, stirring the curtains and shuffling some papers on the nightstand, but nothing—and no one else—moved.

Fine. Callie swung her legs off the bed. If Jack wouldn't investigate, she would.

Early morning light illuminated her room enough to help her grab an older shirt and shorts from her closet. Too tired to worry about shoelaces, she slid on a pair of sandals as she shuffled out of the room. She knew the inside of the lighthouse well enough to avoid the furniture without having to turn on any lights, so she slipped through the house unnoticed, not that the lights would wake up Jack or Ryan. Nothing seemed to bother them.

Stopping in the doorway between the dining room and living room, Callie waited. Where was the noise coming from? The shuffling and bumping noises seemed to float in through the front window. And, was that chattering? What was going on out there?

Making her way through the kitchen, Callie grabbed Jack's giant Maglite flashlight off the refrigerator. It would help her see clearly if she ended up in the woods and would make a hefty club if she needed one.

Callie stepped into the cool, damp morning air. A bubbly layer of dew covered the earth, streaking across the car windows and dampening the deck. Only the frogs, crickets, and birds said hello. She didn't see any cars beside hers, Jack's, and Ryan's. So, who was talking? Maybe she'd imagined it.

The dumpster shook.

Callie jumped. She took a step closer, her eyes never leaving the rusting metal bin. Sure enough, it seemed to vibrate, then move. Her pulse sped up as she walked over, her feet soaked with dew and her palms slick with nervous sweat.

Someone screamed from inside the dumpster.

Was there actually a person in there? A different fear propelled her forward, desperate to help however she could. Callie ran to the blue container and threw back the lid.

"Argh!"

She dropped the flashlight as she smothered her mouth with her hands. Two frustrated-looking raccoons hissed at her as they paced across the trash, one clawing at the side. It didn't take long to figure out why there were causing such a scene. Their weight pressed the garbage bags down so low they couldn't climb back out. They must have climbed the fence to get in, but now they were stuck. Well, she'd let Jack handle them.

The smaller raccoon shuffled away, and Callie's heart sank as it ran across Jack's Maglite. Jack loved that thing. She had to get the flashlight! But first, she had to get the raccoons out.

Not exactly sure what she should do, Callie ran back to the house. In the kitchen, she grabbed some sliced cheese out of the fridge and Jack's keys off the counter, then ran out to the garage. She let herself in and scanned her options. Paint, tools, boxes, half-finished projects. There, in the corner. Jack's scrap box. Several tall pieces of wood stuck out and leaned against the wall. Sorting through the boards, she finally found one that would work, about six inches wide and an inch thick. She pulled it out and stood it on the floor in front of her—about four feet long. It could work.

With the keys and cheese in one hand and the board under her other arm, Callie hauled everything out to the dumpster and leaned the board against the fence. She tossed the keys on the ground before ripping up some cheese and tossing pieces on the plank. Then she slid the board into the dumpster, careful to lean it against the corner closest to the fence. One of the raccoons hissed. She dropped the plank on the edge of the dumpster and ran to the safety of the garage door.

A chipmunk ran along the edge of the fence. Two squirrels chased each other across the parking lot. The raccoons, however, were in no apparent hurry. Callie leaned against the doorframe until the edge cut into her shoulder. She didn't have a watch on, so she wasn't sure how much time had passed, but she didn't care. Her patience had expired. Maybe she should grab some lunchmeat to lure them out. She was just about ready to go back to the house when the board moved.

Callie held her breath as the edge of the board slid left. She gripped the doorknob, ready to rip it off in frustration, but then the wood wedged itself in the corner. Ten agonizing heartbeats later, the first bandit popped his head out over the edge of the dumpster. After some maneuvering, they were both up the board and climbing onto the nearby fence. Without so much as a thank you, the raccoons took their cheese and ran into the woods.

Callie's shoulders sagged with relief. The dumpster was raccoon-less, and she hadn't needed Jack or Ryan to help her figure it out. Now she could grab the flashlight and get back to bed. She actually whistled on her way over to the dumpster.

Pulling out the board, she leaned in. The Maglite had been along the closest wall. Where was it? Oh no. It must have fallen down when the raccoons were moving around. Picking the board back up, she used it to poke around, moving the bags so she could see. There! In the back, near the fence. Perfect. She could use the fence for leverage.

Tossing the board to the ground, she inspected the white pickets for a good foothold. She grabbed the edge of the dumpster and cringed at the slimy texture. She'd have to sanitize her hands later. Until then, she pushed herself up and leaned into the stinky container. The cold metal edge pushed into her stomach as she stretched down. Her fingertips brushed the end of the flashlight, but she wasn't close enough. She made sure her foot was locked in place before shimmying her hips forward. She stretched again. Almost. A little bit further. Just a half an inch.

Something popped.

Callie's naked foot flew up as she tilted forward. She kicked out. Where was the fence? Her shirt pulled tighter. Callie gasped. She pushed out her arms as the bags came closer. Callie covered her head as wet, lumpy plastic crunched beneath her.

Callie collapsed on the floor. Her bedroom had brightened enough that she could identify every blue frill and bauble. Embroidered Bible verses in various shades of blue filled frames that cluttered the walls. A pile of lacy blue and white pillows tried to creep out of the closet where she'd stuffed them. As the sun continued to brighten the room, the paisley wallpaper lightened from gray to gray-blue to blue-gray. It wouldn't matter how much sunshine spilled into the room though. It couldn't cut through the overcast color of the 1980s wallpaper. If she believed in omens, she'd be in trouble.

As she started to relax into the thick carpet, Callie sucked in a deep breath and gagged. Something warm and gooey had soaked into her shirt, and it reeked. She sighed. "I hate this job."

Pushing herself up and off the floor, her foot slipped, throwing her to the ground as her leg crashed into a stack of boxes. Two of them. Something cracked. Callie stifled a scream as she grabbed the nearest pillow and threw it at the closet. "I hate this job!"

Scrambling to her feet, she grabbed her robe off the floor and stomped her way to the shower for the second time in less than twelve hours. In Jack's new office, she plowed into Ryan. Callie stumbled backwards, Ryan steadied her with one warm hand.

"Are you okay?" He rubbed his eyes with the heel of his free hand. His hair stood up, and his clothes were wrinkled. At least they were on even ground this time.

"I'm fine. I tripped." She shrugged off his hand and marched past him.

"It's six o'clock, Cal."

"I know."

"It's Saturday."

She stopped at the bathroom door, her teeth locked together. "I know."

"Why are you awake?"

"Seriously?" When she turned to call him on his lie, he raised his eyebrows. "You didn't hear it?"

"Hear what?"

"The drunks at one o'clock?"

He shook his head.

"The, uh ... couple at three?"

Ryan cocked his head.

She pointed out the window. "The raccoons thirty minutes ago? You really didn't hear that?"

"What raccoons?"

"The ones fighting in the dumpster, which is why I'm wearing something goopy on my shirt."

Ryan's eyes widened. He took a step closer. "You went into the dumpster to chase out two coons?"

Callie crossed her arms. "No, I'm not stupid. But I might have lifted the lid to look in and dropped Jack's new Maglite."

He smiled. "And that's why you went dumpster diving."

"He'd probably send me back to Alma if I lost that thing." Callie shook her head. "I need to be here this summer. I need to talk to Kyle."

The smile faltered on Ryan's face before his mouth stretched into a vacuous yawn. "I'm going to head back to bed. Try not to kill yourself before Jack gets up. He'd miss you."

Callie watched him shuffle into his bedroom. Even on an early Saturday morning, he moved beautifully. She turned toward the bathroom and stubbed her toe on the door frame. It wasn't fair.

Ryan's door clicked shut, so Callie closed herself in the bathroom. She gasped when she saw herself in the mirror. Some leftover mascara blackened her eyes, making her look like the varmints she'd chased from the trash. Ryan hadn't said a word.

Too tired to worry about it, she turned on the shower and waited for the water to heat up. Whatever happened next, at least she'd be clean and flower-scented.

Ryan stared at the ceiling. He had heard the raccoons too. Then he heard Callie open her door and stomp through the house. That memory made him smile. It never made sense that a concert pianist with superior hand-eye coordination could be so awkward at home, but it was one of the many quirks he liked about Callie.

Did Kyle like that about her?

Ryan measured his breaths. He didn't really care what Kyle thought about Callie. His own thoughts about her were confusing enough. As soon as Jack had said she was coming, Ryan knew the summer would be rough. It had potential, lots of potential, but it also had Kyle. How would that affect things?

The bathroom door squeaked open then banged against the wall. Ryan chuckled. He always liked seeing Callie. He just hoped he could convince her it was as good to see him.

"Squirt, you up yet?"

Callie ignored Jack's bellowing as she sat in the dining nook and took another bite of cereal. She checked her phone again for missed calls. Nothing. She dropped the annoying device into her purse. Her brother's footsteps echoed on the stairs as he descended into the dining room.

"What are you doing in here?"

"Eating breakfast."

"Nobody eats in here."

"You should. There's a table. It's convenient."

"Whatever."

"Fine."

He kicked her foot. "What's wrong with you?"

"I'm tired." Callie looked up. She couldn't tell if Jack was wearing the same clothes he had on the day before, but he'd definitely slept in them. She shook her head. "I didn't sleep well last night. This is a busy place."

"You'll get used to it. I'm going into town to run errands today. Want to come?"

Callie looked at her bowl of Fruit Loops. "Can we go grocery shopping?"

"Sure."

"When are you leaving?"

"Late this morning. I have some stuff to do first. We'll probably be in town most of the afternoon. I've got a lot of stops to make."

An afternoon in town. Callie grinned. "We don't have to work today?"

Jack shook his head. "Not here. Too many tourists. It's easier to get things done during the week."

"Then what are you doing this morning?"

"I have some furniture to finish, then—"

Callie's purse buzzed, and she launched herself at the bag. She held her breath and dug for the phone. Her hand touched it, and Callie froze. What if it wasn't Kyle? She couldn't look. She had to. She wanted to. Summoning her courage, she pulled out the phone.

"Mom." Callie tried to ignore the million pieces of her heart that scattered in her chest.

Jack reached out and ruffled her hair. "He'll call."

Callie straightened her hair as she answered. "Hi, Mom."

"You didn't call."

Callie rolled her eyes. "It's good to talk to you too."

"I was worried about you. What if you'd been in an accident?"

"I'm fine, Mom. What are you doing up so early?"

"Your father. He wanted to beat the crowds at the Home Depot."

"At five o'clock?"

Her mom sighed. "It takes him some time to wake up in the morning, you know that."

"Is he keeping you awake?"

"I don't mind. I'll have him take me to breakfast. I just wanted to make sure you weren't lying on the side of the road bleeding to death."

Callie chuckled. "I'm alive and well."

"Hi, Ruth."

Callie jumped at the sound of Ryan's voice. "How did you know it's my mom?"

"Who's there?" her mother asked.

Ryan winked. "I can sense these things."

Callie rolled her eyes. "It's Ryan."

"We'll leave at ten," said Jack. "Don't make me wait."

"Let me talk to him," said her mom.

Callie looked at her phone. She shook her head then looked at Ryan. "My mom wants to talk to you."

He smiled. "Of course she does. I'm practically family." He took her phone, trailing his fingers across hers, sending ripples across her skin.

Practically family? Callie sighed. No one else in the family had ever made her feel like that.

CHAPTER 4

"Oh my gosh, who's controlling the air conditioner?"

Jack rolled his eyes as he followed his sister into the grocery store. He barely noticed a difference, but Callie rubbed her arms like she'd just stepped into a walk-in cooler.

"Aren't you freezing?" She spun around to face him and shoved her forearm under his nose. "My hair's already standing up. If I get any colder it might just fall off."

"Try not to let that happen. I don't want to have to clean it up." Jack sidestepped past her to grab a cart. "Come on. Let's make this quick."

As soon as they started walking, Callie started yammering about something, but Jack tuned her out. He could tell by her tone it wasn't urgent. Instead, he focused on the thumping of his work boots on over buffed linoleum.

Thump, thump, thump through the bread aisle.

Thump, thump, thump past the crackers.

Jack focused on the rhythm of his steps, trying to synchronize them to his sister's chatter. Between his efforts to ignore Callie while keeping a beat, he didn't notice the stack of boxes until his shopping cart plowed into them. Someone popped up from behind the cardboard and grabbed the top box before it dropped.

Stacey Chapman. The short, spastic blonde from church.

She smiled at him. Everything stopped.

The short, spastic, *pretty* blonde from church.

"Hi, Jack!" After replacing the falling box, she stepped closer. Standing there in her tennis shoes, she barely came up to his arm pits. She wasn't any taller than a kid.

Jack nodded. "Hey, Stacey."

"What are you doing here?"

"Uh, shopping?"

Her neck instantly turned pink. He'd never seen anything like it. Her eyes widened, and Jack bit back a smile.

She scratched her arm. "Yeah, I guess I should have figured that out. Do you need any help finding anything?"

"We're good."

"Maybe *you* are, but they've moved everything since I've been here." Callie stepped up beside him. She had to look down at Stacey too.

"You must be Jack's sister." Stacey stuck out her hand, and Callie accepted it. "I'm Stacey. We go to the same church."

Jack sighed. "Come on, Cal. I can show you around."

Callie's fist slammed into his shoulder. "Don't be rude. I wouldn't mind some help."

Stacey smiled even bigger. It made her eyes shine, but it wasn't her eyes that captured his attention. He watched as Stacey's small hand slipped from his sister's grip then patted his forearm. The delicate fingers were soft, warm, and pale against his tanned skin. Something about it made him want to wrap them in his hand and hold them close.

That made him want to run. "Why don't you two shop together?" he said. "I know what I need to get. Get yourself a cart, and we can meet up front in ten minutes. We probably shouldn't stay longer than that—"

"Jack?"

"What?"

Callie's eyebrows were buried somewhere near her hairline. "Are you okay?"

"Stacey Chapman to the service desk, please. Stacey Chapman to the service desk."

"Sorry, I've got to go." Stacey slipped past the grocery cart as Jack hid behind it. She waved at them. "Maybe next time. It was so nice to meet you."

Callie waved. "You too." As soon as Stacey turned her back, Callie glared at Jack. When Stacey disappeared around a corner, Callie hit her brother again. "What's wrong with you?"

Jack glanced down the empty aisle. He took a deep breath. "Nothing. I'm fine. Let's shop."

Stacey hustled to the service desk, her legs moving as quickly as her heartbeat. Why did she have to see him here? Why couldn't he have wandered into the salon, or maybe the art studio? Anything was better than her part-time stocking job. Stacey looked down at her green vest and cringed.

"What can I do for you, Peggy?" she asked as she approached the service desk. When she leaned against the green Formica counter, it blended in with her vest. Great. She looked like the grocery store.

The manager snorted. "Lee called. He's going to be late. Can you stay until he gets here?"

Stacey shook her head. "He's never on time. Everyone knows that. I can stay an hour, but then I have to leave. Next time, schedule him earlier."

"I'll consider it." Peggy stapled some papers together. "I'll talk with Lee about it tonight."

Peggy might have said something else, but Stacey didn't notice. She was too busy watching the tall, leggy brunette pushing a cart around the corner.

Jack's sister was gorgeous. No wonder he never noticed Stacey's stocky frame. He'd grown up with an Amazon beauty at home. He probably thought Stacey looked like an elf.

"Stacey."

"Huh?"

Peggy sighed. "Never mind. Go back to work."

"What?" Stacey turned her attention back to the service desk. "I'm sorry. What were you saying?"

"Just get back to work. Find me when you go on break."

"Thanks." Stacey flashed her boss a smile before heading toward the canned goods aisle. She tried to concentrate on the floor, but she couldn't fight the temptation to look around the store for Jack. She was one aisle away from her stocking station when she spotted Callie rushing toward her.

"Hey!" The giant waved. "Have you seen my brother?"

Stacey's neck heated up. "Uh, no. Did you check the meat counter?"

Callie smiled. "You know Jack well. I'll leave him back there. I'm looking for some bulgur. Do you know if you have any?"

"Bulgur ... is that a health food?" For once in her life Stacey was glad she was already blushing. Callie's presence made her feel short and dowdy. Having to admit that she didn't even know what Callie ate made Stacey feel inadequate too. If the weight of embarrassment could crush her, it would take less than three inches to put Stacey under five feet tall. Then she'd have to shop in the girls' department. Again.

A hand waved in front of her eyes, and Stacey snapped back to attention. "Sorry. My mind wanders."

"Can it wander us over to health food?"

"Sure. This way." Stacey took the lead, striding ahead of Callie's empty cart. "How long have you been in town?"

"Just a day."

"And you're already sick of Jack's food?"

"There's not a lot to eat if you want more than meat and potatoes."

"And beans. I can't believe how much chili those guys eat." Stacey slowed down at the last aisle. "Here you go. There's not a lot, but we have a decent variety."

"Thanks." Callie smiled, but it quickly faded. "Listen, I don't want to be rude, but it sounds like you know my brother pretty well—"

"I don't really," Stacey said. "I'm just observant."

"And you know him from church?"

"Yep. I met Jack and Ryan there a few months ago."

Callie's eyebrows arched a bit. "You know Ryan too?"

"Sure. They've had me over for lunch a couple of times."

"That was nice of them."

Stacey nodded, remembering the warm afternoons at the lighthouse. She smiled. "Those were fun days."

"Why don't you come out tomorrow after church? It'll give us a chance to get to know each other better."

Stacey's spirit lightened. An afternoon at the lighthouse. Then reality set in, and the light faded. "I wish I could, but I have plans for tomorrow."

"Then come by sometime this week." Callie dug into her purse. She eventually pulled out a business card and thrust it into Stacey's hand. "You can ignore the part about piano lessons. My cell number is on there. Give me a call and we can figure out a good day."

"Are you sure?"

Before she could answer, Jack stumbled into the aisle. He glanced between the two women before settling his gaze on Callie.

"Are you done yet? We've got stuff to do at home. I've still got some errands to run, and all of this food is making me hungry. What?"

Stacey looked from Jack to Callie. His sister's eyes were large, then she smiled. She reached out and patted Stacey's hand. "I'm absolutely sure. Call me."

Jack gunned the engine. He squeezed the steering wheel until the vinyl squeaked in his fists. Callie was rambling again. He tried to listen, but his thoughts kept going back to shiny golden hair and a bubbly laugh. That seductive sprite didn't know how she affected him. And Callie had invited her into his house.

"You're going to break that."

Jack looked at his sister. "What?"

She rolled her eyes. "The steering wheel. You can stop strangling it. I think it's dead."

Loosening his grip, the color return to his knuckles. When he thought about Callie's big mouth and that stupid invitation, heat traveled right up his arms and into his cheeks. "Why did you invite Stacey over?" he asked. "You don't even know her."

"That's why I invited her over. She said she knows you and Ryan. I thought it would be nice to have a girlfriend in town, now that Mae's busy."

"It doesn't have to be Stacey. Invite someone else."

Callie's jaw dropped. "Jack!"

"I didn't mean that like it sounds." He rubbed the back of his neck but failed to come up with another way to say it.

"So, you don't mind if she comes over?"

"Yes. No. I don't know. Does it have to be her? Can't you invite someone else to my house?"

"Our house. I'm living there too."

"You know what I mean."

Callie crossed her arms. "Not really. I don't get it. You didn't even pretend to be nice to her. You were practically a jerk."

"I wasn't a jerk."

"I didn't say you were a jerk. I said you were *practically* a jerk. It's like you tried just hard enough not to be a total jerk so no one would notice. If we were kids, Dad would have warmed your bottom for that."

"I didn't mean to be rude." He sighed. "I just don't want to encourage her."

"Encourage her? Just tell her you're not interested."

Jack twisted his hands around the steering wheel, again. That would be the easy thing to do. Instead, he was sending mixed signals and he knew it. It started the first time he invited Stacey out for lunch. The second and third times didn't help.

Callie gasped. "You can't tell her that because you are interested, aren't you?"

He snorted.

She laughed, smacking him on the knee. "Jackson Stephens, there may be hope for you yet."

"Whatever."

All he had to do was stop inviting Stacey over. That would work. It wouldn't look like he wanted to see her, because he didn't want to see her. Not really.

Then why did he suddenly have the urge to go grocery shopping again?

CHAPTER 5

Callie squished another box of macaroni and cheese into the cupboard. Jack was outside doing something, so she was alone with Ryan in the kitchen. The perfect time to get some info. "Tell me about Stacey."

Ryan dropped a can of soup. "Stacey?"

The can rolled across the floor, bumping into Callie's foot. She'd been right. "Something's definitely going on." She picked up the can and gave it back to him. "You and Jack both go nuts when I mention her name."

"It's nothing."

"Yeah, sure. You always throw canned goods around. Now spill."

Ryan put the can in the cupboard. "There's nothing going on. I don't know what you want me to tell you." He motioned to Callie, and she handed him more groceries.

"Come on. I thought Jack still associated girls with cooties."

"He does."

"Maybe he does today, but there was a time when he invited Stacey out here for lunch, so he must have found his cootie catcher."

Callie handed Ryan the eggs. He didn't look at her. When she passed along the milk, cheese, and vegetables, he accepted them all without ever making eye contact. That wasn't like him. While he never looked for conflict, he didn't run from it either. Something was making him uncomfortable, and Callie doubted it was the broccoli.

She also knew what Ryan and Jack thought about her curious questioning. "I'm gossiping, aren't I?"

"No." He flashed a half smile. "But it's your brother's life. It's not really my place to say."

Callie sighed. It was hard maintaining a relationship with a brother who didn't tell you anything. If she didn't already have over two decades of experience with the man, she might scream with frustration. But Ryan was right. It wasn't his story to tell. "I'm sorry." She tossed a loaf of bread on the counter before folding the empty grocery bags. "You would tell me if Stacey's bad news, wouldn't you?"

Ryan dropped a hand on Callie's shoulder and smiled. His skin warmed hers. "Of course. I'd even tell Jack." He winked.

"How chivalrous." Callie swatted his hand away. "Will you at least give me your opinion on something?"

"Depends. Are you going to cook dinner tonight?"

She shrugged. "I could."

"I'll help you."

"You're on."

"What do you want to know?"

Callie squared herself to Ryan. She was looking at his chin. The stubble along the firm jawline darkened his already tan complexion. She'd never noticed it before. That realization did funny things to her insides. Ignoring her stomach, she looked up into his familiar blue eyes.

"Do you think Stacey and Jack could work?"

Ryan crossed his arms. "I think Jack could work with anyone, if he wanted to."

Callie considered Ryan's words. "Do you think Jack would ever want to make it work with … anyone?"

Ryan smiled.

There went those funny tummy things again.

"How about grilled chicken?"

Frustrated, she did the only thing she could think of. Callie stomped her foot. "You're my brother's best friend. You've got to know something."

"We aren't girls."

"What's that got to do with anything?"

"Jack and I don't talk about our love lives while we eat bonbons."

"Are you really that cliché?" She rolled her eyes as she reached past Ryan to grab a cookbook off the counter. "I never gossip with chocolate. Only potato chips. What should we have with the chicken?"

Her phone rang. Callie's heart took off like the raccoons she'd chased away. Digging through her purse, she rehearsed her lines as she searched for the phone. Her summer might be ready to change. She looked at the display.

Alma area code.

Whoever it was, they weren't the kind of change she was hoping for. Callie stuffed the phone into a purse pocket before returning to the kitchen.

Ryan handed her a cookbook. "Not going to get that?"

"No." She dropped the book on the counter and flipped it open. Ryan leaned close. Woodsy. Musky. Masculine. Callie held her breath.

"You okay?" Ryan cupped his hand around her elbow.

Callie couldn't remember how the stomach was connected to the elbow, but when Ryan touched her there, the feelings intensified. She was completely aware of him beside her, pressing in closer to look at recipes. The weirdness spread.

"Callie?"

She jumped back. "What?"

Ryan captured her gaze with his amazing blue eyes.

She took another step back.

"You're pale." He raised a hand. Callie turned away.

She walked to the refrigerator, opening the door and using it as a barrier. "I think I need to eat something." Liar.

"Then let's get started with dinner. Want to finish the menu with me?"

Callie stuck her head in the refrigerator, savoring the cold air on her skin. "You know, I'm not very picky. You decide and just tell me what to do." She grabbed a package of chicken and passed it to him.

Ryan reached for the meat, and their fingers touched. Callie flinched. Her heart flipped. What was happening?

He cleared his throat. "Are you sure you're okay?"

"I think so."

He closed the refrigerator door.

"I'm pretty sure."

He smiled.

Her phone rang.

Callie gasped. "I'll get it!"

Ryan chuckled. "Who else would?"

She ignored him and grabbed the chirping phone from her purse. "Hello?"

"Cal."

Her bones melted. "Kyle?"

"I got your messages." His smooth, bass voice crooned in her ear. "So, you're back in town?"

She looked at Ryan. He pulled assorted jars and bottles out of the cupboards. The phone trembled in her hand. "I got back yesterday."

"Did you have a safe trip? You got here okay?"

"Yeah, yeah. I'm fine."

"Good. Listen, I'm meeting some coworkers tonight for drinks. Do you want to go with us? We can catch up?"

She couldn't control her smile. "Really? I'd love to have drinks with you." Ryan closed the cupboards and looked at Callie. Her heart sank like an anchor. "But I already have plans for tonight." Ryan's eyes widened. "Can I take a rain check?"

Then Ryan shook his head, waving his hands in front of him.

"Wait!" Callie watched Ryan. He pointed at the phone and winked. "I think I can change tonight's plans?" He nodded. "Yes, I can definitely postpone my plans. Tonight will work. Where should I meet you?"

"I'm not sure where we're going," said Kyle. "Why don't I just pick you up?"

Callie's knees wobbled. She leaned against the wall. "Sure, that would be great. What time?"

"We have to finish some stuff here first. I could be there by eight."

"I'll be ready. See you then."

"Bye, Callie."

The air around her buzzed, or maybe it was the phone. It didn't matter. Kyle had called, and he wanted to see her. The very thought warmed her core. She'd already completed the first phase of her plan by moving to Traverse City. Finally, she could focus on the second phase—spending time with Kyle.

"He's coming here," she whispered, looking at Ryan's handsome face. Her heart fluttered. Of course it did, because Kyle had finally called. The flutter had nothing to do with Ryan. Right?

"Kyle's coming here for drinks?" Ryan focused on the cookbook. The news didn't seem to faze him, not that it should.

Still, Callie couldn't help the twinge of disappointment that pricked behind her chest. Why should she be disappointed? Her plan was finally coming together. "He's picking me up. We're going out for drinks with his coworkers." Not her ideal reunion scenario, but could work, if it didn't get awkward.

After all, they'd broken up three years ago. They'd barely seen each other since. The excited buzz in the air turned into a terrorizing zap.

"Oh my gosh." She paced the short width of the kitchen. "I'm going to see Kyle. I need to call Mae. I mean, this is what I wanted, but I never really thought about how I would feel when it finally happened. Things are working out. I should be thrilled, right? And I am. It's just, I was planning on having a good long talk with him, but we're going to be with other people. It could get weird, and I—"

Two strong hands clasped her shoulders, stopping her forward motion and forcing her back into the moment. Ryan looked her right in the eye. "This is what you prepared for. If your plan works, you don't have anything to worry about. It's just drinks."

Just drinks. "You're right." Callie put her hand over her heart, willing it to settle into a slow, normal rhythm. She smiled at Ryan. "Thank you so much. I feel bad bailing on you like this. He's not going to be here until eight, so we can still cook together if you want."

"I can cook chicken by myself."

"That's not what I mean." Her smile faltered when she realized Ryan's hands were still on her. Callie glanced at her shoulder. He dropped his hands. She thought his jaw twitched, but he turned away so quickly that she couldn't be certain. "Are you sure this is okay with you? We had plans first. I don't mind calling Kyle back and rescheduling."

Ryan pulled some tongs out of a drawer. "Don't do that. This is what you've been waiting for. We've eaten together plenty of times before. I'm sure we will again."

Callie knew he was doing the polite thing, but those words from Ryan's mouth sounded more like nails on a chalkboard than a chivalrous offer. "At least let me help you get started. Maybe it'll help me relax."

"If you insist, but you've only got three hours before he gets here."

Three hours to cook dinner and get ready. She could keep her commitments to both men. The thought pushed heat into her cheeks. Why did that sound so scandalous? It wasn't like she was dating both of them, or even one of them. Dinner with Ryan. Drinks with Kyle. Why did nothing about that feel right?

Ryan tried to forget about Callie's date, but she kept running in and out of the kitchen while talking on the phone to Mae. He heard something about her plan, then something about wrenches. She was clearly excited to see Kyle.

Ryan groaned.

Callie and her plans.

She had kept her word and helped him prep some kebobs, but it was more of a hassle than a help. After she had dropped her third piece of chicken and second mushroom on the floor, Callie gave up and sat down to watch. She couldn't focus on Ryan or the conversation for very long, but she wouldn't leave. She stayed to help with the dinner prep, just like she'd planned.

As Ryan walked outside to preheat the grill, he thought back to some of Callie's plans. She'd graduated valedictorian of her high school class, got into her first-choice college, and double majored in music and education. She saved for and bought her car with cash. And Jack never stopped teasing her about her over-the-top, but always amazing, holiday menus.

Most of her schemes worked out exactly how she wanted them to, but Ryan smiled as he remembered some of her less successful endeavors. Using oil-based house paint when she ran out of the right shade of nail polish. Pulling the push mower behind her bike with a string of bungee cords when the riding mower broke. Practicing two hours a day when she tried to teach herself the harmonica, so she could join a blues band.

When Callie set her mind to something, she followed through, no matter what she had to do to make it happen. That determination usually paid off. It took an obvious work of God to pull Callie's attention from her plans. Ryan wondered which way things would work out with Kyle.

Back in the kitchen, he started loading the dishwasher while he made plans of his own.

"Ryan? Can I get your opinion on something?"

He braced himself. "Sure." Maybe. "What do you need?"

Callie shuffled into the kitchen, her phone in one hand and a bunch of blue shirts hanging from the other. "Mae says I should wear blue tonight. Which shirt do you like the best?"

He looked at the hangers full of fabric. "Are you serious?"

"Yes. What do you think?"

One at a time, Ryan grabbed a shirt and looked at it. Blue with sleeves. Light blue with shorter sleeves. Weird blue with straps. Another blue with sleeves. She'd look good in any of them, but that wasn't what she'd asked. Not sure what else to do, he examined each shirt again, his head aching as he wondered if there was a right answer.

"Never mind." She took the shirts back. "You look like someone just asked you to eat a bowl of pigs' feet. I'll pick one."

His shoulder relaxed. "Thank you."

"But you'll tell me how it looks, right?"

"Sure."

"Thanks." She smiled then disappeared before he could blink. The sight of her smiling would never leave his brain, which was why he needed a distraction.

Onions. If anything could take his mind off of Callie's fidgeting and primping, the burning aroma of chopped onions should do it.

He had just finished quartering three large onions when he heard the shower turn on. The water continued to run as he chopped lettuce and peppers, tossing them in a bowl. Setting it aside, he picked up his platter of kebobs and took them out to the grill. Ryan stayed there, and away from Callie, until everything was done. As he pulled dinner off the sizzling grates, Jack emerged from his workshop.

"That looks great," he said, trying to brush the sawdust off of his hands. "I'm starving."

"There's plenty. Grab some plates, and we can eat out here." Ryan turned off the grill. He had just piled sizzling meat and vegetables onto the platter when Jack returned with dishes, the salad, and two cans of soda stuffed into his pockets.

"What's going on in there? Cal said I could have the bathroom in an hour."

"Kyle called."

"He did?" Jack sat across from Ryan at the picnic table.

Ryan lifted an eyebrow. "You didn't think he would?"

Jack shrugged. "The guy disappeared for years. I wondered."

Having aired their opinions on the Callie-Kyle connection, the two men piled food onto their plates. Ryan filled his mouth then spit the scalding meat back onto his plate.

Jack roared. Some tourist's dog barked back.

"Go ahead. Laugh." Ryan cracked open a soda and tossed back his head. The cold liquid bubbled over his tongue, easing the pain.

"I am." Jack continued to chuckle as he leaned forward, blowing loud, long puffs of air over his dinner.

Ryan pushed the food around on his plate instead. He was content to let it take its time cooling. The longer it took, the longer he could sit outside, away from Callie and her excitement.

He wanted to see Callie happy, but he worried about her plan. Not that it was a bad plan, and not that Kyle was a bad guy, but Ryan had been doing some planning of his own, and it started with a talk with Jack.

Ryan watched his friend shovel food into his mouth. Whereas he hadn't even started his meal, Jack was already half done. Perfect. A short interruption would let Ryan speak his peace and give Jack's digestive track a chance to catch up with his mouth.

Ryan crossed his arms. "I need to talk to you about something."

Jack stopped with the fork in his mouth. "'Bow wha?"

"About Callie."

Jack shook his head so hard that a pepper flew out from between his lips and splattered on the table. He grabbed Ryan's open soda and chugged half the can. After he swallowed everything, Jack pointed at Ryan. "Not now. I'm not ready for this." Then he shoveled more food into his mouth.

Ryan's shoulders tensed, but he nodded. It wasn't the best conversation they'd ever had, but it was a start.

CHAPTER 6

Thousands of screaming fans didn't drown out the sound of the couple fighting outside the living room window. Ryan grabbed the remote and turned up the volume. The 1998 Rose Bowl had just started replaying on ESPN Classics when the screen door slammed.

"Jack, they're showing Michigan's last Rose Bowl victory," Ryan said. "You're right on time. They just started the game."

"Not interested."

"Callie?" Ryan muted the game, surprised to hear her voice. He could barely see her frowning in the dark dining room. "I thought Kyle was picking you up."

"So did I." She stomped up the steps. "He's thirty minutes late, and he's not answering his phone."

"Something must've come up."

She slumped onto the other end of the couch, her eyes locked onto the television. "Unless all of the cell phone towers blew up, there's no reason he couldn't call to say he's running late."

"True."

She looked at Ryan. The excitement had faded from her eyes. He wanted to tell her it would be okay, but he didn't have a clue what was going to happen. He decided to stick with what he knew—Callie's coping techniques.

"Want some popcorn?"

Her lips twitched upward but fell again. "I'm not really hungry."

"You've got to be starving. You didn't eat dinner."

"I was too nervous to eat, and I was afraid to get anything on my clothes." She smoothed her hands over her sparkly blue top. Ryan never would have imagined how nice the shirt would look on her. He was glad she picked out her own clothes. Clothes that Kyle wouldn't see, but Ryan could admire.

He un-muted the television and pushed himself off the couch. "I'm making popcorn anyway, so I'll pop some extra for you. If Kyle shows up, I'll give it to Jack."

"Where's Jack?"

"He had a problem with a dining set he's making. He's trying to fix a chair."

Callie shook her head then turned to the game. Ryan watched as she propped her elbow on the arm rest, leaning her head against her hand. Her shiny brown hair moved like silk, falling over her shoulder. The fingers on her other hand lightly tapped her leg in varying patterns and motions. "Can I have light butter on my popcorn, please?"

"Sure."

When he returned with a large bowl of lightly buttered popcorn, he noticed Callie had kicked off her shoes and tucked her feet under a pillow. He handed her a napkin, which she took without looking away from the game.

"Thanks."

He set the bowl between them. "Who you rooting for?"

As he sat back on the couch, Callie looked at him and smiled. "I'll put fifty bucks on the Wolverines."

Ryan shook his head. "Sorry, I never bet against the maize and blue."

"That's a shame. Just between us, they're going to have a few bad years soon. You might want to pick another horse."

"What about you?" Ryan grabbed a handful of popcorn.

Callie took off her watch and bracelet, then unclasped her earrings and set them on the coffee table. "What about me?"

"Maybe it's time to pick a different horse."

Her hand stopped in the popcorn. "Huh?"

Ryan swallowed. "I meant Kyle."

"Oh." She picked up some popcorn and started munching.

"Yesterday you were going to tell me about your big plan, but then Jack showed up. Want to tell me now?"

"The game's on," she said, dropping popcorn on the floor as she waved at the television.

"Michigan wins, 21-16."

Callie chuckled. "Way to ruin it for me."

"You're welcome."

She picked up her watch then sighed. "It looks like I'm staying home tonight." She swung her feet off the couch. "Let me change, then I'll tell you all about it."

Callie adjusted her cotton pajama bottoms before pulling her hair back into a loose bun. She looked at herself in the mirror and shrugged. The faded pink and purple polka dotted shorts and t-shirt didn't flatter her figure, but they were comfortable, and Ryan wouldn't care. He'd seen her in a Strawberry Shortcake nightgown when they were kids. Anything was an improvement over that.

She opened the bedroom door and trotted into the living room, her stomach growling. "Thanks for the popcorn." She plopped onto the couch. "I didn't realize how hungry I was." She grabbed another handful and shoved it all into her mouth.

Ryan laughed.

She tried to smile. "Wha?" A few kernels rolled out of her mouth.

"Nothing. You were saying?"

Callie nodded. She chewed fast and forced the buttery goodness down her throat before helping herself to some more. "Mike proposed."

Ryan stopped mid-toss. His eyes widened. "You're engaged?"

"No, absolutely not." She shook her head for emphasis. "I had been dating Mike for about six months, and out of nowhere, he popped the question."

"And you didn't see it coming?"

"No. When we started dating, we agreed to be casual. We both just wanted someone to hang out with, to watch movies and go to dinner. I told him I didn't want anything serious, and I thought he agreed, but then he got down on one knee." Callie shook her head again as she ate another mouthful of food. "I thought we were fine. We'd kissed a couple of times, but I kept it appropriate. I had no idea he felt that strongly. Having to say no to him was awful."

Ryan finished his interrupted popcorn toss before facing her. "So Mike proposed, and you decided you want to be with Kyle?"

She shook her head. "I stopped seeing Mike immediately, and I apologized profusely. Then, I went back to my apartment and prayed like crazy. I wanted to know what I'd done wrong. Every time I prayed, I thought about Traverse City, so I pulled out my yearbooks and photo albums. After looking through half of them, I knew I needed to come back for the summer."

"And how does Kyle fit into this?"

The heat in her cheeks intensified. "I turned to our senior prom pictures and ... I don't know how to explain it. All of the memories and emotions came rushing back. The more I thought about coming back here, the more I thought about seeing Kyle again. And the more I thought about seeing him, the more I doubted our break up."

Ryan munched some more. "Why?"

Callie licked her lips. "Jack never told you?"

"Not girls, Cal."

She shifted, suddenly uncomfortable. "Kyle and I started dating after prom and dated through most of college, but I didn't want to get married right after graduation. I wanted time to get a job and start my life. I was scared he was going to propose, and I didn't want to say no. And I certainly didn't want to get married, so I dumped him." Guilt pressed in on her, and she squirmed some more. "I never talked to him about it, though. I didn't explain anything. I'm not proud of it now, but that's why I'm here."

"To explain things?"

"And, I hope, to get another chance."

Ryan scratched his chin. "You're sure?"

"I think so." Callie settled deeper into her corner of the couch and helped herself to more popcorn. "I found an old photo album and saw a picture from when we used to have that Bible study in my parents' basement. Remember that?"

Ryan nodded, watching her.

"I found a picture from one of those nights and, well, I don't really know what happened, but I couldn't wait to come here. I just knew this was where I needed to be, so here I am."

"To ask Kyle out. What about your rules? I thought you never asked guys out."

"I don't."

Ryan's brow lifted. "So, how is this going to work? Do you even know if Kyle is interested?"

She flinched. "That was harsh." But also, her deepest fear.

"I didn't mean to be. I'm just looking at this from his point of view." Ryan draped an arm over the back of the couch, angling himself toward her. "You want to go out, but you won't ask him out. I'm wondering how this is going to work. Are you sure about this?"

"What's that supposed to mean?" Callie pushed herself up, crossing her arms and straightening her spine. "It's not like I heard the audible voice of God commanding me to Traverse City, but I know what I felt here," she said, clenching a fist and pressing it against her stomach. "Whenever I looked at that picture, when I thought about coming home, I felt peace. When Kyle and I broke up, he said he'd always be here. I'm assuming he meant it."

"I wasn't trying to be mean, Callie. It's just that you haven't seen him in three years. People change."

Ryan looked at Callie, and she studied him. He was still her brother's best friend. Still a good guy. Still handsome, with blue eyes that she envied. Ryan hadn't changed much, but she had. That gave Kyle a fifty-fifty chance.

She nodded. "I know people change. I'll just have to make sure he knows that I'm here and see what happens."

"That doesn't worry you?"

"Of course it does." Her heart pounded in her chest. A commercial blared from the television. She picked at one of the polka dots on her shorts. "I worry every day that we've changed too much, but I know what I need to do." She once again straightened in her seat. "This is the next step of the plan. I'm sure of it."

Grabbing another handful of popcorn, Callie refocused on the game. The announcers replayed and discussed an earlier play, but her mind was in the past at a Bible study in a basement. She could hear Ryan's prayer, and her heart skipped when she remembered Kyle repeating the words. It had only taken a moment for him to accept the Lord. It took him two weeks before he officially asked her out. Callie smiled.

"Happy thoughts?" Ryan nudged her arm with the popcorn bowl.

"A nice memory."

For the first time in her life, she understood why it had taken Kyle so long to approach her. Nothing scared Callie more than the possibility that he wouldn't be interested.

"I hope things work out for you." Ryan cleared his throat. "You know—"

Her phone rang.

Callie lunged for it. Her breath caught in her throat when she saw the number. She looked at Ryan and her breath caught again. Kyle was on the phone, but Ryan was right there. Something about that tickled her. Another ring.

Ryan flicked her shoulder with his finger. "You going to answer that?"

She swiped the screen. "Hi, Kyle."

"Cal, I'm so sorry I'm late. I'm on my way."

Callie wavered between relief and anger. "It's nine-thirty. Why didn't you call?"

"My phone was in the car, and I couldn't remember your number. I'm really sorry. I'll be there soon."

Callie fingered the hem of her worn t-shirt. Her toes tingled at the thought of squeezing back into her nude pumps. The corner of the couch hugged her with a comfortable arm. "It'll be after ten by the time you get here." She leaned her head against the puffy cushion. "Maybe we should skip tonight and try it again."

"I'd hate doing that. It took us a long time to figure this out. I'm so sorry."

She shrugged, even though she knew he couldn't see her. Her lack of disappointment surprised her, but she didn't let on. "We can figure something out tomorrow."

"Did you want to try again tomorrow night?"

"We could, but I meant that I'd see you at church. We can figure it out then."

Kyle let out a long breath. "I don't think I'm going to make it to church. We've still got a lot to do on this project before Tuesday, so we're going in to the office again tomorrow."

"Oh, okay." This time the disappointment hit her. She filled her hand with popcorn.

"Once we finish this project, I'll have more time, I promise. We should be wrapped up by Tuesday, Wednesday at the latest."

She could handle another couple of days, or more. "Okay. I guess we could—" but the line temporarily muted.

Kyle sighed. "I really need to take this call." Callie heard a car door slam. "I'm so sorry this didn't work. I'll give you a call later this week."

And the call ended.

Callie kept the phone to her ear, just in case she'd missed something. She stared into Jack's office and listened. All she heard was the kitchen door open and close.

"Oh, great! Popcorn." Jack strode into the living room, picked up the bowl, then crashed onto the couch between Callie and Ryan. "What are we watching?"

She set down her phone. Leaning back, she pressed into the couch until she could see behind her brother's head. Ryan was watching her.

"So?" He mouthed.

She shrugged.

He winked.

She smiled. Then she stretched her legs out, swiveling to rest them on Jack's knee.

His face contorted, which made her laugh.

Watching football and eating popcorn wasn't in the plan, but she couldn't complain about her first Saturday night at home.

CHAPTER 7

Jack looked at his sister as Ryan pulled into the church parking lot. She sat silently in the back seat. Hadn't said a word since they left the lighthouse. It finally hit him why. Her eyes were drooping, and her shoulders sagged. "You look tired."

Callie glared at him as she climbed out. "Thanks." She slammed the Jeep door. He cringed.

"Don't take it out on my car." Ryan climbed out of the vehicle and nudged his door closed.

Jack shook his head. "I wasn't trying to be mean, Cal. I was just trying to start a conversation." He just didn't know what else to say. She'd gotten up at least three times during the night, banging around in the living room each time, and hadn't teased him all morning.

"Now?" She looked at him like he'd just grown a third arm. "We had forty minutes in the car, and you wait until we're in the church parking lot?"

Women. The only thing Callie ever wanted to do was talk, and now she was upset that he was trying? "Forget it then." He walked past her. Twenty-seven years, and he still hadn't figured out how to talk to her. She didn't make sense.

Ryan jogged up to Jack. "Play nice, kids. We're at church, after all."

Callie laughed, stepping next to her brother and squeezing his arm. Her fingernails tickled his skin.

First, she was mad—now, she was tickling him. Jack shook his head again. "You're nuts." He poked her in the ribs. She giggled. He still didn't know what had happened, but at least she was feeling better. Big Brother did it again.

The trio had just stepped into the climate-controlled foyer when he heard it. That voice. High pitched. Twittering. Like Beaker from the Muppets. Then Jack saw her. As she chattered with a group of people, her hair shone against her back. She never wore a ponytail to church. He liked that about her.

Stacey, the golden-haired Muppet.

"Hey, Stacey!"

Callie's voice echoed through the foyer.

Jack sucked in a deep breath.

Stacey turned. She smiled. Her eyes matched the pale green color of her shirt. It reminded Jack of oxidized copper, but softer. As she walked toward them, her skirt brushed across her knees.

"Hi, Callie. Ryan. Jack." Stacey joined the group. "It's good to see you again."

Callie reached out and hugged the small woman.

Jack's gut clenched.

"Are you still busy after church?" Callie asked.

Stacey nodded. "I promised to help a friend do some repair work to her house this afternoon."

Jack struggled to imagine Stacey in a tool belt. "What kind of work are you doing?"

"We're going to fix some holes in her walls."

"Drywall?"

Stacey shrugged. "I guess so."

Jack looked at Ryan. His friend's shoulders shook as he looked at the floor. Polite. Jack didn't bother trying to hide his response though. He let loose and laughed. "Stacey, do you even know how to patch drywall?"

"You buy some extra wall panels and put them in the hole," she said. "I'm sure the guys at Home Depot can show me how to do it."

The dam burst, and Ryan's laughter echoed with Jack's.

Callie smacked them both. After years of practice, she hit Jack at just the right spot with enough force that his shoulder ached. "Don't be mean," she said. "At least Stacey's trying."

She was trying. Stacey was always trying, always helping anyone who asked. Jack couldn't remember the last time Stacey didn't have plans to go help someone after church. He'd not been paying attention, of course, but it did seem like she was always babysitting or gardening for someone else. Her home improvement announcements usually sucked him into her schemes, not that he tried very hard to avoid them.

Jack nudged Callie with his elbow. "You haven't known Stacey long enough to know that Ryan and I have helped her with lots of home improvements, and she's never started a job she's known how to do. I swear, we're not laughing at her."

"We're just not surprised." Ryan chuckled.

Jack refocused on Stacey. "Do you need help?"

"Oh, no." She waved her hands. "I'm sure we can figure it out."

"So am I, but I can help you do it in half the time."

"No, no. Your sister's in town. I don't want to intrude on your time together."

Jack snorted. "She's here all summer. In a week, I'll be begging you to intrude."

Stacey's eyes widened. She gave him a funny look. He would have called it a smile if her eyes weren't the size of golf balls. Jack wondered if she was feeling well, and then, oh, no. Those stupid mixed signals.

"I, um, it's just…" He looked for an escape route, but the cavernous lobby offered no sanctuary. There was always the bathroom …

Ryan smacked him on the back. "We should probably go find a seat."

Salvation. "Right. Let's go." He launched himself to the left and away from Stacey. If he was lucky, Pastor Bill would run long today. That would give Stacey over an hour to forget that Jack had practically invited her to spend time with him, and it would also give him some time to figure out why he wanted to.

Pastor Bill said something about love and repentance, then he threw in a little bit about a person's heart. Stacey figured it had been a touching message, but she didn't remember a thing. All she heard was, "I'll be begging you to intrude."

Jack, begging her to spend time with him? She could only hope.

The people next to Stacey nudged her toward the aisle. She hadn't even noticed the service had ended. Without much thought, she gathered her things and moved her legs. The next thing she knew, she was standing in the aisle looking up into the mocha-brown eyes of the handsome lighthouse keeper.

"I'll meet you at the Home Depot in a couple of hours." Jack pointed to Ryan and Callie. "We drove in together, so I'm going to have to get my own truck."

"You don't have to do that," said Ryan. "Callie and I can stay in town and can grab some lunch."

"We can?" Callie looked up at Ryan, and he looked down at her. Ryan smiled. Callie blushed.

Interesting.

Jack tensed. "It'll take us a few hours."

Ryan shrugged. "That's okay. We'll find a way to kill the time." He set his hand on Callie's back and steered her toward the door. "Give me a call when you're ready and we'll come pick you up." He nodded toward Jack. "We'll talk later."

Before anyone could object, the couple slipped out the door.

Stacey tipped her head back, and further back, to look up at Jack. He didn't look happy, but he didn't look angry either. In fact, with the way his forehead crinkled, and his mouth gaped open, he looked quite confused, which only made him more attractive. What was he confused about? Maybe he was questioning his decision to help her. Her heart skipped. Maybe he'd changed his mind.

"You don't have to come with me," she said. "This is really last minute, and I don't want to intrude—"

"Why does your friend need help?" Jack asked, aiming his confused look at Stacey.

"She broke her wrist, and her sister is visiting next week. I offered to give her a hand."

A smile crept onto his face. How could every expression make him more attractive? She smiled back. "So, you offered to help with home repairs."

She nodded.

"But you don't know what you're doing."

She swallowed then shook her head.

"Do you have drywall tape?"

Stacey shrugged.

"Do you have spackling paste? A trowel? Drywall screws?"

The enormity of the situation slammed into her like a truck. She hadn't realized how ill-prepared she was until he started asking questions. She couldn't even look at Jack when she shook her head again.

Jack chuckled.

Stacey's head snapped up. "What's so funny?"

"I'm impressed with your determination to help everyone, even if you don't know how to do it. I offered to help, so let's go. You can return the favor someday when my sister needs to go shopping."

Stacey could breathe again. "Sure. I know how to shop. I can totally help out." She bounced with excitement, though she wasn't entirely sure if it was because Jack agreed to help or because he knew what he was doing.

"That's broken."

Jack sighed. "I know." He picked it up anyway, tossing the half piece of drywall on top of the quickly filling cart.

"Are you sure?" Stacey twirled a piece of hair around her finger. She'd been doing that all afternoon, every time she questioned whether or not they needed a level, or primer, or a nail. Jack had never noticed it before, but he liked it.

He leaned toward her. "This is the cheapest option. We could buy a whole sheet, but we won't need it. This will save us a few bucks."

"Really?" She stopped twirling. "I don't know. If it was my house, I wouldn't care, but I don't want to cut any corners. Maybe we should just get a real sheet."

He laughed. "Stacey, this *is* a real sheet. It's just half of one." Jack grabbed the metal frame of the cart and started pushing. "Remind me, how many walls have you fixed?"

When he looked at her, Stacey's neck and ears glowed pink. He didn't know why she kept doing that, but he liked it. Between that and the Sunday skirt, Jack had nearly driven the cart into more than one display. He reminded himself again that he didn't want to look. She kicked something on the floor and the skirt brushed her knees. Once again, the reminder failed.

"You're right." She looked at her feet. He couldn't figure out why she hadn't looked at him since they left the church, when she'd practically jumped into his arms. Before he could ask, she piped up again. "I don't have a clue what I'm doing. I'm sorry. I trust your experience. What else do we need?"

"That's it."

She finally looked at him. "It is?" She smiled. "I was starting to worry that we'd need half the store."

"Now you sound like my sister." He shook his head. "Worrying about anything you can." Jack maneuvered the cart around a display of paint cans and through the aisles. He shortened his stride, so Stacey could keep up.

"Callie's a worrier? She looks so put together. What does she have to worry about?"

"Nothing, but she worries anyway."

"Are you a worrier?"

Jack looked at Stacey's pretty face. He only worried about one thing these days, and he kept making it harder for himself to forget about it. Especially when he invited himself to help her with another project. And especially when she wore that skirt.

"Jack?"

"Sorry. No, I don't usually worry." They stepped into a checkout lane and unloaded the cart.

They were in Stacey's car with a broken piece of drywall wedged in the back when Stacey spoke again. "Why not?"

"Why not what?"

Stacey snapped open her wallet. She thumbed through the cash. "Why don't you worry?"

"Because God told me not to." She stopped and looked at him like he'd just asked her to recite Newton's laws of physics. In Latin. "What?"

"God told you not to worry?"

Jack nodded. "Pretty much. It's all over the Bible. God knows what he's doing, and he's the best prepared to handle it."

"So, you really don't worry about anything?" Stacey glanced at her wallet. "Ever?"

"I try not to."

She sighed, and her shoulders moved, knocking a few strands of hair loose. Jack cleared his throat. "There are some things that still get me, though."

She nodded, and her hair moved again. "Me too. What did you want for lunch? We can just swing through a drive-thru someplace."

"I thought you hated fast food."

The pink came back. "It's not my favorite, but I thought it might get you going home faster. I've already taken too much of your time, and—"

"Don't worry about it."

"No, really. I don't want to hog your day."

Jack wrapped his fingers around her hand, closing the wallet. He had spotted three bills in there, and none of them was larger than a five. She hadn't flinched when she paid for their supplies, but a simple lunch had her counting cash.

Something heavy settled on Jack's shoulders while something in his heart softened. "Let me buy you lunch."

Stacey flinched. "What? Why?"

"Why not?" Jack wanted to kick himself. Another mixed signal. "It can be my contribution to the cause."

"You don't have—"

He squeezed her hand. "You give everything you have to everybody else. I admire that."

"You do?"

"Yes."

She licked her lips. "And that's why you want to buy me lunch?"

He looked at her wallet, at their hands, at that pretty green shirt that matched her pretty green eyes. "Yes. That's why I want to buy you lunch."

"Well, I ... okay then."

"Okay."

Her hand relaxed, but neither of them moved until Stacey's phone rang. She jumped, then dove into her purse to find the phone. Jack's hand felt strangely empty.

As Stacey searched for her phone, she smiled. A beautiful smile beneath sparkling eyes, surrounded by the softest looking hair. And then there was that skirt.

Jack definitely had something to worry about.

CHAPTER 8

Callie licked pink cream from her lips. Ryan couldn't pull his eyes away. "I'm in heaven." She closed her eyes and turned to face the sun.

"You're at a dairy farm." He popped the last piece of a cone into his mouth as a whiff of dairy air blew past.

As Callie leaned against the picnic table savoring her ice cream cone, Ryan swiveled on the bench, so he could lean back to observe the world. They sat on the nearest section of the main deck at Moomer's Ice Cream shop. They could have walked along the building, past the weeping willow and under the covered walkway to the more secluded tables, but a hand-holding couple had beat them to it. Ryan knew there were a couple more tables back there, but he also didn't want to intrude.

Instead, they settled for the main deck, right by the guardrail. The weather-worn wood kept people safe from the steep hill that led to the cow pasture. Today, the heifers roamed the field, nudging and mooing at each other. The farmer left a trailer full of hay for them to munch on. A barn cat that'd somehow managed to stay white amongst the dirt and cows stalked right through the center of the action, ignoring the dangerous hooves and avoiding the ground-level debris.

Ryan watched a mom and dad lead their small children down a set of narrow steps to another observation deck. Their colorful Sunday-best clothes popped out against the green and brown backdrop.

"This is the best ice cream in the world," Callie said, interrupting his thoughts. "This really might be heaven."

Ryan watched a trickle of pink run down the side of Callie's cone. "In heaven, your ice cream will never melt, but back here on the farm, you're dripping."

Her eyes snapped open. Spinning the cone around, she located the drip and slurped the melted treat from her fingers before biting off the edge of the cone. "This is the best." She flashed Ryan a toothy smile. "I didn't realize how much I missed this."

"It is a uniquely Traverse City experience." He leaned against Callie, brushing his shoulder with hers. She looked at him, their eyes so close. Ryan smiled. "You could have it every day if you lived here."

Callie nodded. "I know. It's probably better for my health that I don't. Thanks again."

She took another big lick from her cone, smiling as if she were enjoying a gourmet feast. Ryan watched every second of it, letting her joy fuel his. "You're so welcome."

"You know, you didn't have to buy my cone. Jack hired me. I'm actually getting paid to make a fool out of myself this summer. I'll be rich in no time."

"I know. I don't mind." He winked.

Callie stopped the cone a few inches from her mouth. Her face squished together for second then she shrugged. "Fine, but I still owe you. Next time it's my treat."

He shook his head. "A lady should never pay."

"This isn't a date."

"I know."

Callie stared at him. Her face squished up again as she slowly consumed her dessert, watching him. Ryan waited. Wondered. When had Jack's little sister become one of his best friends? She didn't even realize it. Of course, he hadn't realized it until recently himself. "What do you want to do this afternoon?"

She shrugged. "I was planning on going home, so I don't have anything planned."

"And you're feeling okay? Without a plan, I mean."

Callie snorted. "I'm fine."

She focused on the cone, and Ryan's eyes zeroed in on her lips, as if his gaze couldn't escape their pull. He needed a distraction. Pushing himself away from the table, he tossed his napkin in the trash and headed down the creaky stairs. He nodded at the small family when he passed them on his way.

His shoes clunked on the dark wood of the lower observation deck, catching the attention of a nearby heifer. She licked her nose with a long, thick, pink tongue. Finally deciding that Ryan didn't deserve her attention, she trudged through the muck, turning her black-and-white rear end toward him.

A soft chuckle reached Ryan's ears. Then he heard the muted clack of heels on soft wood. Callie appeared beside him. She leaned against the guardrail, inhaling deeply. "Is it weird that I like this smell?"

"Only if you buy the air freshener."

"When I was younger I dreamed about moving to the city, but I can't give this up. I love it."

"Thinking about moving back?"

She shook her head. "That's not part of the plan yet."

"But it may be someday?" Hope surged through his veins.

"Possibly. I still need to reconnect with Kyle. If that goes well, we'll have to see." She sighed, still taking in the view. "I wouldn't mind ending up back here."

"Does Kyle know about this plan?"

"Can I confess something to you?"

"Sure."

"It's not really a plan. I mean, I prayed about it and know I'm supposed to be here right now, but I'll be honest. My emotions are so involved that I'm not completely sure what else is supposed to happen. I'm pretty sure this is what I'm supposed to do, though." She glanced over her shoulder at Ryan, her eyes squinting against the sun. "I really do want to follow God's will for my life. I just hope I'm hearing him right."

Callie turned to watch the cows again. He followed suit. He hadn't told her his plan yet either, but he would. Eventually. In the meantime, he had to do something.

Without another thought, Ryan grabbed Callie's hand, wrapping his fingers around her sticky ones. "Let's go."

"Where?" Callie stumbled to keep up but giggled as she trounced up the stairs.

She shifted her fingers in his so that she was holding his hand too. Comfortable. Ryan didn't answer until they stopped beside his Jeep. "I don't know. Where do you want to go?"

"You already bought me ice cream." She adjusted her purse strap. "What else can a girl ask for?"

He opened the door. "Food?" Twenty minutes later, Ryan parked beside a pink and purple sign. Next to him, Callie smiled so wide that he thought her ears might pop right off. He shook his head. "Four hundred restaurants in town and you want to eat here?"

"I haven't had a gordita in years." Callie jumped out of the car. She was already opening the restaurant door before Ryan caught up with her. The heavy scent of grease engulfed them. A teenager behind the counter smiled beneath her purple visor.

"Welcome to Taco Bell," she said. "Would you like to try a value meal?"

"Do you still have cheese gorditas?" Callie practically climbed onto the counter.

"Um, yeah."

"Can I have one, please?"

She shrugged. "Sure."

The young girl went to work as Callie bounced in place. "I'm sure I'll regret it later, but I can't wait to eat one. I haven't been here since we used to come after Bible study."

Ryan thought about those nights in the Stevens family's basement—a group of teens looking for God, not at each other. He didn't know if he'd still be able to do that with Callie around.

As the employee walked back toward them, Callie opened her purse, but he already had his wallet out. Before Callie could even find her money, Ryan dropped a five-dollar bill on the counter.

Callie's face scrunched up. "You don't have to—"

"I know."

Since when had cheesy gorditas become an aphrodisiac? They used to simply be tasty, cheesy high-calorie treats, but in the company of Ryan Martin, each bite made Callie's pulse race.

"Aren't you going to get anything?" Callie asked, squirming in the booth as Ryan sat across from her.

"You think you'll regret that later. I know I would." He leaned back in his seat.

She stopped the gordita on its way to her mouth. "Then why did we come here?"

"Because you wanted to."

She shifted again. "That's it?"

"Yep."

"But what about you? What are you going to eat?"

He shrugged. "I'll pick something up later. Jack'll be a while, so we've got time."

"Well, thanks."

"You're welcome."

Callie took another bite of the gooey snack, closing her eyes to better appreciate the hot, processed flavor. She sighed. "This is fantastic. You must think I've got some type of food fetish, but I honestly haven't had Moomer's or Taco Bell in years."

"I'm glad I could be of assistance."

She tossed the last bit of gordita into her mouth, then crumpled the paper in her fist. "Now what? How long do you think it'll take Jack and Stacey to fix those walls?"

"I don't know, but they'll call." Ryan reached across the table and took the wrapper. He stood up and offered Callie his hand. "Where would you like to go now?"

She didn't have a clue. She'd expected to be home unpacking. What did a person do without a plan? She shrugged. "Let's just get in the Jeep and see where we end up."

Ryan pulled his hand back, his eyes wide. "Are you sure?"

"A little queasy, but I think it'll pass. Does spontaneity always feel like this?"

He laughed and reoffered his hand. "You're just not used to it yet. Give it time."

Callie accepted his hand and found herself standing inches in front of Ryan, her eyes level with his chin. His familiar fragrance tickled her nostrils. He smiled but didn't back up. She scanned up his neck and face until their eyes met. The intensity of his gaze sent shivers across her skin. Their nearness didn't bother her, and that bothered her. She needed to see Kyle.

"Feeling better yet?" Ryan asked, leaning forward until their eyes were level.

"Air." What had happened to all of the air in the restaurant? "I think I need some air."

She darted for the door.

Callie stepped into the bright afternoon sun. A car honked on the nearby street. The air carried the scents of barbecue, spices, and fryers from neighboring restaurants.

Ryan stopped beside her and put his hand on her back. Another chill covered her skin, cutting through the moist afternoon heat. He led Callie to his Jeep, opening the passenger door for her. She climbed in and reached for the belt, which he had already pulled forward. All she had to do was grab the nylon strip.

Instead, she looked at him. That strange intensity looked back at her. She didn't recognize that look, but something about it—with the hint of a smile on his lips and his nearness to her—startled her senses.

So did the piercing ring tone.

Ryan handed off the seatbelt as Callie answered the call.

"Callie, it's Kyle." The sound of his voice hit her like a cold June wave in the Grand Traverse Bay.

"Kyle. I didn't think you'd call."

"I'm sorry. I should have called sooner. I *should* have called the other night. I could give you a list of reasons why I didn't, but it doesn't matter. I just want you to know that I'm sorry."

The temperature in the car spiked. "Don't worry about it. It's good to hear from you."

"Thank you, but I shouldn't have made you worry. I'd like to make it up to you. How about dinner?"

"Dinner?" The air left her lungs again. "I, I'd lo…" She watched Ryan climb into the Jeep. "I'd like that."

"Why don't we shoot for Friday? I'll pick you up at seven."

"Sure. Sounds great."

"Thanks for the second chance. And Cal?"

"Yeah?"

"I can't wait to see you again."

Callie's head spun as she hung up the phone. She had to close her door, but there was already a shortage of air in the Jeep.

Ryan had ended up in the driver's seat while she was distracted. He reached over and touched her shoulder. "You okay?"

She pulled the door in and nodded. "Kyle apologized and asked me to have dinner." An expected excitement tingled in her toes. The heavy disappointment, however, surprised her.

Ryan slid his sunglasses onto his nose. "That's great." He backed out of the parking spot. "Looks like today's the day for creating happy memories at Taco Bell."

Happy, and completely confusing.

CHAPTER 9

Jack stared into the garage looking for inspiration. He had no idea what he was going to have Callie do.

Unlike Stacey, who easily handled every project Jack threw at her, Callie was a klutz. He wanted to keep her away from anything sharp, pointed, scalloped, most things with moving parts, a few things with stationary parts, and all things electrical. Ladders were iffy. He'd gladly let her use one if it kept her away from the more dangerous objects, but he wouldn't mind keeping the ladders in the garage too. He needed something safe, like weeding, but the township had the garden club doing that.

Maybe Stacey was available to help. She'd learned to spackle and hang drywall in one afternoon. He chuckled, remembering how she had cheered when she knocked in her first straight nail, looking more like a middle-school cheerleader than a responsible adult.

"What's the plan?" Callie stepped beside him.

Busted. Think fast. Scanning the walls, his gaze hit the paint cans. He pointed toward his work bench at the far end of the garage. "Grab a wire brush. I'll get a tarp."

"Tarp?" Her face perked up. "What are we doing?"

"We're not doing anything. *You* are going to repaint the garage."

Ryan checked his watch. Half an hour late. Marshall said he'd call thirty minutes ago. Slim chance he'd call now. He'd always been one of Ryan's biggest fans, but Marshall was also incredibly loyal to his graphic designer and not ready to give Ryan a chance. Still, Marshall called Ryan for bids, raving about his skills while never committing. What did it say about Ryan that he kept submitting them?

Closing the browser on his laptop, he swiveled in his chair, turning his back on the tan-colored office to enjoy his second-story view. The parking lot wasn't the best scenery, but a line of sugar maples stretched across the far end of the lot, and he couldn't complain about all the natural light. Not all of the tenants in the building had such a wide window.

Thump.

Ryan's flimsy door rattled. Someone must've come up the front stairs. He'd know for sure if his door had a window like the other offices, but at least he had his view.

BOOM! BOOM! BOOM!

The plywood door shook. Ryan checked his calendar. Nothing scheduled after Marshall's phone call. As he stood, the door opened.

"Do you want me to build you a better door? This thing is awful." Jack strolled in, his heavy boots scuffing across the high-traffic carpet.

"You can make me one, but I'm not paying you for it. That's why I pay rent." Ryan sat back down.

Jack dropped into one of Ryan's wooden guest chairs, plopping a brown grocery sack on the desk. The aroma of spicy garlic wafted into the room.

"Thai Café?"

"Ming's."

Either way. "What's up?"

"Nothin'. I was in town to pick up some parts for the mower and got hungry." He reached into the bag, pulling out four different containers. "I figured I owe you one, since I sort of stuck you with Callie on Sunday."

That was not anything he needed to apologize for, but Ryan wouldn't say no to free food.

The desk phone jingled. Ryan checked the caller ID. Of course. Marshall. "I have to take this." Jack didn't even look up from his lunch as Ryan lifted the receiver. "This is Ryan Martin."

"Ryan, Marshall. Sorry I didn't get back to you earlier."

"Not a problem." After three years of submitting bids to the man, Ryan didn't expect any less. "Do you have any questions about my proposal?"

"Everything looks great. As always, your work is amazing."

Bad sign. That's how all of the conversations started. "But you're not ready to switch."

"I really am impressed. I even told your father at the club last weekend, but I've been working with Gibson Miller for years."

Ryan tuned out the rest of the speech. He'd heard it before. As Marshall rambled, the thick scents of sweet, sour, and garlic surrounded him. When Marshall neared the end, Ryan recognized his cue. "I can appreciate your loyalty, Marshall. Thanks for giving me the chance to bid on the project."

When he finally hung up, Jack was shoveling a forkful of noodles into his mouth, his head shaking. "Ypp ma fhht fslsmn." Noodle bits shot onto the floor.

Ryan grabbed the nearest carton and dug in, picking a piece of noodle off the top. "Sorry, I don't speak slob."

Jack laughed. "I said you're the worst salesman. You just thanked a man for not hiring you."

"I'm not a salesman. I'm a designer." Ryan's stomach growled, his mouth watering.

"You've got to be more aggressive."

Another speech he'd heard a dozen times. "My work speaks for itself. Marshall will come around."

"It's been years. Push him hard or let it go."

Ryan dug into the salty, sweet chicken. Just what he needed. He should probably let Jack finish the lecture, since he did feed him. "I appreciate the advice. I'll think about it." After lunch.

Jack snorted.

Ryan stopped his fork. "What?"

"You and I had the stomach flu together six times in grade school. I know more about you than I care to admit. You're not going to think about it, so just say so. You don't have to play nice around me. I've seen you puke."

His stomach stopped growling, but something in Ryan's chest rumbled. "Maybe you need a refresher course. There's nothing wrong with manners. People still say please and thank you."

"Yeah, after they get the job, not after giving it to someone else."

"I'm not going to take business advice from a guy who considers good work clothes as those with the most stains."

"Just because I've never worn a suit to work doesn't mean I don't know how to get a job. I've never lost a job I was qualified for. I had to fight for the park superintendent job."

"There were only two applicants."

"I got the job building the new furniture for the peninsula library."

Ryan huffed. "You work for the township. It made sense to hire you."

"It doesn't matter why they hired me, the point is they did. I stayed on them until I got an answer, and then I convinced them to hire me."

Jack pulled the takeout container from Ryan's hands. "Are you going to eat this?"

"Yes, I am." He took it back.

Jack laughed. "At least you'll fight for something. Next time forget the garlic chicken. Go for the job."

"Says the man flashing me his navel."

Jack looked down, tugging at his shirt. He poked a finger through the hole and smiled. "At least I'm consistent."

"And you bought lunch." Because of Callie, which made him curious. "Where'd you leave your sister today?"

"She's working at the lighthouse."

Ryan stuffed a juicy piece of meat into his mouth. "I didn't think you were really going to make her do anything."

"I wasn't, but she insisted."

"What did you find for her to do?"

"It's perfect. She's stripping paint off the garage. There's no way she can mess this up."

CHAPTER 10

Blood dripped on the tarp. Again.

"Seriously?" Callie mumbled as she grabbed the red-stained rag from her pocket. The knuckles on her right hand had finally stopped bleeding after repeated scrapes along the wall, but not before creating a colorful spot on her once-favorite khaki shorts. That's what she got for trying to look cute while doing manual labor.

Now a red streak painted her left forearm. She wouldn't have gouged it with the edge of the brush if she hadn't lost her balance after slipping in a puddle on the tarp that Jack laid down. Technically, it was his fault.

The blood traveled down Callie's arm, snaking its way across her skin. That was a lot of blood for a little scrape. As the shock of it wore off, the stinging started and spread, burning along the cut and numbing the rest of her arm. Maybe not such a little scrape. This definitely warranted a trip to the first-aid kit. Holding the rag against her arm, Callie left the tools in the yard and headed toward the lighthouse.

The small group of people approached her. She'd never met this group of six people, but she recognized them from previous trips to the lighthouse. Two older couples and a young, smiling couple. The young brunette pointed and chattered, her arms flailing as she talked. One woman nodded continually. The other looked like she'd eaten a spicy pickle. The men appeared to be absorbed in their own conversation, though the shorter, balding one occasionally pulled at his collar.

Callie didn't need to talk to them to know what was going on—wedding planning. Her arm throbbed. A quick look at the rag almost buckled her knees. Between the blood and water, the cloth was turning pink.

The group moved toward the fence, so Callie hurried. She just had to make it to the lighthouse first. Each step vibrated up her spine and into her arm. Lengthening her stride, she reached the gate at the same time as the nodding, dark-haired woman. Callie smiled, but she put her foot in front of the gate, stopping its path. "I'm sorry, ma'am. This part of the park is private property."

"We won't take long," she said. "We just want to see if the lighthouse will be big enough for the bridal party."

The gate pressed into the side of Callie's foot, but she didn't move. "The lighthouse is a private residence. It's not available for public use."

The bride stepped forward, her brows crinkled. "But we were told we could have our wedding out here."

"At any public area in the park, yes, but not inside the fenced-in area."

The bride sighed and turned to the other women. The taller man was demonstrating a golf swing. The towel dampened under Callie's hand, so she checked the gate latch before heading toward the deck. If she could just get a bandage on her arm—

"Excuse me."

So close. Callie turned to the group following her on the other side of the fence. "How can I help you?"

The nodding woman approached her. "How long will it take to build a rail?"

"A rail for what?"

"For the steps."

"What steps?"

The woman rolled her eyes. "The steps down to the shoreline."

An image of the worn, wooden slats popped into Callie's mind. A section of the eastern beach sat at the base of a small dune. It wasn't difficult for most people to climb, but several years ago Jack had installed steps at the township's request. She'd hiked up and down the gently sloping stairs several times, never once needing a handrail. "I'm not aware that we're planning on putting one in."

"Then how's my daughter supposed to get safely down the stairs?"

Callie's mind spun, and heat seared her arm. She grimaced but managed a smile. "I suppose her father could give her away."

"And how do you suggest he keeps his balance?"

One of the men finally looked up and approached the conversation. He looked at Callie and frowned. "Miss, are you okay?"

Callie looked at him, but the throbbing crept up her arm and started pulsing in her brain, blocking out everything else.

"For crying out loud, Virginia. Look at the poor girl. She's white as a sheet, and her arm's bleeding." He reached a hand toward Callie. "Can I help you inside?"

Callie shook her head. "I just need to get this cleaned up." Virginia said something, but Callie was already up the deck and letting herself inside.

She stumbled through the house, forcing back the queasiness as she struggled to focus. When she finally made it to the bathroom, she leaned against the vanity, resting her arm on the sink. She pulled back the rag, shuddering.

The torn, red skin on her arm flashed before her. The bathroom started spinning.

Callie sank to the ground. She dropped her head between her knees. Her eyes closed. She focused on breathing. In and out, deep and slow. In and out. In and out.

"Callie?"

In and out. Deep and slow.

"Squirt?"

Boom, boom, boom. Someone walked toward her.

Deep and slow. In and out.

"Callie!" Jack pulled on her arm.

The bathroom spun. "I'm fine. I got a little dizzy when I saw the blood, that's all."

"Cal, this needs stitches."

She heard the faucet turn on. A warm cloth wiped across her arm, stinging slightly, but soothing the ache. The water started running again. Seconds later a cold wet cloth landed on the back of her neck.

"I was scraping like you told me to, but I lost my balance. Give me a sec." Callie sucked in one giant breath. As she let the air slip out past her lips, she lifted her head and opened her eyes. "I think I'm good. I'll be fine."

Jack shook his head. "You're not fine. Let's get you to the hospital."

"I'm fine. I probably don't need stitches."

"Not if you don't mind a deep, festering cut."

Callie shivered. "I'd rather get stitches."

"Good." Jack grabbed her right forearm with one hand and stuck the other in her arm pit. With one effortless motion, he stood them both up.

As he led her through the house, guilt piled onto her shoulders. "You don't have to go with me. You have work to do. I know how to get to the hospital."

"You passed out in the bathroom, Squirt."

"I did not. I just don't handle blood well. You know that."

"No arguments."

Callie leaned against her brother. "I'm not a child. I can handle stitches."

"I know you can." They stepped outside. "Tell me what happened?"

She squinted in the sunlight. "I slipped on the tarp and stuck myself with the wire brush."

Jack sighed. "When did you have your last tetanus shot?"

Her stomach rolled. Stitches *and* a shot? "Great."

Callie turned her arm, examining the bandage as she settled onto Jack's hammock. The tight gauze squeezed her forearm as the ropes pressed against her legs and back. She swung her foot down until it touched the ground then pushed off. Sea gulls glided overhead. A few more clouds drifted along. She rocked back and forth. Her head started spinning. The last thing she needed was to make herself seasick. She dragged her foot and anchored the hammock.

A light wind rustled by, stirring the leaves overhead. Their soft shuffle blended with the murmur of tourists wandering around the park. Callie closed her eyes. Warm air. The lapping surf.

SQUAWK!

She jumped, looking around for the obnoxious bird. She spotted it directly above her, suspended by the clouds. It squawked again. She looked at the ground for stones, not that she'd really throw a stone at a helpless bird.

SQUAWK!

But a warning shot might help.

SQUAWK!

Maybe a nice pile of ammunition would scare it away. Rolling out of the hammock, Callie scanned the ground as she made her way to the northern fence. She leaned against it, watching the waves tickle the sand as they rolled in and out. A dozen or so people waded in the rocky water, stepping carefully around hidden rocks. Callie's foot still remembered the pain of discovering those rocks as a kid. Back then she had to be in the water. These days it was enough to listen to its song.

SQUAWK!

Unless it kept getting interrupted. Turning her attention to the ground, Callie looked for a projectile. She didn't have anything else to do anyway. Jack made her promise not to touch anything until he came home. She'd already ignored that and put away the wire brush and tarp. He couldn't possibly be mad about that. He might have something to say about her assaulting seagulls, though.

By the time Callie finally found a pebble, she looked up into an empty, bright blue sky. Figures. Another unsuccessful venture. Tossing the stone toward the water, she returned to the hammock.

The rest of the summer couldn't be as bad. Jack would let her stay but probably out of obligation. Callie didn't want to do that to Jack. He needed someone who could actually help him. He could hire a teenager to paint the garage. It didn't need to be her.

Suppose she'd been wrong. Maybe she'd misunderstood, and she wasn't supposed to be in Traverse City. It wasn't too late to go back to Alma, regroup, and return to normalcy. That had to be better than three months of getting in Jack's way and waiting for Kyle. Kyle wasn't responding to her presence the way she'd hoped. Failure and rejection would definitely ruin her summer, but she didn't have to take Jack down with her.

Flopping around in the unsteady hammock, she pulled the phone out of her pocket without flipping over. Small victory. Speed dial six.

"Y'ello, this is Lee."

She smiled. "Hi, Mr. Foreman. It's Callie Stevens."

"Miss Callie! I can hear you smiling, but I'm not buying it. What's wrong?"

"Nothing's wrong, Mr. Foreman." Liar. "I was just calling to check on my apartment. Is everything okay?"

"My niece is all moved in. We really appreciate you subletting the place."

The smile faltered. "Your niece?"

"She's going to help take care of my Tilda this summer."

"Tilda? What happened to your wife?"

"Surgery on her knee. She's going to need some help in the garden and with the regular chores. We don't have a lot of extra room here at the house, so we appreciate you letting Alice bunk at your place for a few months. And I think she appreciates the privacy."

Deep, steady breaths. "That's great, Mr. Foreman." Just great. She couldn't kick out the caregiver of her landlord's wife ... could she?

"Made Tilda downright chipper when she heard Alice was coming. I think they may actually be looking forward to this."

Of course they were. Apparently, her apartment was the place to be, and now Callie couldn't be there. Reality slammed into her like the waves beating on the shore. Lee and Tilda needed Alice's help. Callie didn't even hesitate. "Call me if you have any questions or problems with the apartment, okay?"

He cackled. "That's my line. You take care of yourself, and we'll see you in a few months."

"Yep. See you then."

The line went dead.

So did Callie's hopes of escape.

CHAPTER 11

"Look at you, enjoying your summer."

Jack. Callie arched her spine, leaning back to stare at the inverted image of her brother. "What are you doing here?"

"I live here." He strolled through the yard toward her. "How's it going?

"I'm stuck."

He held out a hand. "Do you need help getting up?"

"I'm pretty sure I can find my way out of a hammock, thanks."

"Then I'm confused." Jack pulled a green Adirondack chair through the grass, marking a trail through the vibrant blades. He stopped beside the hammock and sat. "How are you stuck?"

"I can't leave Traverse City."

"Still confused."

Callie sighed. "I called my landlord today. He's already sublet my apartment."

Jack straightened. "You want to go back to Alma?"

"I wanted to give you an out."

"An out? What are you talking about?"

"Look at me." Callie swung around, thrusting her arm in his face. "My first day alone and I've already got stitches. You don't need this. You had big plans for the summer. I'm just going to make a mess. You're better off hiring someone else."

Jack leaned forward, his eyebrows furrowed. "What about your plan? I thought you had other reasons for being here."

"It's not working out."

He snorted. "Sissy."

The muscles in her back tightened. "Hardly. I'm just trying to do the right thing."

"For who?"

"For you, dummy"

"Really?" He leaned back and crossed his arms.

"Yes, really." Callie crossed her arms, too. The motion shifted her center of gravity, tossing her forward. Callie tried to disengage her arms, but the hammock wobbled. Her knees slipped through the holes in the rope. Jack's arm wrapped around her waist, plucking her from the hammock and setting her on the ground. "See? I'm a disaster. You're going to get less done with me than you would without me."

"I'll survive. Why would you want to go back to Alma?"

"I told you." She dropped back onto her bottom. "This job isn't working out."

"It's only been a day."

Callie raised her burning arm. "And I've already got stitches."

"Fine. Quit."

"No."

"I'm no good at this stuff, Cal. I'm not going to figure out what you want to hear. Tell me what's going on, or I'm getting off this merry-go-round."

Callie picked a piece of grass and twirled it around her finger. "Do you really want to know?"

He leaned back. "Does it involve men?"

She nodded.

"I changed my mind."

Callie smiled. "Then you'll just have to trust me."

"Don't worry about it. You can stay with me while you figure it out." Jack gave her a quick pat on the head before pushing himself out of the chair. "And just because things aren't working out the way you thought they would doesn't mean they aren't following God's plan. He doesn't have to run everything by you."

"Yeah, yeah." But life would be so much easier if God would clue her in every now and then.

"I'll be in my workshop if you need me." Jack waved behind him.

Maybe Jack was right, and God had a different plan. That possibility shook her, literally—a nervous shiver slid down her spine.

Do not worry about tomorrow, for tomorrow will worry about itself.

Her life's verse. Mae quoted it to Callie on a regular basis. A framed print hung on her bedroom wall. Great time to recall those words. Callie repeated the verse once, then again. Deep breaths. Relax.

Pebbles crunched. An engine whirled. She listened to a car creep along the driveway. Looking up, she recognized the grill of the vehicle when it peeked out from around the trees. Relaxation ran in the other direction.

Ryan was home.

She sat on the grass pouting, her eyebrows pulled together over a crinkled nose. It was adorable. Ryan loosened his tie as he walked straight to the side yard. Changing could wait. He put his laptop case on the chair across from Callie and sat down in front of it. She picked at the grass.

"Long day?"

"No."

"Hard day?"

"Sort of."

"Looking forward to tomorrow?"

"Not really."

He leaned toward her. She smelled like fabric softener and antiseptic. "Want to talk about it?"

She glanced over at him. "I spent the afternoon at the hospital." Callie held up her arm. "Five stitches."

"What happened?"

She sighed and looked away.

He bit back a smile. "We don't need to talk about it."

She looked at him again. This time she batted her eyelashes and smiled. "How was your day?"

"Pretty uneventful. Spent hours in front of my laptop trying to please my clients." He nodded at her arm. "Not nearly as exciting as your day."

Callie cocked her head. "If you do all of your work on your laptop, why do you have to go into an office? Can't you graphically design stuff from home?"

Ryan smiled. "Sometimes I do, but it's good motivation to keep regular work hours."

"I can appreciate that. I live and die by regular work hours."

"Planning everything out?"

"Lesson plans don't write themselves."

A piece of hair dropped down over Callie's eye. She tried to blow it out of her face, but the wind worked against her. Ryan watched her until she noticed his attention. Her cheeks darkened. He gently wrapped his fingers around Callie's wrist and pulled her arm towards him. He brushed his finger over her bandage. "Should I assume you're taking the rest of the night off then?"

"I, uh …" Goose bumps popped up on her skin. He rubbed the spot again. She shivered. He liked it. "I'm, ah … I'm off for the rest of the night, possibly the week."

"What are your plans?"

Callie leaned against the chair. "I … I don't know yet. Right now, I'm stuck at the end of the peninsula with sea gulls, tourists, and a throbbing arm."

"It'll get better." Ryan pulled off his tie with one hand. "Soon enough it'll be too hot for a shirt and tie, and you'll be lounging on the beach while you decide what to do."

Callie watched his hand as he worked on his top button. As he popped open the second button, her cheeks flushed. Ryan stroked her bandaged arm again. She yanked it from his grasp and tucked her hair behind her ear. "I don't really want to sit on the beach all summer. I want to work. I *need* to." Callie attacked the grass again.

Ryan bent over, leaning close enough that his lips brushed Callie's ear. "Whatever you decide to do, I enjoy having you here."

She shivered.

"Life certainly would be boring without you."

"Yeah?"

"Yeah." Neither of them moved. The afternoon sun baked his back. Sweat beaded on his neck, but Callie's nearness kept him rooted to his spot. "I hope you stay."

She leaned back, looking him right in the eye. "I … I …" Her eyes flickered down just before she jumped up, stepping away from him. Thankfully, she was able to do what he couldn't—put some space between them.

Ryan stood, stepping toward her. Despite her apparent discomfort, Callie never moved. Maybe she was feeling it too. He reached for that piece of hair that kept blowing around.

A horn honked.

They both jumped. Ryan snapped out of his haze and away from Callie. He looked at the car in the driveway, immediately recognizing the coupe. Callie's gasp suggested she did too. Jack stepped out of the garage, wiping his hands on a rag before stuffing it in his back pocket. He looked at Ryan and shrugged.

The car door opened.

Callie stepped beside Ryan. "Kyle."

Meticulously styled hair. Clean, square jaw. Perfectly pressed clothes. And somewhere, behind the aviator sunglasses, light-brown eyes looked in Callie's direction. She'd stared into them dozens of times. Now, Callie held her breath. Kyle had practically ignored her for two weeks. Of course, he'd show up when she was sweaty, dirty, and bandaged. Perfect.

Jack moved first, walking toward Kyle with his hand extended. Kyle accepted it. They shook. They talked. Kyle removed his glasses. He was looking at Callie.

She swallowed.

Her brother said something else, then smacked Kyle's arm. They nodded and turned toward her. Jack veered into the garage, but Kyle walked toward her.

Callie straightened her shirt then brushed off her shorts. The dull ache in her arm reminded her to check for blood stains. When she looked up again, Kyle was in the yard. Two weeks of prepared speeches slipped from her mind. Her stomach jumped.

"Callie."

Her knees wobbled. "Kyle."

Ryan stuck out his hand. "Good to see you again, Kyle."

"Thanks. You too."

Those soft brown eyes shifted, looking at Ryan before zeroing back in on Callie.

Her tongue went numb.

Kyle stepped closer.

Callie tried to move. Something must have happened, because someone touched her arm. She looked down and saw Ryan's hand. "What?" she asked, focusing on his face.

"I said I'll let you guys catch up. I need to talk with Jack anyway."

Though she'd dreamed about it for weeks, the sudden reality of time alone with Kyle paralyzed her. She wasn't ready to be alone with him. She grabbed Ryan's wrist. "Are you sure you don't want to chat with us?"

"I really do need to talk to Jack." Ryan patted her hand. "You guys have fun." He released Callie's arm, leaving her unprotected and vulnerable. She crossed her arms over her chest.

Callie watched Ryan walk away, tie in one hand as he rolled up his sleeves and abandoned her in the yard.

It's Kyle, she told herself. Just Kyle. The man she had once thought she would marry ... until she panicked and ran away. Nothing at all to worry about. Beautiful, brown-eyed Kyle Berg.

"You look good, Cal."

"Thanks." She squeaked then cleared her throat. "So do you."

He stepped forward. She took a deep breath.

"It's good to see you again." Kyle reached back and scratched his neck. "I was really surprised to hear from you."

"Yeah. I ... uh ..." What? "I wasn't sure if I should call, but after I did it was too late to change my mind, and then I figured I should just go with it, but I wasn't really sure what I'd say when we saw each other again, and—"

Kyle chuckled.

She blinked. "What?"

"You're rambling. I think I miss it."

"You do?"

"Yeah."

Great, she was a natural rambler. Dang it. They stood there, staring at each other. Her nerves jumped, but she managed a smile.

Kyle moved forward then walked past Callie and toward the fence at the far side of the lawn. "I wondered what this would be like."

She turned to join him. "The lighthouse in June?"

"No. Seeing you again."

Disappointment stung Callie's heart. "Is that why you drove out here? Morbid curiosity?"

"Not morbid, but curious. I figured you'd have a script all planned out."

"I did." She stopped beside him, resting her hands on the rough, worn fence posts.

Kyle looked over his shoulder at her. "And?"

She shrugged. "I just can't remember it right now."

He smiled. "Well then, let me start. I want to apologize for the other night."

"You already called for that. Why'd you drive all the way out here?"

"I told you. Curiosity."

"Wanted to see if I got fat, eh?"

He laughed. "Wanted to see what would happen when I saw you again."

So did she. Callie's throat clenched. "Are you mad?"

"Mad?" He turned to her. "About what?"

She wrapped hear arms around her waist, trying to protect herself from his much-deserved anger. "Us. Me. Calling you after all this time."

"No, of course not."

"You're not?" She dropped her arms. "Not any of it?"

"Did you want me to be mad?"

"No, but I thought you might be the littlest bit upset."

He smiled. "It's been years, Cal. We're good. I should get going, though."

"Already?"

"I'm actually on my way to a meeting. It's on the peninsula, so I thought I'd drive up to see you. I didn't want Friday to be the first time we saw each other. Are we still on for Friday night? Dinner?"

Callie nodded. "Yep. Don't worry about picking me up though. I'll meet you downtown. Why don't we go to the Kitchen?"

"Sounds good. I'll see you there." He slid his aviators back onto his nose, then turned and walked away.

Callie stood there, watching him leave. Her emotions shifted, matching tempo with the nearby waves. God wanted her in Traverse City, and Kyle was one of the reasons why. He had to be … right?

Once again, doubt slithered through her brain. What if she was wrong about Kyle? Again? As she watched him leave, someone else moved into her sight line.

Ryan, walking around the garage.

Palpitations.

Callie pressed her hand over her heart. She should ask her mom if anyone else in the family had cardiovascular issues.

Weak-kneed, fast-pulsed, and utterly confused, Callie headed toward the house. Whether or not she understood what was going on, she always knew how to calm herself down. There was a Bible in the blue room that literally had her name on it, and somewhere on the desk sat a giant bag of M&Ms.

CHAPTER 12

Callie sprayed another corner of the living room window with lemon-scented Windex then wiped it down with a fistful of paper towels. She might not be valuable to Jack outside, but at least she could help him inside and clean the house. The layer of dust suggested he didn't waste much time cleaning, so she wasn't sure how much he'd appreciate her efforts. Still, cleaning kept her safe and kept her busy. She'd spent almost two hours polishing his furniture.

And now, all the downstairs windows were clean. Time to head up. Tossing her paper towels, spray bottle, and a few rags into her bucket, she went straight to the window at the top of the stairs. She needed a few pumps of the bottle to cut through the grime, but she didn't mind. Once she was satisfied the remaining spots were on the outside of the window, she turned toward Jack's room. Going there next made sense, but the metal staircase in the middle of the hallway grabbed her attention.

When was the last time she'd taken a minute to enjoy the view from the lantern tower? With everything else going on, she hadn't even thought of those steps since she'd been home. Leaving her bucket on the floor, Callie grabbed both handrails. She swiveled to the left as she side-stepped her way up the steep, narrow stairs.

Hot, stuffy air enveloped her as she stepped into the cupola. She squinted in the light. Sweat beaded on her shoulders and rolled down her back where sunlight kissed her body. Callie flipped two locks and cranked open a window.

She sucked in a fresh breath as Mother Nature performed for her. Sunlight danced across the surface of the water. Seagulls glided through the air. Birds twittered and chirped as the waves kept time. Even the chatter of the tourists added a syncopated, dissonant harmony. Callie closed her eyes to absorb the song. Soon her fingers started their own dance as her mind set Dvorak's *Romance* to the tempo of the waves, and her hands played through the piece on their own.

One. Two. Three bars.

With each imagined note, her body relaxed. Her mind calmed. Playing the piano was way more effective than chocolate. When she opened her eyes, blues and greens stretched out around her as far as she could see. As a child, she was sure she would be able to see the Upper Peninsula from the top of the lighthouse, but she'd underestimated the grandeur of the bay. Or maybe she'd overestimated her own size and abilities.

Not just the expanse of the bay prevented her from seeing, though. A decade's worth of dirt had layered itself on the glass. Stepping quickly down the stairs, Callie returned with her supplies and doused the panes. One section at a time, the view sharpened. As she wiped away the impurities, the colors brightened. The view hadn't changed, but her perspective did. How much clearer would it be after she cleaned the outsides of the windows?

"Cal? Where are you?" Jack's muffled voice reached her.

She retreated a few steps to yell down. "Up here."

"Why?"

"Cleaning windows."

"Why?"

She sighed. "Why not? What else am I supposed to do?"

"Put your shoes on and meet me outside. We've got work to do."

Callie nearly slid down the steps in her excitement to get to work. Jack wasn't giving up on her! She rushed down to the main level, emerging in Jack's office. She left the bucket of supplies on his desk before pulling on her tennis shoes. By the time she made it outside, Jack was climbing into his truck. She climbed in beside him, and they were off.

The wind tossed her hair around, but Callie didn't mind. She was on her way to work, which was all she wanted. As they continued to drive, Dvorak's music continued to play in her head, providing an unconventional soundtrack for the trip.

"What song are you playing?"

"What?" She looked at Jack, a little unnerved that he had read her mind.

He pointed at her left hand. "Your fingers are moving. You've been playing air piano since you were a kid."

Callie smiled. "Dvorak's *Romance.*"

"Is that the piano and violin song you played at your graduation thing?"

"Yes. I'm impressed you remember."

"It's hard to be related to you and not learn a few things about classical piano music."

"You did come to all of my recitals."

He shrugged. "It wasn't my favorite music, but I wanted to support you. You always seemed like you enjoyed it."

"I did. I do, actually." Nothing helped her calm down as well as playing a few songs. Closing her eyes and letting her fingers move in their memorized patterns. She could use some of that calm. Maybe Jack could help her make it happen. "Do you have access to Mom and Dad's storage unit?"

"Yep."

"Is the piano in there?"

"And all of the other furniture they promised you. Don't you have a key? It's all your stuff."

"I have it someplace."

He sighed. "Cal—"

"I know, I know. You can lecture me about losing keys later. Do you think there's room in the lighthouse for the piano?"

Her brother snorted. "Are you kidding me? Even if we could fit it through the front door, and if we could somehow squeeze it through the dining room, where would we put a piano? Do you want me to get rid of my desk or the couch?"

Callie slouched in her seat. "You're probably right. I was just wishing I could play. I've never gone three months without playing."

"What about that electronic piano you have?"

"It's not the same. The digital keyboard sounds okay but doesn't have the same feel. Besides, I locked it in my storage unit in Alma. I didn't think I'd need it." As she said the words, she realized her fingers were once again tapping out chord progressions on her thighs.

"Why do you need a piano? Did you find a job playing for someone?"

"No, I just wanted to clear my head."

"Nothing else will work?"

She shrugged. "Chocolate isn't working. Sometimes it helps to go for a drive, but my fingers are antsy."

Jack nodded. "I get it. Sometimes I just need to build something."

"Maybe you could teach me to—"

"No."

"It would give me something to do with my hands."

"Like cut them off? No."

"I guess I could call the local churches. Maybe someone would let me stop by and play. Before I bought my keyboard, there was a church in Alma that let me use one of their pianos. I had to volunteer to play with their choir, but at least I could practice. I guess it wouldn't matter if I went to a different church for a few weeks."

Jack sighed again, and she could almost hear him rolling his eyes. "I'll see what I can do about getting the piano out to the house."

"Really?"

"Don't mention it. Let's just focus on the job, okay?"

Jack turned off the two-lane road and pulled into the small parking lot. Though the mid-morning sun was already warm, the park was still quiet, which he'd expected on a weekday morning. These were the days he loved the most, when he could tend to acres of parklands with only the birds, the breeze, and the bay to bother him. He parked his truck near the pavilion at Archie Park and admired the shoreline view.

Callie jumped out of the truck and walked around to his side, yammering about something.

If only it were just him, the birds, and the bay.

"Thanks again for letting me work with you today. Honestly, I was a little nervous about being on my own outside."

He pointed at her arm. "Are you keeping that clean?"

She rolled her eyes. "Yes, Dad. I actually like putting a wet cloth on it. Helps with the itching."

"When are you getting the stitches removed?"

Callie shook her head. "Don't have to. They dissolve on their own. You have me all day."

Jack twisted the steering wheel in his hand. "Fabulous." Maybe she'd stay out of trouble if he stayed within helping distance. They'd worked well together in the past. There was no reason to think they couldn't do it again.

"So, what are we doing today?"

"Repairs." He slid out of the truck and let her close the door behind him.

She followed him across the driveway to the long wooden building. "What are we fixing?"

He unlocked the old barn doors. "Everything. The family who rented the park yesterday had too much fun. I took a few complaint calls but couldn't get out here until today." With a little effort, he pushed the giant sliding door out of the way. It creaked in protest.

"Holy cow!"

"Yeah." Jack walked around the rectangular building and unlocked the other door. It groaned along its track as he slid it open. Callie stood in the doorway across from him, her face twisted as she scanned the pavilion. Somewhere beneath the piles of garbage were a solid concrete floor and ten pine picnic tables. Glassless windows lined the top portions of most of the walls. Normally, he'd open them for the extra sunlight, but even the lightest breeze would swirl through the building and scatter the trash. Better to wait until he got the mess cleaned up, so it didn't spread to the farthest corners. How could anyone leave so much junk without even bagging it up?

Counting to ten, he stood beside his sister and checked for broken tables. He spotted three. Park signs littered the ground. Empty beer and soda cans jostled in the breeze. The scent of spoiled food wafted around them.

Callie stepped inside. "I hope you got a deposit."

"Yeah, me too."

She looked at him, eyes wide. "You didn't get a deposit?"

"Commissioner's friends. I'm not sure what they collected, if they collected anything." Jack watched a mouse dive under a plate. "But I'll make sure they get the bill." He walked up to stand beside his sister, crossing his arms while he calculated the damage.

She kicked a can that had rolled against her foot. "Where do we start?"

"We've got to clean up before we know what else needs to be done."

Callie nodded. "Why don't I do that? I can't get into too much trouble bagging garbage."

He nodded. "I'll get you some gloves and garbage bags." Some clear liquid dripped off the nearest picnic table and splashed in a puddle below it. "And some industrial strength cleaner."

Stacey squinted against the early afternoon sun. If she had been able to find her sunglasses, she wouldn't have almost clipped that mailbox, but she was already late and didn't want Jack to have to wait for her. When she finally pulled into Archie Park, she checked the clock. Only ten minutes later than expected.

She parked next to Jack's truck and had barely turned off the engine before she was out the door and walking toward the pavilion. Her pulse quickened with each step. She hoped Jack wouldn't mind the new delivery girl.

"Stacey!" Callie popped out from behind a post. "What are you doing here?"

Stacey raised the white paper bag. "Delivering lunch."

Callie's eyebrows slid up her forehead. "Did Jack order from the grocery store?"

"No. There's a sandwich shop not far from here. A friend of mine owns it, and I was helping him out today."

"You're a delivery driver too?"

"Not usually, but when I saw that Jack had placed an order, I volunteered."

Jack stepped into the pavilion through the opposite door. "Is there anybody in Traverse City you don't help?"

She shook her head. "It was just for a few hours. Your delivery is actually my last job for the day."

"Last job at the deli or last job all day?" he asked, walking toward her. Her pulse surged faster than it should have for a girl in her good health. He stopped in front of her. When his arm reached for her, she gasped. Jack gave her a strange glance before taking the bag from her clutched fingers.

"Your lunch." Her ears nearly burned off her head. "I'm sorry. You must be starving. I hope you don't mind, but I brought out a sandwich for myself."

"Of course, we don't mind." Callie grabbed a sandwich from Jack and plopped herself on a table top. "If you're done for the day, you're welcome to hang out here and keep me company. Jack's not much of a conversationalist."

Stacey looked at Jack, waiting for him to approve the invitation, but he was busy unwrapping his sandwich. Callie ripped hers open, then winced. Jack sighed as he offered her his. After they swapped sandwiches, he sat next to Callie on the tabletop, took a bite, then finally looked at Stacey.

She hadn't meant to stare, but she wasn't sure yet if she was welcome to stay.

Jack shrugged. "We'll be working, but you can stay." He took another bite, forcing bread and meat into his cheeks until they bulged. "You don't have to do anything."

Stacey beamed. "I can help. I've got some work clothes in my car. Let me just get changed."

Jack shook his head, visibly forcing his food down his throat. "You don't have to work."

"No, it's okay. I have to go to my car anyway. I forgot your drinks."

CHAPTER 13

When Stacey returned, Jack wondered if a dying man had ever refused a lifesaving sip of water. Not that he didn't want the water. It was the blue-eyed blonde in the black shorts and peach golf shirt. No one should look that cute in an ugly uniform, but she did. That bothered him.

Stacey disappeared for five minutes before she bounced back into the pavilion with another bag and a gigantic smile. She'd changed into jean shorts and a faded t-shirt. Her hair was in a ponytail. She looked even cuter, dang it.

"Sorry, I forgot to bring these over." She sat on the other side of Callie. "I hope they aren't too warm."

He took the first bottle she offered. "It's fine."

"So..." She snapped open a soda. "What can I do to help?"

"I'm almost done sanitizing everything, then I have to apply another coat of something to the picnic tables," said Callie. "Jack thinks it's the safest job for me." She offered up her arm for Stacey's inspection.

Stacey laughed. The cheerful sound grated on Jack's nerves.

He chugged a mouthful of water, then picked up his sandwich. "Why don't you two work together? Let me know when you finish, and I'll find something else for you to do."

They nodded, then turned toward each other. Callie started talking, and it didn't take long for them to settle into a giddy discourse about sandwiches and cleaning supplies. Jack relaxed, knowing they would keep each other occupied for hours, maybe long enough to finish out the day. He didn't care if their chatter slowed them down, so long as they left him alone.

An hour later, Jack smiled when he heard Callie telling the story of the first time she had used a nail gun. Thanks to her, there was a row of shingles on his parents' garage that would survive a typhoon.

"Argh!"

The familiar sound of Callie in pain sliced through the air. Jack dropped his tape measure and ran into the pavilion, his heart racing. Ignoring Stacey, he ran right for his sister. "What happened?"

Callie sat on the ground rocking back and forth while she squeezed her left forearm.

The air stalled in his chest, pressed down by an undetermined amount of anxiety. "Again?"

She nodded, her breaths hissing between her teeth.

"It's my fault," Stacey said, mopping up a puddle of green liquid. "I swung the bucket and hit Callie's arm. I spilled cleaner everywhere."

The anxiety eased, and Jack exhaled. Nothing debilitating. He carefully cupped Callie's injured arm, not wasting a second before pulling the saturated gauze away from her wound. She turned her head, squeezing her eyes shut.

Blood oozed around the nylon stitching. Jack quickly scanned for a clean rag, but Callie had done a good job emptying the place. He doubted he'd find anything, much less something quasi-sanitary. Looping his thumb through a hole at the bottom of his shirt, he pulled. Cotton ripped. He slid the pocketknife off of his belt and cut off the edge of his shirt. It couldn't be any dirtier than anything he'd find in his truck.

Callie sucked in a deep breath. "Do I need new stitches?"

Jack grabbed her bottled water and dumped it over her arm. The blood washed away quickly, leaving thin pink trails over her skin. He dabbed the cut with his shirt. "No, they look okay. You might have pulled them a little, but you don't need to go back to the hospital. If I were you, I'd give this a good clean and wrap it again with a fresh bandage."

Stacey leaned over Jack's shoulder. "I'm so sorry."

Callie shook her head. "It's not your fault."

"Yeah. She would have found a way to do it to herself eventually." Jack laughed. He stood up, and Stacey backed away from him, then he caught the scent of vanilla. Figured that she would smell like dessert.

Callie reached up for some assistance. "I might have avoided injury." He grabbed her stable arm and pulled her up. She took his shirt scrap and wrapped it around her stitches. "I'll run home and take care of this. I should be back in about an hour."

Not if he could help it. Jack crossed his arms. "I don't think so."

Callie blinked. "I guess, I mean, well … I could try to make it back faster, but there have been a lot of cyclists on the peninsula this week. It'll probably take me twenty minutes to get home. Then I have to clean up, wrap my arm, change clothes—"

"Whoa." Jack help up a hand. Leave it to his sister to turn yard work into a fashion show. "Why do you have to change clothes?"

Her eyeballs nearly popped out of her head. "Because you dumped water on me." Jack followed Callie's gaze toward her legs. Yep. A giant wet spot, right on her shorts. "I can come back after I change, but it'll be another twenty minutes. That already puts us at an hour. I'll hurry, but I don't think I can do it much faster than that."

"I don't want you to hurry back. I want you to take the afternoon off."

"What?" She looked at him as if he'd just suggested she join the circus. That emotion didn't last long before Confused Callie turned into Confrontational Callie. Anchoring her feet and clenching her jaw, she looked so much like their mother. Jack braced himself for the same kind of stubbornness. "No."

"Yes."

"Jack—"

"Callie."

"Jackson!" She stomped her foot.

He sighed. "Calista."

They stared at each other. Not their greatest argument ever, but it served its purpose. He didn't want to upset Callie, but he also didn't want her to hurt herself again. Then again, she was an adult. She could decide what she wanted to do. He just needed to figure out a way to make her want to do something different.

Vanilla.

The scent pierced through the stink of the pavilion as Stacey tried to sneak behind him. It might have worked if he wasn't so aware of her presence, which suddenly delighted him. "You're right." He tucked his hands into his pockets. "You didn't work yesterday afternoon. You should at least finish out today."

Callie's posture eased. "Really?"

Stacey stopped her non-discreet desertion.

"Yep. I'm paying you to work. You should work."

Callie smiled.

He would never understand women.

"Thank you." She let her arms relax. "I can do this, I know it. I just don't want to disappoint you."

"I know, Squirt. And I don't want you to spend your entire vacation working. I just thought that, since Stacey's here, you might want to cut out early and go ..." Where? Did he have to suggest something? Jack raked his brain for ideas. "Well, you could go do ... girl stuff together."

There was that weird look again, except this time Stacey swung around and gave it to him too.

He looked between them. "What?"

Callie raised an eyebrow.

He waited.

She narrowed her eyes, studying him.

Stacey giggled.

Both Stevenses looked at her.

"Oh, don't mind me. This is fascinating. I don't have an older brother, and I always wondered how it worked." She nodded. "Go on."

When had he gone from being a caring older brother to afternoon entertainment? The longer Jack stood there, the less he cared what his sister did. He just needed to get back to work. There were plenty of jobs to fill the afternoon, with or without Callie. She could—

Callie erupted with laughter.

He stepped away. "Are you okay?"

"I'm fine." She looked at Stacey. "I wouldn't exactly consider this fascinating, but I can see how it's entertaining."

Back to that again. Jack glanced at the little blonde as she smiled, tilting her head to look up at him. He fought it, but the corner of his mouth popped up. She giggled again. A chuckle rumbled in his chest.

"I'm sorry you had to witness this." He waved a finger between himself and Callie, "but I'm glad we could amuse you."

"Me too, but I really should take care of this." Callie grabbed her arm.

Jack pulled the truck key out of his pocket. Had they actually agreed on something? "I expect you back in an hour." He tossed her the key. She managed to catch it.

"An hour." She smiled. He forced it. She rolled her eyes. "And I'll bring some extra clothes, just in case Stacey and I want to leave early to do girl things. Don't run off without me."

Heat coursed through his veins as Callie walked away. He'd never run off with Stacey. Not without her permission, of course. Not that he wanted her permission to run off with him. He'd never even thought about that until Callie had to mention it.

Great. Stacey's hair, eyes, and smile already distracted him. Now, he wouldn't be able to eat vanilla ice cream or drive around without thinking about her.

He needed to refocus. The busted siding wasn't going to fix itself. Grateful for the distraction, Jack headed back outside.

Stacey jumped in front of him and smiled. "I'll help out until Callie gets back."

This was not the kind of distraction he needed.

After circling around the park for ten minutes, Stacey finally found Jack at the farthest end of the pavilion, hanging trim. "I'm done cleaning." She looked up at him, into his intense eyes. Captivating eyes. Beautiful eyes. There was something else she wanted to tell him. Something brown? No, that was the color of his eyes.

"Thanks, but you really don't need to stay. Go on home."

"That's okay, I don't mind. Besides, Callie should be here soon. We might actually take you up on your offer and go do something."

Jack scrubbed his hands over his face. Great. She'd be spending more time with his sister. "Stacey—"

"Jack." She jammed her fists onto her hips. She might not have a big brother, but she certainly understood Callie's frustration with hers. "You helped me plant Grandma Luce's garden, put a new starter in my car, taught me how to change my oil, and helped me with Chloe's drywall. The least I can do is fill in for Callie until she gets here." Stacey looked at her watch. "That's only thirty minutes."

"I can handle the work. I expected this sort of thing."

Stacey's arms dropped to her sides. "You expected this? You thought she'd dump soap on her stitches?"

"No. I expected her to miss a lot of work."

"Then why did you hire her?"

He shrugged. "She's my sister. I needed help. She wanted to spend the summer here."

"But you don't really want her to help?"

Jack smiled. "Callie has amazing musical coordination. She can play a dozen different instruments better than I could ever play one, but her brain malfunctions when you put a tool in her hand. She gouged her arm out with a wire brush. A *wire brush*."

Stacey tried to imagine that one but couldn't. Maybe Jack had a point. "So, why don't you tell her you don't need help?"

"I can't. I spent a *lot* of time praying about this—a lot—and I knew I was supposed to hire her, at least part-time. I hired someone else to do the actual work that needs to be done."

"Does she know that?"

"No, and she doesn't need to." He picked up the nail gun.

"So, you're lying to your sister?" That didn't seem very brotherly.

Jack pressed the gun against the thin piece of wood but didn't pull the trigger. "I guess. I hadn't thought about it that way." BAM! BAM!

"Why don't you just tell her the truth?"

"I didn't think it mattered." He let the gun drop, swinging his arm back as he looked down at Stacey. "She knows her own faults. I don't need to point them out. Besides, I never told her she was my only assistant. She's getting paid for the work that she does. So's the other guy. I just don't have to follow him around everywhere."

"Oh." That seemed sort of brotherly. Stacey just stood there, partly because she didn't know what else to do, and partly because she didn't want to move. For the briefest moment, she thought she smelled something fresh and soapy, but her nostrils still stung from industrial-strength cleaner fumes.

Though she could stand there all day enjoying Jack's company, even if they were both sweaty messes, Stacey started to squirm under Jack's steady gaze. "Is there anything else you'd like me to do?"

Jack shook his head. "Callie should be back soon, so you don't need to start any major projects, but you'd save me some time if you emptied the trash containers and checked the bathrooms."

"You got it, boss."

He nodded.

They looked at each other.

Jack swung around and pressed the nail gun to the wood.

BAM! BAM! BAM!

Stacey sighed. Garbage and toilets. That would keep her mind from wandering. She headed toward the nearest trashcan.

"Stacey?"

She spun, her heart anxious.

He nodded. "You're just about the nicest person I've ever met."

Heat. Heat and disbelief coursed through her arms and legs. "I, um ... ah ..."

"I just thought you should know."

He turned around before she could reply.

BAM! BAM!

Collecting garbage had never been so much fun.

CHAPTER 14

Ryan tapped his brakes. His side mirror bounced against the door. Reaching through the open window, he grabbed the limp accessory as he stopped the car. The current repairs were going to cost him enough. He didn't need to do any more damage.

He cut the engine and climbed out, trying not to look at the crippled front end. He hadn't even shut the door before Jack came trudging out of the garage, some type of carving tool in his hands. Ryan fell into step beside him, happy to get as far away from the disaster as possible.

"What are we doing for dinner?" Jack asked.

Ryan unbuttoned his collar. "Why do you always ask me that? I never care."

"I know, but since I make you cook most the time, I figure it's polite to ask. See, I listen to you. Using my manners."

"Call Emily Post."

"Is that a new client? Oh wait, this isn't the right size." Jack stopped and spun around. He was sure to notice the Jeep.

Ryan took bigger steps. Maybe he'd make it inside before—

"What happened to the Jeep?"

Or not. Ryan rolled his neck, loosening his shoulders before Jack dumped a colossal lecture on him. He turned to confront the mess. "It's nothing."

"Your bumper and quarter panel are smashed, and the mirror is hanging on by a wire. Literally."

"Yeah, I noticed."

"You okay?"

"I'm fine, it's just the Jeep."

BEEP! BEEP! BEEP!

A shiny yellow Mini Cooper whipped into the parking lot.

Ryan groaned. Not now.

"You know the Mini?"

"Missy Tate. She's the accountant in the office next to mine."

The driver's door swung open. A poof of yellowish hair popped out thirty seconds before the rest of her. She waved, her pink claws flashing in the sun. Missy wobbled across the parking lot on shiny high-heeled shoes. Only the gray suit implied any sort of professionalism.

Jack strolled toward Ryan. "What's she doing here?"

"I have no idea."

"Do I need to be here?"

"For what?"

"I don't know. She looks ..."

"Intimidating?"

"Plastic."

Ryan stifled a laugh. "She's smart. Be nice."

"Hey, Ryan!" Missy tiptoed over, bringing her cloud of perfume with her.

The heavy scent surrounded him, immune to the breeze. "Hi, Missy. What are you doing out here?"

"I was on a conference call in my office when I saw that jerk sideswipe your car. Since I couldn't run out after him, I wrote down his license plate number for you." She smiled at him, holding out a piece of paper.

Ryan stared at the number, conveniently written on a personalized note pad that included Missy's email and phone number. "Thanks, but you could have just called."

"That's okay. I didn't mind the drive." She stuck a hand out toward Jack. "I'm Melissa Tate."

"Jack Stevens." He shook her hand

"The lighthouse keeper?"

"Park supervisor is more accurate, but yeah."

"That's so interesting. Ryan keeps telling me he'll give me a tour, but this is the first time I've been out here." She flashed a smile between the men.

Jack slapped a hand on Ryan's shoulder. "Since you drove all the way out here, why doesn't he show you around now?"

No way. Ryan stuffed the paper in his pocket. "I should probably take care of this first."

Missy's smile faltered. "I could wait until you're done, in case you have any questions about what I saw."

"No, thanks. It could take a while. You've already driven this far. I'd hate to keep you here longer."

"I don't mind. I have some free time tonight."

Yes, she was a good accountant, but obviously not as smart as Ryan had thought. They stood there staring at each other. He suddenly understood how a deer felt in the crosshairs.

"You know, I could show you around." Jack stepped up. "I know more about the lighthouse than Ryan does, anyway."

"That's true." Lighthouse keeper, park superintendent, superhero best friend. Ryan's shoulders finally relaxed. "I'll go take care of this while you show her around. Thanks again, Missy."

Jack smacked Ryan's back again. "Can't wait for dinner."

Ryan stirred the Hamburger Helper. Grilled burgers would have been better, but he could still hear Missy outside. Man, that woman couldn't take a hint. By the time Jack walked in, Ryan was dishing up dinner.

Jack took his bowl. "Not exactly what I was expecting."

"I never claimed to be June Cleaver."

"Another client?"

"Just eat."

They took their bowls into the living room and sank onto the couch. Jack grabbed the remote and flipped to ESPN. "What did the cops say about the license plate?"

"I didn't call."

"Why not?"

"I'd already talked to the police before I knew who hit me, and I've already called my insurance company. There's no reason to get anyone else involved."

Jack muted the TV. "Someone else already is involved. He hit your car. You need to call that in."

"Thanks, but I've got this under control. I've got full coverage. I'm fine." Ryan stole the remote and changed the channel.

Jack actually backed off. Finally, someone who could take a hint. Ryan turned up the volume and focused on his dinner.

"What's the deal with that girl?"

"Missy?" Ryan shrugged. "She's just my office neighbor."

"She asked a million questions about you."

"I hope you lied."

"What?" Jack grabbed the remote and the noise died. "What's wrong with you?"

"Let it go."

"Your Jeep's a wreck, and you just asked me to lie for you. Not the time to let it go. What's up with you?"

"Nothing. I'm not in the mood for a lecture."

"Who's lecturing?"

Ryan laughed. "It's coming."

"Fine, then forget it." Jack reclaimed the remote. ESPN flipped back on, loud and distracting. They finished their dinner while baseball highlights flashed across the screen.

The sportscasters bantered, but the silence in the living room grated on Ryan. Stupid conscience. "There's nothing to tell. Missy keeps throwing herself at me. I'm not interested."

"Tell her."

"I don't want to embarrass her. Maybe she's just being friendly."

"She drove twenty-five miles to give you a license plate number."

"She'll figure it out eventually."

"And you have to call the cops about the Jeep."

"I thought we'd moved on."

"We can't. You're being stupid."

"Mature."

"You suck at confrontation."

"You're confronting me now, and I'm not avoiding it."

Jack snorted. "Yeah, I'm confronting you while you hide from Accounting Barbie and won't turn in a criminal."

"I'm not hiding from anyone. There's no need to hurt her feelings or get someone else into trouble."

"He hit your Jeep!"

"Yeah, and it'll cost him to get his fixed. My insurance will cover mine. It's fine."

"You know, you're confusing politeness with pushoverness."

"That's not even a word."

"You know what I mean." Jack jumped off the couch, his spoon and bowl clanging in his hand. "Maybe I'm rude sometimes, but at least I know when to step up to the plate."

Ryan's pulse surged. "If I need to, I will."

"Whatever. Someday you'll want something bad enough that you'll break your stupid rules."

The jerk left before Ryan could respond. Not necessarily a bad thing, since Ryan didn't know how to respond. Polite reason obviously didn't work, so he reached across the couch and took back the remote. He had the news back on by the time Jack returned with another full bowl.

"The game starts in ten."

"The news will be over by then."

Jack dropped onto the couch, laughing.

"Now what?"

"I'm glad you can stand up to someone. I just don't know why it always has to be me."

CHAPTER 15

For the second day in a row, Callie didn't die. She didn't even hurt herself. With Jack by her side, she survived another day on the job. Dinner with Kyle was the perfect way to celebrate her productivity.

She stood in front of the mirror examining her outfit. It wasn't quite right. Something about the cut of the shirt? She tugged at the hem, then the neckline. That didn't work. Was it the skirt? Maybe she should just change. And what about her hair? Callie pushed her fingers through it, pulling it out, then up. Her stomach clenched. Nothing helped.

Of all the days not to drop a hammer on her foot. Why couldn't she have gotten hurt today? Then she'd have an excuse for her appearance or being late ... or canceling. Nervous energy rolled in her stomach. Callie leaned against the wall and breathed. In through the nose, out through the mouth. She needed a few minutes at the piano to work off her nerves.

Not that she had anything to be nervous about. It was just dinner with Kyle. Nothing she hadn't done before.

Although a night at home suddenly didn't sound too bad either. She could watch some TV. With Ryan. Her nerves jumped, but in a different way. It wasn't a way she wanted to think about while getting ready for dinner with Kyle.

Someone knocked. "Cal?" Jack poked his head in through the open bedroom door.

She looked at his reflection in the mirror. "Yeah?"

"You good?"

"I think so. Why?" She looked down at her clothes, then back at her brother. "Be honest. Is this a bad outfit? I don't know if I should change the whole thing, or maybe just the shirt? Maybe I should reschedule."

Jack took a step back, eyes wide. "So, you're not good then?"

"I don't know." Callie tugged at the hem of her shirt. "I'm a little nervous, that's all. Did you want something?"

"There's a couple of breadsticks left. Do you want one?"

Callie stopped adjusting her clothes. "So, it's not a bad outfit? Do you think I need a breadstick?"

"Well ... do you want one?"

Did she? It was hard to tell if her clenching gut was hunger or nerves. A snack shouldn't hurt though. She hoped. Maybe half a stick.

Jack rolled his eyes and walked away. "If you ever decide, they're in the kitchen."

She ran after him. "Sorry. I was thinking. Thanks for the offer."

Jack dropped into his arm chair and picked up a magazine. "You're welcome."

She dropped onto the arm of the sofa. "I don't know why I'm so nervous."

"Uh-huh."

"It's Kyle, you know. I think I'm just expecting him to be mad, to let me have it. I would deserve it."

"Uh-huh."

Callie watched Jack flip through a *Sports Illustrated*. His preoccupation didn't deter her.

"Do you think this is a good idea?"

He flipped another page.

She flicked the cover.

Jack dropped the magazine on his lap. "I'm too tired for this, Cal. Just tell me what's going on, because I won't figure it out."

She leaned forward. "Do you think this is a good idea? Me going out with Kyle? I mean, every time I think about Traverse City, I think of Kyle. But we already ended this once. And I don't think it was a coincidence that I felt like moving back here after I stopped seeing Mike. I just keep wondering if I made a mistake with Kyle. Why else would I be here? And what if I'm overthinking things again?"

Jack smacked her knee with his magazine. "It's just dinner, Cal. Don't read into it. Enjoy it."

"What if—"

"Cal." He leaned toward her.

She leaned a little closer, studying his face, searching every feature for some type of assurance. He smiled. "You've already made the plans. Just eat dinner and come home."

Eat and run. Callie nodded. "I can do that." Her stomach growled.

"And eat a breadstick."

"I can do that too." She stood up. "No more overreacting. Or overthinking." A car door slammed. She jumped. "Is it ever quiet out here?"

"Only in the winter." Jack opened his magazine. "You've got a long drive into town, Squirt. You might want to take two breadsticks."

"Good idea." Callie picked a pillow off the couch and threw it at her brother. "And don't call me Squirt."

Callie stood outside of the restaurant and prayed like a toddler—wild and with no clear direction. Maybe she shouldn't have eaten that last breadstick. Now, her unsettled stomach clenched around a giant lump of processed dough. That would be enough to make her queasy on a good day.

Ugh. Kyle always ran late. Maybe she had time to run to the store for some Tums. She checked her watch.

"Sorry I'm late."

Callie's heart dropped onto the doughy mass. Kyle stood in front of her, gorgeous in khaki pants and a crisp, blue button-down shirt. Way more casual than her. She smiled. "You're not that late." Not by his standards. By Kyle Standard Time, he was still ten minutes early.

"But I'm still late, and I shouldn't be. I've been doing better about being on time. I know how much that used to annoy you." Kyle gave her half a grin then offered his arm. "Ready to eat?"

"Of course." She wrapped her hand around his biceps, letting him lead her into the restaurant. They got their table, ordered, and were nibbling on appetizers before Callie's nerves started to settle down. Kyle's words finally began to register.

He popped a brie-smeared cracker into his mouth, then leaned back in his chair. "So, how long are you in town?"

Callie licked a crumb from her lip. "Through August. School starts after Labor Day, so I need to be back before then."

Kyle nodded. He twirled a shiny butter knife between his fingers. "Still teaching downstate?"

"Yeah." Callie dropped her hands in her lap. She tapped out Rachmaninoff as she struggled to relax. "I've got a great gig at an elementary school. I get to teach instrumental classes to the older kids while my colleague does all of the singing with the little kids."

"You don't like singing kids?"

Callie laughed. "Everyone likes singing kids but teaching them is something entirely different."

Kyle smiled at her. The waitress leaned in to refill her water glass. It was a good time to get to the point, but where to start? How've you been? How's the family? Did you miss me? I think you're the reason I'm back in town?

Before she could decide on a topic, Kyle set down the knife. "Why'd you call me?"

Her heart skipped. "Why?"

"Yeah. I haven't heard from you in almost three years. Why now?"

The restaurant chatter echoed in Callie's ears as she struggled to find the words. "Well ..." The woman next to them complained about her husband's spending habits. The couple behind her read the menu to each other, struggling over unusual words. And somewhere nearby, someone cackled loud enough to interrupt every other conversation in the room.

Every conversation except hers. Kyle politely watched her, his hands clasped on the table.

"Well ... I wanted to see you."

A waiter carried something sizzling and savory past their table. Callie's stomach moaned. She reached for another piece of goat cheese.

Kyle's fingers wrapped around hers. A shiver rippled up her arm.

"Help me out," he said, adjusting his gentle grip. "You left with no real explanation. I mean, I'm happy to see you, but I need to know. Why did you call me?"

Callie studied Kyle. There was no fire in his eyes. No anger in his voice or his touch. He was as calm as he'd been earlier in the week. The only thing she saw was confusion. She had prepared herself for yelling. This hurt just as much. "I'm so sorry. Some things happened that made me realize I didn't like how I ended things. We spent a lot of our lives together, and then it was just over. I didn't handle that well, and I'm sorry."

Kyle squeezed her fingers. "Thank you." He released her hand.

Disappointment replaced his touch, but relief also lifted her spirit. At least he didn't hate her. They were okay ... ish. That was good enough for her. Maybe it was time to open up. "I felt like God was calling me home this summer, so I called Jack for a place to stay," Callie said. "The more I thought about coming home, the more I thought about you."

Kyle froze.

"I mean," Callie cleared her throat. "I wanted to apologize to you for how I left. It was selfish and immature, but I also wanted to see you again. We have a lot of history. I guess …"

Kyle leaned forward, his brows cinched together.

The waitress reported that their food would be out soon.

What was Callie supposed to do now? This was the part of planning that she hated. The variable. Not knowing made her anxious. She grabbed another piece of cheese.

Kyle pushed the plate toward her. "Still eating when you're upset?"

"I'm not upset." She stuffed the cheese into her mouth, then followed it with a cracker. "Just thinking."

"Trying to figure everything out?"

She nodded.

"Why don't we just eat dinner and not worry about it?"

She sighed. "I've been telling myself that all day, but then my brain kicks in. I tried to prepare for this, but it's not really going how I'd planned, so I'm not sure what to do now."

Kyle chuckled. "How much chocolate have you eaten?"

"Just a bag of M&Ms."

He cocked an eyebrow.

"It might have been a large bag of M&Ms."

Another layer of anxiety washed away as Kyle smiled at her, and they enjoyed a moment of comfortable silence.

Their food arrived, and Callie savored every moment of the entrée and the company. Three years of separation faded into a memory as they caught up on everything from work to family.

"Jack didn't tell me I'd be living with him and Ryan," Callie said as the waitress cleared their plates. "After being on my own for three years, this is an adjustment."

Kyle smiled. "I miss those guys."

"Before this week, when was the last time you saw them?"

"We've seen each other around town, but I haven't talked with either of them since a few weeks after we broke up." He leaned back against his chair. "It was a little awkward."

Because of her. "I'm sorry."

He shrugged. "I had no idea why you left. The last thing I wanted to do was call your brother to talk about it. I didn't know what you'd told him."

"Didn't you ever run into each other at church?"

Kyle chuckled, but the sound caught in his throat. "I know it's juvenile, but I *really* didn't want to confront either of them at church, so I, ah …"

Joined a cult? Lost faith? Callie held her breath.

"I switched churches." He shifted in his seat.

"Oh, well, that's not a big deal." And totally something she would do. "You don't have to be embarrassed about it."

"I'm not. It's more that I'm disappointed in myself. I shouldn't have been so concerned about what might happen. I acted childishly."

Someone bumped into Callie's chair, but she ignored it, intrigued by Kyle's obvious discomfort at having distanced himself from her brother. She'd never seen him so unsettled. It tugged at her heart, but also surprised her senses. They'd known each other since their freshmen year in high school, and she was still getting to know him. "Did you think Jack was going to beat you up in the sanctuary? Then again, we are talking about Jack."

Kyle sighed. "I wasn't going to tell you." The corners of her lips popped up even as she willed herself to stop smiling. He pointed at her mouth. "*That* is why. I know. It's ridiculous. I just didn't know what else to do. Jack and Ryan are pretty intimidating."

"Intimidating?" Callie laughed. "That's not a word I would use to describe them."

"Well, you've never been the boy who asked you out. Trust me. They can intimidate."

"The boy who asked me out? What do you mean?"

"You didn't know?" Kyle cocked his head.

"Obviously not." A mixture of emotions bubbled up inside. Callie didn't know which one to grab on to. "What happened?"

"They cornered me after our first date. I was still in the driveway."

Anger pushed past all of Callie's emotions and reached the surface first. "They did what?"

"They told me to be careful, suggested that I pray about it, and told me you were a princess who deserved to be treated like one. Then they told me horrible stories of people who disrespected royalty. I especially liked the one about the German monk who spent his life doing hard labor for not opening the door for a young queen. I haven't been able to verify that one."

Heat radiated from Callie's face and neck. If she had known about it years ago, she still would have been humiliated. Thank goodness for small favors. "I'm going to pummel them. Both of them."

"It wasn't that bad, Cal."

"You didn't deserve that. I am so sorry."

"Don't be. It's not your fault." Kyle shrugged. "They were just looking out for you."

"That's very kind of you. I'm sure they'll appreciate your understanding after I'm done with them." A waitress walked by, and Callie tapped her on the arm. It wasn't their waitress, but she didn't care. "I'm going to need a dessert menu, please. Quickly."

"Don't be mad at them, Cal. I might have done the same thing if I had a little sister."

"Maybe. I get Jack, but what's Ryan's excuse?"

Kyle chuckled. "He's always had a soft spot for you."

The dessert menu arrived, but Callie ignored it. Ryan had a soft spot for her?

It was definitely time for some chocolate cake.

CHAPTER 16

Finally. It was just Jack and Ryan at the lighthouse, and a dozen or so tourists. Time for the talk. Ryan made his way to the garage where Jack stood at his workbench. Ryan took a long, deep breath. "What would you say if I asked Callie out?"

Jack paused. "Out where?"

"On a date."

Jack put a chisel in his toolbox. Something in there must have grabbed his attention, because he was suddenly interested in organizing every nut and bolt. Ryan waited as Jack dawdled. Finally, the metal lid slam shut. "Why?"

Because she's smart, beautiful, funny. Because the thought of her with Kyle made Ryan cringe. Because he looked forward to seeing her every day, and he wanted to make sure he had that opportunity for as long as possible. Valid reasons, but probably not the right things to tell Jack. Ryan leaned against the door frame. He shrugged. "I like her."

"She's dating Kyle."

"She's just having dinner with him."

Jack hauled the toolbox off of his work bench and let it bang on the floor. He kicked it under the bench before turning toward Ryan.

They stared at each other. Somewhere in the garage a cricket chirped. The stench of sweat mixed with the crisp scent of sawdust. Ryan waited for his best friend to say something, but Jack just stared. Ryan felt like one of Jack's pieces of raw wood, as if he were being scrutinized and analyzed to find the best place to stick the chisel.

Ryan's gut clenched, but he forced out the words he'd promised to use if necessary. "I won't do it if you don't want me to." And he meant it, even though it would probably give him an ulcer.

Jack whipped off his hat and scratched his head. "I might need to think about this."

Ryan nodded. At least it wasn't a no.

"Do we have any steaks left?"

"I picked some up last weekend."

Jack tugged the hat back over his head, then nodded. "I need to finish cleaning in here. You can start the grill."

Anything to put himself in Jack's good graces. "Sure. I think Callie picked up some asparagus. I'll toss that on the grill, too."

"Sounds good. I should be done in about twenty minutes."

"All right."

Jack grabbed a broom. Ryan took that as his cue. When he stepped out of the garage, he sucked in a chest full of fresh air. It hadn't gone as well as he'd wanted, but at least Jack hadn't punched him, not that Ryan thought Jack would actually punch him. Very hard.

Ryan took most of the responsibility for the awkwardness on himself. He should have talked with Jack earlier. Then maybe he'd be eating with Callie instead of eating with Jack.

When he finally made it across the yard, Ryan opened the grill and fired it up.

It was still bright outside, but the clouds were coming in and the temperature was dropping. The weatherman predicted partly cloudy skies overnight—he might finally be right. A great night for a fire. Getting one started would help distract Ryan as he waited for Jack.

While the grill warmed up, Ryan headed toward the woodpile. Someday he'd convince Jack to move the pile, but right now he didn't mind hiking over to the farthest part of the yard. It kept him moving. That kept his mind off Callie. And Jack.

What could he possibly be thinking?

What in the world was Ryan thinking?

Jack shoved the broom across the floor. Some of the sawdust moved forward. The rest of it jumped into the air before settling back onto the floor where he'd just swept. If he didn't calm down, it'd take him twice as long to clean up, not that that would be a bad thing. He could use a few more minutes before he had to face Ryan.

How pathetic. One stupid conversation and life was suddenly so complicated that he had to "face" his best friend.

Why did Ryan have to ask about Callie?

Jack always knew it was possible, but he never wanted to think about the actuality of his sister and his best friend. It shouldn't bother him. If he had to pick a guy for Callie, Jack would want someone like Ryan—he had a solid faith, good job, and great work ethic. But why Ryan?

Then again, why not?

Jack pushed the broom.

Poof!

As the dust settled, he tossed the broom in a corner and rested against his workbench. Leaning back, he pushed open a window, letting out some of the stale air. Usually the smell of his workshop comforted him. Now, it would forever remind him of the day Ryan wanted to date Callie.

And why shouldn't they? Ryan was the best guy in the world. He hadn't really dated anyone in a couple of years. Maybe that was because he liked Callie.

Jack moaned. If he thought about it too long, he'd convince himself of a hundred different reasons why Ryan and Callie should and shouldn't date. They'd find him in the garage tomorrow morning still sweeping and thinking.

"Okay, God, what do I do?"

A breeze slipped in through the window and blew at Jack's hair. Something bumped against the side of the garage. Jack leaned toward the window and listened.

Thump. Thump. Thump.

Someone was at the woodpile. Probably Ryan. The guy who wanted to date his sister.

A chipmunk scurried across the floor, leaving a trail through the sawdust as it ran for cover. Jack shook his head. He'd already plugged every crack he could find in the decades-old garage. Hopefully the little guy snuck in through the door and not another hole. Just in case, he'd set up a couple of live traps.

Pushing away from the workbench, Jack reached up to the rafters and pulled down a wire cage. It hit a box, knocking it to the floor. The cardboard container barely made a sound when it landed in the pile of sawdust. Jack kicked it over. Empty. One of Callie's moving boxes.

She wasn't going anywhere for a while. Even if she wanted to leave, there was no way she'd spend the summer in Mom and Dad's retirement community in Arizona.

Ryan, however, had options.

Jack tossed the trap onto the workbench, picked up the box, and headed outside.

Heat waves rose from the grill. A pile of wood sat by the fire pit. No Ryan. Jack had just reached the fence when the screen door squeaked, and his friend stepped out with a plate full of beef.

Jack held up the box. "You have to move out."

"What?"

"That's my condition." He let Ryan walk past, then followed him to the grill. "It's too weird to think about you and Callie. If you think this is what you want to do, fine, but you can't be living in the same house as my sister and dating her at the same time. So, you have to move out."

Ryan settled the steaks on the hot grates, muting their sizzles when he closed the lid. "For how long?"

"As long as she's here." Jack passed off the box. "And you need to be out before you ask her. If she says no, it'll be weird the rest of the summer. And if she says yes," Jack pointed a finger in Ryan's face, "you get the same treatment as any other guy she's ever brought home."

Ryan smiled like he'd just won a brand-new John Deere tractor. "I'll start packing tomorrow."

"Where are you going to go?"

He shrugged. "I'll stay in a hotel until I figure it out. Thanks."

"Whatever. I'm going to wash off this sawdust. Don't overcook my steak."

Jack walked away, trying to forget Ryan's obnoxious smile. If spending time with Callie made him happy, good for him. Probably good for Callie too. Not much rattled Ryan. Maybe it would rub off.

CHAPTER 17

The fire crackled, casting shadows across the grass and against the lighthouse. Ryan had a fire going the night before when Callie had returned home from her date, and it looked so nice she decided to have her own. The nights were already staying warmer longer, and the humidity was rising, but the bonfire danced in front of her and her visiting, ready-to-pop best friend. Almost a perfect night. She sighed happily. "Dinner was wonderful."

"Really?" Mae kicked off her sandals as she balanced her pregnant body on the edge of an Adirondack chair. Her blonde Shirley Temple curls swayed as she did. "Then why the heavy sigh?"

Callie twirled her marshmallow over the orange flame. "What would you think if I told you someone has a soft spot for you?"

"Depends on who it is." Mae smooshed two graham crackers together. Marshmallow and chocolate oozed out the sides. She wedged the s'more into her mouth. "This is heaven."

Callie passed her roasting stick to Mae.

"Oooh, thank you."

Callie couldn't help smiling as she watched her friend. Normally, the low chairs were perfect for Mae's petite frame, but she didn't look nearly as comfortable with an eight-months-pregnant belly. She obviously couldn't focus either, as she downed another campfire treat. She'd just licked the last bit of marshmallow off her finger when Callie leaned toward her. "So, tell me. What you would think?"

Mae chewed a few times before trying to answer. "I think you're avoiding my question by asking your own." She spat crumbs onto her extended abdomen. Shaking her head, she brushed them to the ground. "I am so ready for this guy to make an appearance."

"I thought you weren't going to find out the sex of the baby."

"We didn't, but I never had cravings like this with the girls." Mae didn't bother with the chocolate or graham crackers this time. As soon as she had room, she stuffed the toasted marshmallow into her mouth. "It's got to be a boy."

Callie smiled at the thought of a miniature Charlie Raven running around. With his mother's brains and his father's Chris Martin looks, he'd be quite the catch. If he was a mini-Charlie and not another mini-Mae, like Ruby and Becca. Those two kept their mother on her toes. They were the secret to Mae having only gained twenty-five pounds by the end of her third pregnancy.

Callie wondered what she'd look like when she got pregnant. Would she keep her figure like Mae or puff up like a pastry?

Not that it mattered. She wouldn't be getting pregnant until she got married. She'd have to get engaged for that to happen, and one dinner with Kyle didn't quite constitute a commitment. And the revelation of the supposed "soft spot" set a whole new set of wheels spinning.

Callie leaned over and brushed some missed crumbs from Mae's leg. "I hope you have a boy. Charlie could use some support at home."

"I agree. Now, back to this depressing, wonderful date. What happened?"

"First, answer my question. What does it mean to have a soft spot for someone?"

Mae shrugged. "I guess it means someone likes you but in some sort of different way. I told you, it depends on the person. My dad has a soft spot for you, but you're like another daughter. Why? What does this have to do with your date?"

A breeze swirled the air. It stirred the fire, blowing smoke and ash in Callie's face. She closed her eyes against the burst of heat and listened to the logs crackle and pop.

So, possibly, Ryan liked her but in a different way. That didn't resolve anything. He could have a soft spot for her, like she was his sister. *Ugh.*

When Callie opened her eyes, Mae was watching her marshmallow rotate over a flickering flame. "I can still see you," Mae said, never taking her eyes off the marshmallow. "I'm a mom. I don't have to be looking at you to know what you're doing."

"Wow." Callie snapped off a piece of chocolate bar and slid it into her mouth. "Do your kids ever get away with anything?"

"All the time. That's why I lie about seeing everything. Now tell me what's going on."

"Kyle told me that Ryan has a soft spot for me."

"What?" Mae turned so fast she nearly whacked Callie with a flaming marshmallow. Callie blew it out and pushed the stick back toward Mae.

"He said Ryan has a soft spot."

Mae's face scrunched up. "What does that mean?"

"I don't know. That's why I asked you."

Mae tugged the charred puff off the stick and ate it.

Callie gagged.

"That could mean anything, Cal."

"I know, Mae."

Callie reloaded the stick. She'd been counting on Mae for some help, but her sugar-crazy, hormonal excuse for a best friend just sat there staring at the fire while she nibbled on a cracker.

Callie sighed. They sat together in relative silence. No chatter. No traffic. Just croaking and chirping and crackling.

She ignored her conflicting emotions long enough to perfectly roast her marshmallow. At precisely the right moment, she pulled back a light brown, crispy masterpiece. The toasted exterior crunched when she squeezed, and the sticky interior stretched when she pulled. She blew on it twice, then popped the piece of perfection into her mouth. Sweetness and smoke melted on her tongue.

Mae cleared her throat.

"What?"

"Okay, I get why the whole soft spot thing is confusing, but what about dinner with Kyle? Can we focus on that for a second?"

Callie smiled. "I told you, it was wonderful."

"Be more specific. Was the food wonderful, or was it the conversation, or was there good music?" Mae leaned back, stretching her legs and rubbing her belly. "You know, I don't get to go out on many dates anymore. The smell of something usually makes me sick. You're my avatar. Tell me all about it."

"He took me to the Kitchen. We had an exotic cheese tray, salads, I ordered the filet, and a chocolate lava cake."

"Mmmmm." Mae closed her eyes. "Go on."

"He told me about his job at the resort. Apparently, they're creating a new marketing campaign, which is why he's been working late and had to cancel the other night. He still sails in the summer and skies in the winter. I told him about school and my job here—"

"Skip to the part about the soft spot."

Callie's pulse quickened. "Did you know Ryan and Jack threatened Kyle after we started dating?"

Mae laughed. "No, but it doesn't surprise me."

"Apparently, they attacked him after our first date. I was *so* embarrassed when he told me." The heat returned to Callie's cheeks as she remembered the conversation. "I can imagine Jack doing that, but when I said Ryan didn't have a reason to say anything, Kyle said Ryan had a soft spot for me. So, tell me what that means?"

Callie leaned back, mimicking Mae's stance. Callie hoped Mae was getting some type of deep revelation because Callie didn't have anything, other than ash in her hair.

"Are you interested in Ryan?"

"As in ... dating?"

"Yes."

Callie shivered. She'd never seriously considered dating Ryan, the same way she'd never seriously considered owning a unicorn. "I've never really thought about it," she said. "We had a lot of fun Sunday—"

"What?" Mae popped up like a whack-a-mole. "You went out with Ryan on Sunday?"

"Not really. Jack had some stuff to do after church, so we waited around to give him a ride home."

"Where did you wait?"

"We had lunch, went on a walk, talked a lot. It was no big deal."

Mae squealed. "Pretty much what you did last night."

Callie's core temperature spiked. The similarities hadn't escaped her attention.

"Wow. You've been here less than a week and already scored two dates. Looks like you're on the good end of feast or famine."

"You'd think."

"Is that what this is about?" Mae reached over and clamped her hand on Callie's arm. "Are you upset because you and Ryan went out?"

"No, Mae, I'm not." Callie leaned toward Mae. "And please keep your voice down," she whispered. "Ryan is inside, and I really don't need him overhearing your guesses."

"I'm not guessing." Mae whispered loud enough for the fish to hear. "I'm just figuring this out. You had fun last night, but you feel bad because you went out with Ryan too."

"No, and I really don't want to talk about this right now."

"Callie, there's nothing to worry about. You're not committed to either of them."

"Please." Callie snagged Mae's hand and pressed it between hers. "Not now."

"I just don't think you need to worry. Kyle's not going to care that you had lunch with Ryan. It's not a big deal."

"I know it's not, but what is a big deal is the fact that I had just as much fun with Ryan as I did with Kyle, and I wouldn't mind doing it again. I cannot be thinking like that if I'm here to fix things with Kyle."

Callie let Mae stare at her while her heart thundered in her chest. There. She'd said it. She liked hanging out with Ryan. She even compared it to her dinner with Kyle. She silently prayed to God that no one was lurking around the lighthouse listening to their conversation.

"Would it be a bad thing to have a few dates with Ryan?" Mae finally asked.

"That's not the point. Entirely." Callie hopped up. "Ryan has always been a friend. He's like a brother. We've never thought of each other that way." She grabbed a large stick from the ground and started poking the firewood. Maybe the heat would hide her blushing.

"Just because you haven't thought of it before doesn't mean you can't start thinking about it now."

Callie's heart thumped wildly. She had been thinking about it, but she didn't want to think about it. It didn't fit into her plan. She'd already figured out how the summer should go, and she hadn't planned on Ryan. Callie turned back to her friend for help. "What am I supposed to do?"

Mae scooted herself forward, twisting a little as she adjusted her footing, then pushed up on the chair arms. With a hearty grunt, she plopped back into the Adirondack chair. "A little help." She waved her hands in front of her.

Callie laughed but grabbed Mae's sticky hands and planted her feet. Mae groaned. Then she was up.

"Whew." She leaned over and snatched up the bag of marshmallows. "Everything takes so much effort these days." Two sugar puffs disappeared in her mouth. "Anyway, I don't see why you can't just see what happens. Why do you need to have everything planned out and ready? Just enjoy the summer."

"I know. I need to let go. Let God."

"Oh good, you remembered. After having these conversations for the past fifteen years, I'm glad I don't have to repeat *everything*."

Callie grabbed the rest of the s'mores ingredients and headed toward the house. "Do we really keep having this same conversation?"

"Only every time you come up with the next great master plan." Mae waddled up beside Callie and pointed back over their shoulders. "Shouldn't you do something about the fire?"

"It'll be fine. It won't take us long to put this stuff inside and strap you into your car."

Mae snorted. "That's what you think. You'd think they could create a car seat for the pregnant woman. Nothing about driving is comfortable for me right now. I think my arms have shrunk."

Callie chuckled. "Want me to drive you home?"

"No way. I'm driving ten under the speed limit these days just so I can have a few moments of silence before facing the girls again. I swear, those two are determined to kill themselves."

They reached the deck, and Mae handed Callie the marshmallows. "I'm not going up any stairs that I don't have to. I'll just wait here."

Callie rushed into the kitchen and dropped everything on the counter. She heard movement in the other room, but she went outside.

Mae was already at her car, lowering herself into the gray bucket seat. The gravel driveway grated beneath her feet until she finally dropped onto the leather. "Okay, now let's review this before I leave. You had a great time with Kyle."

Callie closed the car door. "Yes."

"You had a great time with Ryan."

"Yes."

"It is impossible to perfectly plan out your future, so you will stop trying to control and understand everything."

"I, um ..."

The screen door slammed, stealing Callie's attention. She turned in time to see Ryan rush across the deck and into the side yard. His lean body moved effortlessly across the grass.

Pain ripped through Callie's elbow. She looked down at Mae pinching her skin.

"What was that for?" Callie jumped away from the car, rubbing her abused skin. "I'm already a mess."

"Just trying to help you focus. Scrap the plan, Cal. It's okay not to know what's going to happen next." Mae leaned as far out the window as her petite and pregnant frame allowed. "Bye, Ryan!"

"You can go now." Callie massaged the tender spot on her skin.

The engine roared. "I hope to have a baby the next time we meet."

"You're not due for three weeks."

"Yes, but I can hope." Mae shifted. "I'll see you Sunday!"

Callie waved her good arm. She watched until Mae's taillights disappeared around the first corner. When Callie turned back to the yard, Ryan waved from beside the fire pit. Maybe modifying the plan wasn't such a bad idea.

CHAPTER 18

Ryan kicked the rogue log back into the fire pit, then stomped on the grass, killing any flame's chance at surviving. With another quick kick, he nudged the singed lawn chair a little further away from the unstable bonfire.

The crunching of Mae's tires across the pebbles faded into a cadence of soft steps. By the time Ryan looked up, Callie was already crossing the yard toward him.

She smiled. Her skin glowed yellow in the firelight. "Mae says hi."

"Sorry I missed her. I should have come out earlier."

"I would have invited you out, but we needed some girl talk."

Hair. Shoes. Kyle. "Never mind then. I hope you had fun."

Callie laughed. "Girl talk isn't that scary." She closed the gap between them, then stopped within arm's reach.

Through the rich flavor of smoke, Ryan caught a brief whiff of something flowery. He remembered the fragrance from the day Callie arrived. Just like she had on that day, she stood in front of him, lovely and familiar, but this time she was examining the ground. He watched her drag her foot across the dark, flattened grass.

"What happened here?"

Ryan kicked the ground near her foot. "Your fire tower collapsed. I happened to look out the window as a log rolled off the pile and into the chair."

"What?" Callie dropped to all fours, pulling the chairs closer to the light and inspecting each one. "Oh, no!" Her hair whipped around when she looked up at Ryan. "Did I ruin it?"

He squatted and looked at the chair legs with her. He ran a hand across the singed paint. "I doubt it. I don't think the log was hot enough to burn through the paint. A quick cleaning, maybe repaint it. A new coat would definitely work."

Callie moaned. "Great. If he wasn't mad enough before, this should send Jack right over the edge."

"Why? All they need is a little paint."

"These were his first chairs," she said, sliding onto one of the seats. "Don't you remember? He made them in high school. He loves these things. They're his inspiration. They helped him realize that he wanted to be a carpenter. They—"

"I get it." Ryan raised a hand and nodded. "Jack likes these chairs."

Callie plucked a twig from the grass and tossed it on the fire. "Do you realize that everything I've done since I got here has been a disaster?"

"Everything?" Even dinner with Kyle?

"Everything."

Ryan pulled the other chair closer to the sulking beauty. He sat. The flames flickered, stirring the light. Yellow and orange hues danced across Callie's cheeks. Her lips sagged, pouting. He held back a smile. She would think he was laughing at her circumstances. She wouldn't understand how cute she looked.

Turning his eyes back to the fire, Ryan refocused on the conversation. "So, dinner didn't go well?"

"Oh, no. That was actually very nice."

"Then not everything has been a disaster."

"I guess, but my work has been, and now I'm ruining things in my free time." She rolled her head to the side, looking over at Ryan. "I want to help Jack, not be a burden."

"You're not."

She snorted. "Says the man who doesn't work with me." She slid down in the chair, sinking until she was hanging off the edge, practically sitting on the ground. "It's okay. I can admit it. I'm a klutz. I stink at my job."

"Don't let the first week get you down." Ryan reached for her hand but remembered his promise to Jack. He tucked his hand back behind his head. "You've got a lot of summer left. It'll get better."

"I've already maimed myself with a paint scraper. It can't possibly get much worse ... unless I poke out my eye with a foam paint brush."

Ryan tried to picture the scenario. Nothing about it triggered his sympathies. No matter how he tried to imagine a debilitating sponge-tipped accident, he couldn't muster up any fear for Callie. Instead, he laughed. Then laughed a bit more. As he chuckled, he saw the corners of Callie's mouth perk up. Finally. Progress.

"You might not be as handy as Jack, but I don't think your sight is in any danger," he said. "Have a little faith in yourself. Anyone who can play a piano like you do can't be a complete klutz. You'll figure it out."

Callie pushed herself up and leaned toward Ryan, resting her arms on his chair. "You should have been a cheerleader. You're really good at this."

Then she hit him with a full-watt smile. Ryan's blood surged.

He leaned forward, leaving just inches between them. "Not really, but you make it easy. I'll cheer you on anytime."

Callie flinched, but she didn't move. Her eyes widened, and as they stared at each other, something changed. She swallowed. Her eyes glanced down, then back at him. Ryan glanced down. His eyes stopped at her lips. His pulse raged.

When he looked back up, Callie's eyes fixed on his. She watched him, studied him. Were her emotions as confused as his, or was he simply seeing himself reflected in her eyes?

"Soft spot," she whispered.

"What?"

Before she could answer, a car door slammed.

Callie jumped to her feet. The murmur of late-night tourists floated toward them. Grabbing a long, charred stick, Callie poked the fire and turned her back on Ryan.

What was he doing? Ryan scrubbed his hands over his face. He needed to talk to Jack again. The move was taking longer than Ryan had hoped, and he wanted to share his intentions with Callie. Maybe he and Jack could come to a different arrangement.

Callie cleared her throat. "I haven't told Jack yet, but I don't like living in Alma."

Ryan hands stilled. "You don't?" He hopped up and stood beside her. "Why not?"

She shrugged. "I like my job and everything, but I miss Mae. I miss the beach. I miss seeing you guys." She sighed. "Alma's just not the same. I didn't realize it until I got back here."

Ryan watched Callie poke at the fire, drawing the branch through glowing red coals. He thought about her living with Jack, about football games and eating popcorn on the couch, teasing each other as if nothing had changed, but wanting it to. He'd never noticed how nice she looked in a ponytail before or how comfortably they could talk about anything. It would be nice to have her closer to home.

"It would?" she said.

"What?" Ryan looked down at her. Callie's eyes were the size of softballs. The stick dropped to the ground. "What are you talking about?" he asked.

She blinked. "You said it would be nice to have me closer to home."

Every muscle in Ryan's body tensed. "It would be ... nice."

Callie stared at him. Then she stepped closer. She licked her lips. Why did she have to lick her lips?

"I had a really nice time with you on Sunday," she said. "I wouldn't mind doing it again."

Ryan's eyes flickered back to her lips. "Neither would I."

She watched him. Firelight danced in her eyes. The scent of flowers teased him. Somewhere someone laughed, but beside Ryan and Callie, only the fire dared speak, sizzling and popping in the silence.

"Ryan?"

"Yes?"

"Thanks for Sunday." She grinned.

Jack. I promised Jack.

Ryan took a deep breath, closed his eyes, then moved. "You know, I think the fire is under control." He stepped back and stuffed his hands into his pockets. "Just make sure you douse the wood when you're done. I think I left the television on, so I'd better go back inside."

Before she could respond, he dashed across the yard and through the gate.

Space. He needed space.

The warm evening air chilled his skin as he walked away from the fire. Until he got out of the lighthouse, Callie was a friend. Just a friend.

If only he could convince his emotions to believe it. It wasn't easy to do, especially after the way Callie had looked at him. Ryan had just climbed the deck stairs when Callie's face popped back into his head. The way she smiled at him. The way she licked her lips.

He spun around and jumped off the deck, jogging toward the garage. Callie's empty boxes were still in there. If he didn't sleep, Ryan could be packed up and ready to move by morning.

CHAPTER 19

Callie circled the power washer, inspecting every nut and bolt, not that she'd really know if anything was wrong. "Is it safe?"

"For you." Jack handed her a pair of goggles. "Put those on." With one fluid motion, he yanked on the cord, and the engine roared to life. "Make sure you keep the water moving. Don't hold it in one spot for too long. And don't point it at anyone."

Callie watched as Jack blasted paint chips off the garage. "This is amazing! Why didn't you just let me use this in the first place?"

"I've never seen anyone maim herself with a wire brush before. I didn't think it would be a problem. Besides, I was trying to keep you busy. This shouldn't take you longer than an hour or two."

"Excellent." She adjusted her goggles. "What should I do when I'm done?"

Before he could answer, her pocket vibrated. Jack offered her the washer wand, but Callie stepped back. "Let me just see who this is, okay?" Jack shook his head, but he cut the engine. She smiled and pulled out her phone.

Caller Unknown.

"Hello, this is Callie."

"Hi, Cal."

"Kyle." A wave of nervous excitement buckled Callie's knees. She leaned against the garage. "What a nice surprise."

"Thanks. I hope I'm not interrupting anything."

"No, not at all. I haven't started working."

Jack cleared his throat.

"Yet. What's up?"

"One of my coworkers has tickets to see *West Side Story* tonight at Interlochen, but her kids got sick, so she can't go. If you're interested, she said we could have two tickets."

Callie jumped away from the wall. "*West Side Story?*" Only the greatest musical of all time! "I'd love to. What time?"

"Seven. If you want, we can pick up dinner first. Say five-thirty?"

An evening of the Sharks, Jets, and Kyle Berg? How could she have ever doubted God's reason for calling her home? Callie looked at Jack. "How long will this take me? Do you think I'll be done in time to go out to dinner and a show tonight?"

"Sure. You'll be done in a few hours."

Pure joy seeped through her veins. "I'm free." She smiled. "Where should we meet?"

"Why don't I pick you up at the base of the peninsula at five? We can decide from there."

"Perfect. I'll see you then."

Another night with Kyle. And *he* had called *her*! Things were looking good for the plan.

"I'm having dinner with Kyle," she said, smiling at Jack. He shrugged. Then she shivered. Wet cotton clung to her back where she'd leaned against the wall. Better water than blood. Of course, there was plenty of time left in the day for that. "Did you want me to do anything else today?"

"No. Just make sure you clean up before you leave. This is the township's equipment. With our luck, someone will actually walk off with the power washer if you don't put it away."

"Clean up. Got it."

"And keep track of your hours if you want to get paid. I forgot about that before." Jack pulled his hat lower over his eyes. "Sorry."

"No problem. Do I need a time card or anything?"

"No. Just write down your hours somewhere. I'll verify them for you."

"I haven't worked a full day yet. Is that going to be a problem?"

"I hired you as a part-time employee. As long as you don't work more than twenty hours a week, we're fine."

"What?" Callie's smile faltered. "I thought I was your assistant."

"You are. I never said this would be full-time work. I doubt I can even find enough work for you to do for twenty hours a week. Besides, it's your summer vacation. I thought you'd enjoy the break." Jack winked, then smacked her on the shoulder, like she was one of the boys. "Don't be a drama queen."

Drama queen. Callie's jaw clenched as she bit back evil words for her sloppy, dirty oaf of a brother. He didn't need to remind her of her occasional emotional variances.

He laughed. "Calm down, Squirt. You're getting that constipated look."

Her jaw dropped. "Jackson!"

He laughed harder, pulling the keys from his pocket. "I'll be gone all day. Call me if you need me."

And support his drama queen accusation? Hardly.

Callie twisted the water out of her ponytail. The strengthening breeze carried droplets onto the lawn. It also chilled her to the core. Of all the days to use a power washer, it had to be overcast and windy. Not a great day to wash the building. It wasn't a great day to do much of anything outside. That didn't stop the tourists though.

She'd already caught an escaped dog, given directions to three different couples, and answered as many questions about lighthouse history as she thought she could fake her way through. Even with all of the interruptions, though, she was still on schedule to meet Kyle on time.

"Excuse me? Would you mind taking a picture of us?" Callie turned around and found an older couple, this one in matching skin-tight blue biking outfits. They looked like any number of couples from her parents' retirement community.

Callie smiled at them. "Not a problem." She nudged the washer wand away with her toe. The cyclists passed her their camera, then posed by the fence. Before Callie had taken two shots, another couple walked up and waited. As she handed back the first camera, Callie accepted a Nikon from the new couple.

Four photo shoots later, the rain started. Tourists darted to their cars, trying to stay dry. Callie just sighed. Her clothes couldn't absorb much more water anyway. She meandered back toward the garage.

Paint chips littered the tarp and surrounding grass. Jack would probably excuse the mess in light of the rain, but Callie had promised to clean up. She wouldn't let him down.

She was reaching for the washer wand when she noticed her hands—dry skin, chipped nails, a few cuts and scrapes. If her hands looked this bad, what did the rest of her look like? The tarp crackled under her as she walked over it toward the garage door, then peeked at her reflection in the door window. Streaky make-up. Dark roots. Loose hairs clinging to her face and neck.

Ugh. No one deserved to see her looking like that. She didn't have time to do anything about the hair color, but she could handle her hands and make-up.

In two heartbeats Callie had her phone open and the speed dial working. She stepped into the safety of the garage as the salon answered. "Tiffany, it's Callie Stevens."

"Callie! Welcome home. Enjoying summer break?"

"As much as I can. I'm working in the rain right now and realized that I could use some pampering."

"Did you want to schedule a cut or color with Brooke?"

"Maybe later. Right now, I'm hoping you have an opening this afternoon with Nanette for a manicure, and maybe a quick blowout."

"Nanette's booked, but Stacey had a cancellation. I can put you down for three o'clock."

"Stacey?" Stock girl, deli driver ... nail tech? It couldn't be. "Stacey Chapman?"

"Yep. Do you know her?"

Obviously, not well enough. "I've seen her around."

"Everyone does. She'll be free in about an hour. Would you like me to pencil you in?"

An hour to clean up, then spend some one-on-one time with the mysterious Miss Chapman? "Absolutely."

CHAPTER 20

Callie opened the salon door and stepped into the calming familiarity of earth tones. Heels clacked against hard wood. Hair dryers blasted. The scent of coffee and chemicals tickled her nose. She spotted Brooke blow drying someone's hair and waved when her high school classmate saw her in the mirror.

Brooke set down her hair dryer and rushed over to give Callie a hug. "It's so good to see you. Why don't we schedule your hair cut while you're here?"

Callie returned the hug before stepping back to examine herself in the mirror. She combed her fingers through the straight blown tresses. "Is it really that bad?"

"No, but I was out of town the last time you were here. I haven't seen you since before Labor Day."

Callie smiled. "That's your fault. You were the only person here who'd touched my hair since you got your license." She turned back to her friend. "You know I'm only here Memorial Day, Labor Day, and Christmas break. You'll just have to plan your vacations around me. That was the first time Dawn's touched my hair in over seven years."

Brooke laughed. "And she did a great job. Here comes Stacey. I've got to finish Mrs. Wessell's blowout, but don't leave without making an appointment. I want to catch up, and there's a highlighting technique I've been using that will work great with your hair."

As Brooke walked away, Stacey stepped up to the front desk. Like everyone else in the salon, she wore all black. Unlike her previous outfits, however, Stacey wore a figure-flattering blouse, a skinny metal belt that showcased her trim waist, and a pair of canary yellow pumps that nearly made Callie drool. Wave after wave of long blonde hair rolled over her shoulders and back.

Stacey smiled. "Shocking, isn't it?"

"Isn't what?"

"You're nice, but I know how ugly my other uniforms are. I don't always look like a teenage bag girl. Come on. We're this way." Stacey led

Callie into the manicure room. Not only did she look different, she walked differently too. Taller. Confident. Comfortable in the salon.

"So, you're a nail tech too?"

"Yep. This is my favorite job, though." Stacey motioned to a chair. "I'd love to do this full-time someday."

"Why not now?"

"I can't, not until I finish my apprenticeship, anyway. I have two more months before I'll be fully licensed." Stacey reached for Callie's hand. Callie hesitated. Stacey laughed. "I've been doing this for almost a year. You're safe, I promise."

Callie narrowed her eyes but couldn't completely hide her grin. "If I lose a fingernail, I want free polish."

"I'll give you three."

"Deal." Callie shoved both hands at Stacey.

"You won't be sorry." Stacey dabbed some oil on her palms, then massaged it into Callie's skin.

Callie closed her eyes and slouched down in the chair. "That feels great."

"Thanks. You'll be just as happy with the rest."

"You were really working here last year?"

"Yep. I started in August and will finish in July."

"And then you'll be a cosmetologist?"

"No, I'll be a nail tech."

Callie opened her eyes. "You don't want to be a cosmetologist?"

"I'd love to, but I really can't afford the full two-year internship. I love doing nails the most, so they created a one-year program for me." Stacey pressed and pulled the tension out of Callie's fingers while skillfully avoiding the scattered scrapes and bruises. Stacey hadn't lied. She was good. Too bad she couldn't do it for a living.

"Is this an unpaid internship?" Callie asked.

Stacey rubbed and nodded.

"That's why you work at the grocery store."

Stacey nodded again and set Callie's hand in a dish of warm water. "And it's why I work at the art studio. Occasionally at the deli. And for any friend who will give me a few hours here or there. I work twenty hours a week here, so I fill in my days wherever I can."

"Well, I promise to stop in and use your services again before I go back to school. I forgot how great this feels."

"You don't pamper yourself often?"

Callie chuckled. "All of the time, but I can't always afford to pay someone else to do it for me. I usually save my money for the things I can't do for myself."

"I'm glad you decided to treat yourself today." Stacey began massaging the other hand. "Is there any special reason why you decided to come in?"

Callie's heart fluttered. "I have a date later."

"That's wonderful! With Ryan?"

The flutter skipped a beat. "Ryan? Uh, no. With Kyle. Why would you think that?"

Stacey shook her head. "I don't know. I just, I guess … I'm not sure why I thought that. I've heard a lot about you from Ryan. I guess I thought you guys were an item, although he probably knows you because of Jack, right? I mean, you're his sister, so, of course, Ryan knows you. You've probably known each other for years."

Callie sat in awe as Stacey continued on without breathing. "Wow."

Stacey's hands stopped moving. "What?"

"Now I know how Jack feels when I ramble." In less than five seconds, Stacey's entire neck turned pink. "I don't mean that as an insult," said Callie. "I'm impressed. I'm glad to know there are others out there who can keep up with my talking speed."

Stacey's lips twitched, working their way up into a half smile. "Thanks. I think." She shuffled Callie's hands around, then focused on her nails. "So, you were telling me about your date. Who's Kyle?"

This time Callie's face warmed up. "He's sort of the reason I came home."

"Your boyfriend?"

"He was my boyfriend, a few years ago."

"What happened?"

There was more to the story than Callie had time to explain during the twenty-minute manicure. She went with the abbreviated version. "Things didn't work out, so we broke up."

"And now you're going out on a date." Stacey sighed, smiling. "That's kind of romantic."

"Kind of." Hopefully. But enough of that. This manicure was an excuse to get information. Time to turn the tables. "What about you? Are you dating anyone?"

"No. Tell me more about Kyle. Why did you break up?" Stacey's eyes never left Callie's hands.

"It just wasn't the right time."

The file scratched quickly and expertly across Callie's nails. "The right time for what?"

"To get married."

Stacey looked up, her eyes wide. "You turned down his proposal?"

"No. Kyle never proposed, but I was afraid he would. We were both graduating from college, and it seemed like the next step. I just wasn't ready for it."

"But you are now?"

"Maybe, but it's not really an option now. We're just having dinner. It's nothing serious."

Stacey flashed Callie a quick smile. "But it never hurts to put your best fingers forward."

"Absolutely."

The filing resumed. "I still think it's a romantic idea, the two of you picking up again. Even if you just stay friends, it's a happy ending."

But not the ending Callie was counting on. There was more to her trip than just being friends with Kyle, not that she wanted to be talking about her dating habits. Stacey's dating habits were what intrigued her. "You're quite the romantic. Why aren't you seeing anyone?"

"It's not really my choice." She switched hands again, drying then filing. "I'd love to date someone, but it's a two-way street. You can't make someone love you, you know? Besides, I know God's got a plan for me. I just have to wait on him."

"Well said."

"I mean, look at you. You've been waiting. Maybe after all of this time it's right for you and Kyle. If not, at least you know you're ready."

"Yes, but Kyle and I aren't actually dating. We're just going out to dinner tonight."

Stacey cocked her head, spilling her hair onto the table. "How is that not dating?"

"Technically it's a date, but we're not a couple."

Stacey nodded, but her brows pinched together. "Whatever happens, it's great that you and your ex can stay friends like that."

Yeah. Friends. Would God really call her back to Traverse City for that? Patching things up with Kyle seemed so obvious, but only to her. Stacey assumed Callie was with Ryan. Of course, all she knew was Callie's long history with Ryan. It was the more recent history, however, that made her pulse kick.

Stacey jiggled Callie's hand. "Color?"

"What?"

"Polish?"

"Huh?"

Stacey pointed at the rainbow display. "Sorry to interrupt your thoughts. What color nail polish do you want?"

"Oh!" Callie grabbed an iridescent white and handed the bottle to Stacey. "My mind was wandering to places I'm trying to avoid. I'd rather hear about how you and Jack met."

Stacey fumbled the bottle, dropping it into the water dish.

Callie tried to hide her smile. She'd known there was more to the story.

"That's not much of a story." Stacey dried off the little bottle. "We met at church. He invited me out to the lighthouse for lunch a couple of times. That's all."

Lunch? With a girl? "That doesn't sound like my brother."

"He doesn't usually eat lunch?" Stacey set the polish aside and grabbed a clear base coat. When she twisted off the top, a sweet, stinging scent greeted them.

"Yes, but he doesn't usually invite women to the lighthouse. Were you and Jack dating?"

Callie lurched forward when Stacey pulled on her hand. "Sorry," Stacey said, her neck turning pink again.

"Oh my gosh, you were. And I keep bringing it up. Stacey, I'm sorry." How could she have missed the signs?

"Don't apologize. We weren't dating." Stacey swiped the clear coat over the rest of the nails. "I think your brother is wonderful, and confusing, and he and Ryan have become two of my best friends. They've really helped me get to know God. They're so smart about the Bible."

Stacey managed to finish the first hand before dropping her hands to the table and looking up at Callie. "My family has a long history of bad relationships, but I'm not like them. I don't date because I don't want to get distracted. That was a lot easier before I started going to church, because none of the guys I knew before thought about anything but themselves, and some of the guys at church are so different. But I still don't want to do anything stupid, so I've turned that over to God and I'm letting him tell me what to do, and I'm just trying to keep praying and let things work out, because I don't want to get distracted with a relationship that isn't going anywhere."

Callie stared at the sincere, confused eyes looking back at her while she processed Stacey's explanation. Distractions at church? "So you like Jack?"

"I didn't say that."

"You sort of did. Listen, I get it. Jack's a good guy. My dad beat that into him when we were kids—"

"You know," Stacey leaned forward, her neck now a brilliant shade of red, "this is a little awkward."

"I'm sorry. I shouldn't have pushed so hard. You don't know me, and—"

"And you think I like your brother."

"Yes."

"It doesn't matter, though, because I don't want to get distracted." Stacey shook her head but smiled. "Maybe we need a new subject. Jack told me you're a music teacher. Tell me about your job."

Twenty minutes later Stacey knew all the horrors of third-graders with recorders, and Callie's fingers sparkled. Stacey escorted her client to an empty chair, giving her a quick hug.

"I'm so glad you came in today," said Stacey. "Come in again before you leave. You can tell me more about Alma."

"I will."

"Melissa will finish up with your hair. Have fun on your date tonight."

Callie smiled and sat on the soft-leather seat. "I will."

Before she walked away, Stacey leaned down, her long hair brushing against Callie's cheek. "Please don't tell Jack what I said," she whispered.

"Of course not." Callie wouldn't say anything, but maybe she could find another way to help Stacey and Jack see what she'd already figured out.

CHAPTER 21

As Jack pushed the wide orange cart, one of the wheels wobbled. Then it squeaked. Continuously. He considered swapping it for a different cart, but it was already after five, and he hadn't been back to the lighthouse all day. Though he trusted Callie's ability with a power washer, he wanted to make sure he had enough daylight left to fix any of her mistakes. He needed to shop fast.

The cart squeaked through the aisles. Jack searched for the few things he needed to install new sinks at the township hall. He quickly filled the cart, then headed toward the front of the store. That's when Stacey walked in.

He almost didn't recognize her. The black clothes and fancy shoes made her look older and professional. She wore her hair down at church, but not like this. It curled and moved around her shoulders and back. Not for the first time he wondered if it felt as soft as it looked. She saw him and smiled. Before he knew how it happened, they were standing together in the lighting aisle.

Jack nodded. "You're not going to try to build a house, are you?"

Stacey laughed. "No, I'm just here to pick up a few things for my apartment. I need to replace a couple of outlet covers and a light fixture."

"Did you talk to your landlord about it?"

"Yep." She crossed her arms, tipping her head back and grinning. "I told him I'd do it if he'd knock some money off of next month's rent. He agreed."

"Have you worked with electricity before?"

Stacey narrowed her eyes. "I've installed two ceiling fans, thank you very much. You don't need to worry about me. I'm not a child."

She spun around, whipping her hair through the air. Her heels clicked on the concrete floor as she sauntered away, not looking anything like a child. Maybe that's why Jack's mouth opened before he could stop himself.

"Do you want some help?"

Stacey stopped. She looked back at him, her chin in the air. "I don't need your help. Thank you."

Jack pushed his cart after her. "I'm sure you don't need my help, but I'm offering. Haven't we had this conversation before?"

Instead of answering, Stacey shoved the cart aside, so she could walk right up to him, hands on her hips. She said something, but Jack didn't hear it. He'd expected her to smell like perfume and hairspray, like Callie did when she got dressed up, but as she moved closer, she reminded him of cinnamon rolls and ice cream. Stacey's hands dropped to her side as she looked at him.

Jack watched his own hand reach out and brush aside a stray piece of her hair. As soft as feathers. "You could probably remodel the entire apartment yourself, but I'd like to help you."

She swallowed. "Why?"

"Because I can't resist a woman in a tool belt."

Her neck went pink.

He smiled. "Why do you keep trying to say no?"

Then red. Stacey grabbed a piece of hair and twisted it through her fingers. "Because I don't know what to think about you, and I'm afraid to find out. I'm a bad judge of character when it comes to men, and I don't need to make another mistake."

Something weird clenched in his gut. "You think I'd be a mistake?"

"No, I ... why do you care?" Her fingers paused. "This is why I don't know what to think about you." Releasing her hair, she poked Jack's shoulder. "*You* are a confusing man, and I am a hopeless romantic. Every time you offer to help me, my mind goes crazy and I start imagining things, but then you don't talk to me for a week, and I have to remind myself that life isn't a romance novel, at least not for me, and I don't need to know how this is going to end, but I at least want to know the next step, so I can either move on with my life or keep hoping." Stacey huffed. Her eyes, closer to his than normal, shifted, scanning his face as he processed her words.

"I'm confusing you?" He didn't even know how to process that tirade.

She nodded, her hair bouncing forward with each movement.

Jack pushed it back over her shoulder. "I'm giving mixed signals."

She pushed his hand away. "I know."

"I don't know what else to do."

"Well, I don't want to wait around while you figure it out." She waved her finger between them. "I've done this before. Some guy doesn't know what he wants, so he wants everything until he decides there's something better for him out there, and I won't do it again. You should probably take some time to figure out what you want, and I should probably give myself some space." She pulled her purse closer to her chest. "It's not me, it's you."

The words smacked Jack in the face. "It's what?"

Stacey smiled. "I need a light fixture. I'm sure I'll see you at church."

Jack just stood there holding onto his cart as Stacey disappeared around the corner. She was right. It *was* his fault. She scared him, excited him, challenged him to be a better man, and she didn't even know she was doing it. Did she?

The faint clicking of her heels almost faded away before he snapped back into the moment and chased after her. He found her examining outlet covers when he rounded the corner.

"You can't run away now," he said, stomping up to her. "Talk about confusing. Why would you tell me that?"

Stacey's hand shook as she put the covers back on the shelf. She locked her fingers in front of her and stared at the ground. "I'm so embarrassed," she whispered. "I can't believe I just said all of that."

"Me neither." He crossed his arms. "But you said it, and now you won't even look at me."

"Can we pretend like this didn't happen?"

"Normally, I'd love to, but I'm just as confused as you are. What do I need to do to fix this?"

"Nothing. I get it." She finally looked at him. "You're not really interested in me, but I keep sucking you into these stupid projects. Then I read into everything you say and do, and now I'm blaming it on you. I'm sorry."

"Why?"

"For guilt-tripping you into things." She wrapped a piece of hair around her finger. "And for getting emotional about it. Now will you please leave me alone?"

Jack shook his head. "You're not guilt-tripping me into anything. I'm the one who offered."

"I know, but it's confusing. Why did you touch my hair?" She practically hissed at him, stepping closer. "Are you just trying to mess with me, or are you really thick, because one second I think we're getting along great, and then I think you can't wait for me to leave, and most of the time I think you just feel sorry for me."

Jack couldn't focus with her that close. "What do you want from me?"

She shook her head. "I don't know. What do *you* want?"

To help her with her light fixture. To touch her hair again. To be ten years younger. Jack's chest tightened. "Are we really having this argument in Home Depot?"

Stacey moved back, her shoulders relaxing. "No. I appreciate your offer to help, but I can't handle—" she waved her arms between them "—this. When you know what you want, give me a call. Goodbye."

Once again, she walked away. Her goodbye rotted in Jack's gut like a cheap, greasy burger. If Callie were there, she could explain Stacey to him, but he was on his own. And that goodbye sounded so final. He still didn't know exactly what was going on, but he knew he didn't want Stacey walking away from him. He had to do something. Before he could reconsider it, Jack yelled after her.

"I want to ask you out."

The hours of nail polish fumes must be affecting her brain, because Stacey was imagining things, or at least hearing things. Did Jack just ask her out? She sucked in a shaky breath, crushing her purse against her chest. She needed a hearing aide, and possibly a defibrillator.

"Ma'am, can I help you find anything?" Stacey stared at a round man in an orange vest. "Are you finding everything okay?" he asked.

She leaned toward him and lowered her voice. "Is there still a tall man in a baseball cap standing behind me?"

"Yes, ma'am."

"Oh." She leaned back. "Okay. Then I'm fine." Except for the shortness of breath. And the possible hearing loss.

The employee walked away, and Stacey turned around. Jack stood there looking like a lost toddler. She walked right up to him, stopping when she was far enough away to that she couldn't hit him but close enough to see his dilated pupils. She looked him in the eye. "Did you just say what I think you said?"

He swallowed. "Yes."

Angels sang. "Then ask me out."

"I want to, but I can't."

"Why?" She stepped closer. "This isn't getting any less confusing."

Jack adjusted his hat and looked around. "What happened to my cart?"

"You didn't bring it over here, and don't change the subject."

Jack walked back the way that he came, but even in heels, Stacey was quicker. She stopped in front of him, nearly causing a collision. "Now who's running away?"

"I need to find my cart."

Rolling her eyes, Stacey almost plowed over another employee when she ran back down the lighting aisle and dragged Jack's stupid cart behind her. Maybe this would get him back on track. He met her halfway. She stood toe to toe with him, the cart securely behind her.

"There you go. Now ask me out."

"I, uh …" He scratched his neck.

"Are you just toying with me?"

Jack's eyes shifted from her eyes toward her ear. That's when Stacey realized she'd wound a piece of hair all the way up her index finger, right next to her ear. He smiled.

"Don't try to charm your way out of this, Jack." She released the captive hair. "Please. I need to know if this is going anywhere. I deserve that much at least."

He glanced around. After every other customer and employee disappeared, he cleared his throat. "Callie's six years younger than me. When she was a freshman in high school, my dad sat me down for a talk. He told me I couldn't ever date one of her friends until they graduated from high school, even if they were already eighteen. He didn't want anyone using her to get to see me at home, and he didn't want me or my friends using her to meet girls. I respected that. I didn't want to disappoint my dad, and I didn't want to hurt Callie, so I told myself I would never date anyone Callie's age. Ever."

Stacey let the full weight of Jack's words sink in. He didn't date younger women. Period. Then reality crashed into her like a Mack truck. "How old is Callie?"

"Twenty-seven."

"Four years older than me."

He nodded.

People walked around them as they stood in the middle of Home Depot, finally communicating. The gentleness around Jack's eyes, the softness of his jaw, the nearness of his whole being assured Stacey that he struggled with the truth he just shared with her. Joy filled her heart that he finally trusted her enough to be honest, even if it tightened the noose around their doomed relationship.

Standing tall, she nodded. "So, that's that." She stepped away, but Jack grabbed her hand.

"Would you stop walking away from me?"

"Hey, you walked away too."

"I know. I'm sorry. This whole thing is a big mess. That's why I wanted to avoid this conversation." Stacey pulled her arm, but Jack held tight. "But I don't really want to avoid it. I want to ask you out, just not right now."

"Are you two finding everything okay?"

Stacey looked over her shoulder to see the same old, chubby man smiling at her.

She smiled back. "We're sort of in the middle of something. If you walk away right now, I'll let you tell me everything you know about light fixtures, but if you don't leave immediately, this man may *never* ask me out. So, give me five minutes, okay?"

Jack chuckled. The old man gave her the thumbs up as he turned around. Stacey faced Jack again, and his smile nearly melted her knees. His hand slid down her arm to capture her fingers. She'd never known hand-holding could be so exciting. Stacey never wanted it to end.

"Please. Give me some time too."

"So you can get over your fear of younger women?"

He squeezed her hand. It pumped up her pulse. "I'm getting used to the idea, but I can only handle one change at a time."

"What does that mean? What do you want to do?"

"Help you around your house. Sit by you at church. Maybe go to a ball game together."

Each suggestion broadened Stacey's smile until she was sure her ears would pop off. "Okay."

Jack winked. "Thanks. Now let's get your light fixture."

"No way." She spun Jack around and pushed him out of the aisle. "I finally have permission to talk to you. Let's get out of here before Mr. Light Fixture comes back."

CHAPTER 22

Callie stood in the parking lot watching so intently for Kyle's black sedan that she didn't notice the tan SUV until it stopped in front of her. Her heart thudded, and she threaded her keys between her fingers as she backed up against her car.

The back passenger window rolled down, and Kyle sat there smiling at her. Callie's hand relaxed. "I hope you weren't waiting long."

"Not at all." She leaned forward, peeking into the vehicle. A thin, dark-haired man waved at her from the driver's seat. She turned back to Kyle. "Did you want me to drive?"

"No, I thought we'd all go together. These are my co-workers, Ian and Rachel. They took the other two tickets for tonight."

The other tickets? Callie's mind raced back to their conversation. Kyle hadn't actually said they'd be the only two going. As her hopes for the evening fizzled, she put on her best smile. A double date wouldn't completely ruin the evening.

Kyle opened his door, then slid over to the other side of the seat. Callie climbed in.

Ian reached back, offering her a long, narrow hand. With his rectangular glasses and button-down shirt, he could have walked right off the pages of J. Crew. "Nice to meet you. I get to play chauffeur tonight."

Callie shook his hand. "Thanks."

He nodded before turning around and pulling out of the parking lot.

"I'm Rachel," said the other passenger. A curtain of glossy auburn hair swung around the front passenger seat. Emerald eyes. Ruby lips. Creamy skin. Callie smiled at beauty incarnate.

"I'm Callie."

"I'm glad you could join us. Kyle said you're a fan of musicals." Rachel smiled at Kyle.

He smiled back.

Callie reminded herself not to overreact. "I'm a fan of music in general. What about you?"

Rachel shrugged. "I like plays, but I'm more excited to spend some time with Kyle and Ian outside of work. We've been on this project together for almost six months, and it's always conferences or business luncheons. Seeing everyone outside of our natural habitat should be fun."

Callie looked between Rachel and Ian. Only conferences and business luncheons? "So, you two aren't ..." Callie motioned between the seats.

Ian laughed. "No, but it's not for a lack of trying. I just keep telling her no, but she's persistent."

The trio laughed together. Callie forced a smile, but she wasn't exactly sure why. She looked at Kyle for an explanation. He was busy laughing.

"For the record, I've never asked Ian for more than a pencil," said Rachel. "He's a happily engaged man."

"Oh, congratulations," said Callie. "Is your fiancée meeting us there?"

"Not tonight. She's in California visiting her sister."

Callie nodded. So, it wasn't a double date. Just a bunch of coworkers trying to get to know each other better. How did she fit into the mix?

"Someone needs to decide where we're eating," Ian said as he wove the SUV through summer rush hour. "I'm going to have to pick a lane soon."

"Greenies Café?" Rachel said.

Kyle shook his head. "We lunch there once a week. What's the name of the place Ted took us to last week? The one with the fish?"

Rachel cringed and stuck out her tongue. "I don't want to go anywhere that reminds me of Ted."

Callie couldn't find a good place to pipe in as the trio debated and laughed about all of the places that reminded them of this work day or that work event. By the time they pulled into a familiar parking lot, Callie had almost convinced herself to never eat out again—each meal apparently came with a side of emotional baggage.

She climbed out of the back seat and looked at an unfamiliar building. The terracotta walls and giant sombrero were gone. Now the restaurant looked like a giant, square heifer. "When did Little Foots close? They had the best tacos."

"Last summer." Kyle stepped up beside her and offered his arm. "This is actually the second restaurant to be here since then. I hear they have great hoagies, but no one stays in this building long. We should try a sandwich before they move or close shop."

"With a name like Holy Cow, I'm guessing it'll be the second option." Rachel sauntered ahead of them.

Ian said something to her. She smacked his arm and laughed.

Another inside joke. Before Cal could slip into self-pity, however, her phone chirped. Thankful for the interruption, she dug the phone out of her purse and flipped it open.

"Need 2 talk. Call me. ASAP. Jan"

Callie checked the number. The same Alma number that had been calling her for the last couple of weeks. If she'd known it was her co-worker she would have answered earlier. Too late now. Of course, Callie normally wouldn't interrupt a night out for a call from Jan, but if things continued as they were, a text conversation might salvage the evening.

Kyle patted Callie's hand, pulling her back into the moment. "Are you okay?"

She dropped the phone back into her purse and nodded. "I just didn't realize we were riding with anyone else. That surprised me, but it's not a big deal."

"I wasn't trying to surprise you."

"It's okay, really."

When they stepped onto the sidewalk, Kyle stopped moving. Callie stopped beside him and looked up at him. He pressed her hand where it rested between his hand and his arm. "We won't talk about work all night, I promise. That was one of our goals for tonight."

An evening with goals. Not exactly romantic, but Callie couldn't argue with that type of planning.

The restaurant door whooshed open, jingling the bells on its hinge. Rachel popped her head around the solid wood. "You guys coming?"

Kyle dropped his arms and motioned for Callie to walk ahead of him. She stepped into the clangy atmosphere and back to reality. It wasn't a date. She was the tag-along. Depression threatened to party-crash the night, but she focused on where they were going. *West Side Story*. Nothing could ruin the evening.

When Rachel and Kyle stepped in line beside Callie, Rachel had her perfectly manicured hand on Kyle's shoulder as she gave him her magazine-worthy smile. Kyle smiled back.

Well, almost nothing could ruin the evening.

"That was amazing." Callie smiled as she closed her eyes, listening to the rich harmonies that replayed in her mind.

"I knew you'd enjoy it." Kyle chuckled, his familiar baritone blending with the imaginary tunes. "You haven't stopped smiling since we left."

"I can't help it." She opened her eyes, looking at the handsome man beside her. "This whole night has been wonderful."

"It has, hasn't it?" Rachel's face peeked out from the other side of Kyle. Well, not the whole night.

"Maybe not wonderful, but I sure appreciate the ride home." An older man smiled back at them from the front seat. "I can't believe my spare was flat too. It would have taken forever for a wrecker to get through that traffic."

"Not a problem, Phil." Kyle leaned forward, patting his neighbor's arm. "I'll take you back tomorrow before work. Save you the cost of a tow. Did you enjoy the show?"

"I didn't get to see it. I was just working late and got caught in the traffic."

"I didn't realize you still worked there."

As Kyle chatted with their additional passenger, Callie's mind wandered. Every now and then Kyle turned his head just right and she could see the little scar on his jaw where he'd cut himself shaving in high school. He told her that he'd shaved for her, having heard a rumor that she didn't like facial hair. She didn't even know his name at the time.

Callie couldn't hide the smile that crept up.

Kyle's rich voice rang in her ears. Ian laughed at something. Rachel yammered. The group slipped into a friendly conversation. Callie tried to focus. She should contribute. Kyle turned toward her, smiling that crooked smile. He leaned into her and winked.

Focus. Focus!

Ian pulled the SUV into the church parking lot, right next to her car. How did they get there so quickly? Callie willed her legs to move.

"Thank you so much for the tickets and for the ride. I had a great time."

Ian offered a hand into the back seat. "A pleasure."

Phil nodded.

Rachel smiled. Perfectly straight and white. "It was so nice to meet you. I hope we run into each other again."

"That would be nice." And it probably would, but Callie didn't need to admit that. Instead, she opened the door and slid out of the vehicle. When she turned around, Kyle was climbing out behind her. Something shifted in her chest. "Thanks again for the invite."

"I couldn't go to Interlochen without you." His arms wrapped around her. Callie's body responded without thinking, remembering the strength of his chest, the clean scent of his skin. "Drive safe." His arms loosened.

The warmth of his arms clung to her skin. "You too."

He climbed back into the SUV, right next to Rachel. The supermodel leaned forward, patting him on the knee. They both looked at Callie, waving. Like a beautiful, happy couple.

CHAPTER 23

Callie rolled over again. Any minute now she'd fall asleep. She had to. She'd been up most of the night trying to figure out whether or not her plan was working. She still wasn't sure, but she knew one thing for certain—lying in bed and hoping to fall asleep wasn't working. Kicking off her covers, Callie popped out of bed, exhausted but fully awake. The clock said five thirty. Too early to start working around the house, so she pulled a hoodie on over her t-shirt and blue pajama shorts before slipping her feet into a faded pair of flip flops. Shuffling through the house, she grabbed a muffin on her way out the door.

Blessed silence greeted her. Not a car in the visitor's parking lot. No tour groups or family reunions. Callie closed her eyes. The gulls chattering, crickets twittering, and a few frogs picking up the bass line. Nature's song.

The crisp air bit at Callie's legs, but she ignored it as she shuffled through the damp grass toward the shore line. She bit into the cranberry walnut muffin. Tart but sweet. Soft yet crunchy. Different but delightful. Maybe she could make all of the seemingly contradictory parts of her life blend together as nicely.

As she stuffed the last bit of breakfast into her mouth, Callie refocused her attention on the rippling surface of the bay. The early morning sun painted the waves, tempting her into the frigid water. Before she could talk herself out of it, Callie dipped her feet in the water, flip flops and all. The waves crept in and out, tickling her toes and enveloping her feet with slimy, wet sand. She stepped farther in.

With each step, the water deepened, chilling more of her feet, ankles, shins. The waves kissed her knees as Callie reached a large pile of smooth rocks. An early-morning sunbeam peeked through the leaves on the trees, illuminating the largest boulder. She waded toward it and sat.

The sun had warmed the stone, so she pulled her freezing feet up to rest on the hard surface. Callie stretched the sweatshirt over her legs, simultaneously drying and warming them. A rough night with Kyle was no reason to give herself hypothermia.

Not that it had been a rough night, per se. Everything about the evening had been lovely—the perfect, friendly night out. Not part of the plan but not terrible. She'd been thinking about what happened all night though, and she still didn't have any clarity. Maybe she needed a new perspective.

She pulled her phone out of the hoodie pouch and punched at the screen. *R u up yet?*

A frog croaked.

The phone dinged.

Yep. Baby's boxing with my bladder. What's up?

Callie didn't bother trying to spell it out. She hit Mae's speed dial and waited.

"You're up early." Mae yawned. "I'd still be sleeping if I didn't have to share organ space with my son."

"'Still sleeping' would imply that I ever fell asleep."

Mae gasped. "Calista Marie, are you just getting home?"

"No, of course not. I've been here all night. I just haven't been sleeping."

"Are you alone?"

"Mae!"

Her friend laughed. "I couldn't help myself. I'm sorry. So, tell me—what happened?"

Callie rehashed the date, from the invitation to the pick-up to the amazing performance to the drop-off at her car. She included every detail while leaving out as much emotion as she could. By the time she finished, the sun had climbed a bit higher, heating her chest and shoulders.

Mae hummed. "Sounds like a fun evening. What did I miss?"

"Nothing. It was just me, Kyle, and his co-workers, all hanging out. Part of the gang." After a second's pause, Callie heard Mae's slow exhale.

"Oh, no."

"Exactly."

"It wasn't a date?"

"Not a date."

"Callie …"

"One of the gang." Callie sighed. "Just friends."

Saying that sounded so final. Her greatest fear vocalized. She looked up, searching for the disaster that was bound to find her. A seagull with the stomach flu? A stray Frisbee blowing in from down shore? With all of her bad luck thus far, surely something miserable was about to happen.

Instead, the sun moved higher. Beautiful. Blinding. Distracting.

"I'm sorry, Cal. I don't know what to say." And there was Mae, pulling her back into reality.

"Neither do I." Callie blinked, turning away from the morning star. "I didn't know what seeing Kyle after all of this time would be like, but I didn't expect this." She'd even tried to prepare herself for a beautiful redhead, for the woman Kyle might be dating. Somehow that was easier to deal with than 'just friends.' Those words stung like the icy bay on her skin.

Mae cleared her throat. "Cal, will you be honest with me?"

"Of course."

"Brutally honest."

"Um ... okay?"

"I mean I *really* want you to think about this. Don't just blurt out the first thing that comes to mind."

"I've got it. Honesty. Contemplation. What do you want to know?"

"What bothers you more, that Kyle might not be interested in dating you again, or that you might be wrong about why you're back in Traverse City?"

Kyle. Right? But she promised to think about it, so Callie let the sun do its magic while she meditated.

Kyle. The one-that-got-away getting away again. Okay, maybe he wasn't the one-that-got-away, but he was definitely the one she let go and was starting to reconsider. She'd been so certain back then—absolutely confident she'd made the right decision when they broke up. The technique she'd regretted, but never the outcome.

Was that Mae's point? "I really do miss Kyle," Callie said.

"But is that why you're so upset?"

Of course. Sort of. Everything about Kyle was familiar. Comfortable. She looked forward to seeing him again. But if she was really honest, she felt the same way about Ryan. That thought did weird things to her pulse. "Maybe not."

"Good. Admitting that you have a problem is the first step."

Callie's shoulders tensed. A problem? "I don't have a problem."

"A compulsion then."

"What compulsion?"

"You had to know what was going to happen this summer," said Mae. "You couldn't just come home, enjoy yourself, and let God work things out. You picked the most reasonable solution and ran with it."

"Because it made sense. Why is that so wrong?"

"It's not, honey, but everything about God doesn't have to make sense."

"I know, I know. God confounds the wise."

"Oh, good. You've been listening. I don't have to repeat the whole speech."

Callie sighed, thankful she wouldn't have to sit through Mae's therapy session again. It wasn't the lecture that bothered Callie. But Mae always went back to the Bible, and Callie couldn't argue with that. "I just like to be prepared."

"I know you do, but it's okay to be surprised every now and then."

It was, but the surprise wasn't what bothered Callie. She could handle a surprise. What really bothered her was the mistake. What if she was never supposed to be in Traverse City to begin with? If she was wrong about Kyle, maybe she was wrong about the whole summer. And if she'd misunderstood that simple command from God, what else had she messed up?

By the time Callie came back inside, Ryan and Jack were both up and getting ready for work. Ryan went to the office. Jack insisted that he didn't need any help, so Callie sat on the couch to read a book. Three hours later, she woke up with a crick in her neck.

Grabbing the book from the floor, she set it on the table as she checked her phone for messages. Kyle hadn't called, and she wasn't really interested in calling him. No news from Jack, so he was either working in one of the parks or out in the garage. He basically only came inside to eat and sleep these days. Leaning back, she pushed aside the curtains and looked outside. The overcast skies didn't make for good beach days, and the thought of all the tourist traffic made her want to avoid going into town.

Grabbing the remote control, she flipped through channels. Lots of nothing to watch. There had to be a better way to pass the time. She was considering calling Mae when the front door opened.

"Squirt! Come on out!"

"Jack?" Callie tossed the remote onto the couch and headed outside. She got out there just in time to see Jack's backside disappear around the far side of the garage. She'd known him long enough to follow, but she wasn't sure if she should hustle or not. Well, if he wasn't going to give her any clear guidance, she was going to take her time. After all, the temperature was perfect, even if the clouds were hiding the sun. By the time she reached the corner of the garage, Callie was considering moving her pity party outside. At least then, she could get some fresh air.

She rounded the corner. Jack was rearranging boxes. "What do you need?"

He didn't look back, he just pointed to the opposite wall.

Callie turned. Her piano! She ran to it and slid onto the bench, her fingers hovering over the shiny white keys. "Can I play it?"

"You better. I took two whole days to make room for it out here."

Fingers trembling, she brushed the smooth keys. They begged to be teased, but before she played even one note, she ran to her brother and threw her arms around his waist, pressing her cheek against his back. "Thank you so much. Thank you, thank you, thank you."

He turned so he could hug her back. "I was sick of watching you mope around the house. Maybe now, you'll have an outlet." After a quick squeeze, he patted her back. "Now go play something."

She hadn't brought any music with her, but she doubted her parents had touched the piano since she moved out, so she rushed back to the bench and lifted the lid. Sure enough, assorted books and pieces of sheet music filled the space. She grabbed the first piece of Mozart she found and sat down. Her fingers practically vibrated with excited energy as she placed her hands over the keys.

Closing her eyes, she inhaled. On the exhale, she touched the cool keys. Softly. Slowly. Chords filled the packed garage. As her fingers moved, her shoulders relaxed. Up and down. Left and right. Wave after wave of music wrapped around her. She didn't need to look at the sheet. Her fingers instinctively knew the way as they danced across the keys. With each note, her troubles faded. The movement. The harmonies. The essence of the song reached into her heart telling her all would be okay.

She played the final notes, then let her fingers rest on the keys, holding them in place as if she could press out another second of beauty. When she opened her eyes, Jack was leaning against the wall beside her, his arms crossed, and his head cocked to the side. He smiled at her the same way he had when she graduated from high school, and then college. Her cheeks heated.

"You are truly talented, Squirt. I hope you make good use of that piano this summer."

"I will, I promise. I can't thank you enough."

He mussed up her hair as he walked by. "You don't have to thank me. Just keep playing. And maybe grill up a few steaks for dinner."

CHAPTER 24

Jack handed Callie another black plastic bag bulging with garbage. Her nose crinkled when she grabbed the sack, but she didn't complain. She hadn't complained much in the past few days—since he'd delivered the piano. For the most part, she was content to work around the house, but yesterday she started asking about working with him again, so he thought he'd bring her along for garbage day.

The smell hardly affected him anymore, but Callie plugged her nose before tossing the bag onto the pile in the back of his truck. They had a couple of hours yet before noon, then the sun would really cook the trash beyond a point that even he could handle. They had to work fast.

"Make sure it's on there good." Jack pulled off his cap and examined the flimsy black tower. "We've got to haul these to the trash compactor. The township board won't increase my budget, so I get the cheap bags, but I don't trust them." He wedged his head back into the old hat. A hair cut would probably help the cap fit better, but he'd missed his appointment when he took Callie in to get stitches. That had been a couple of weeks ago, but who had the time to reschedule?

His sister stood on her tiptoes examining the pile, tugging and adjusting the bags. The first layer sat securely under the rest of the bags, but the top two teetered a bit. She pushed them around, then shrugged. "Drive carefully?"

Jack chuckled. She was finally starting to sound like herself. "I'll tie them down with some rope before we leave. Follow me."

He hiked through the overgrown lawn to the tiny brown maintenance shed. Someday he'd convince the board to replace the outdated structure. In the meantime, the barn doors stuck together as he yanked on the handle. When they finally creaked open, waves of stuffy hot air rushed out.

Callie stepped up beside him. "Whoa. It's a sauna in here." She used the hem of her sleeveless pink shirt to wipe the sweat off her face. "Are we going to be in here long?"

"Nope. We just need to get the mower and weed wacker."

She groaned.

Jack chuckled. "I'll use the whacker. Do you remember how to handle the mower?"

Callie examined the massive grass-covered machine. She'd spent ten summers mowing with their dad, but this was a newer model. Better steering, more power. Bowers Harbor Park included three acres of public property. The commercial-sized Toro sported a sixty-inch deck. He'd given her a quick ride and demonstration once before, but that was two years ago. He fully expected to reexplain it all.

Instead, Callie smacked him on the back. "I'll figure it out." She stepped onto the machine, plopping herself down on the cracked vinyl seat. The whole thing bounced as Callie shifted around, playing with the handles.

Pressure started to build behind Jack's eyes. Maybe he should mow the lawn later.

But then Callie turned the key, firing up the engine. She smiled, giving him two thumbs up. The engine thundered in the shed. "I've got it!"

Jack grabbed some ear protection from a hook on the wall and tossed them to Callie. "Be careful!"

She snapped them over her ears and nodded, but he was sure she couldn't hear him. He felt better for warning her, though. She waved then shifted the mower into gear.

The pressure subsided as Jack realized he didn't really have to worry about Callie. She easily drove the machine out and around the shed. She'd always been good with a mower. The grass would be fine.

Jack yelled something as she rolled out of the shed, but Callie had no idea what. If it was important, he'd chase her down. She steered the mower right around the shed, getting a feel for the controls. Between the angry roaring and the bone-rattling vibrations of the engine, it took most of her concentration just to stay in the seat. After a few laps around the mud-colored building, however, her confidence peaked. She could do this.

She took the final turn, driving straight toward Jack's back. Callie yelled, but he wore a set of the same ugly ear muffs that she did. Her fingers strangled the control levers as she shifted and pulled to save her brother. The machine spun, but not before the edge of the deck clipped the heel of Jack's boot. Before the mower had even stopped, Callie swiveled in the seat to make sure Jack was okay. He just stood there shaking his head.

Callie's shoulders relaxed.

Jack pointed at his eyes.

Huh?

He took off his safety glasses and waved them at her.

Oh, her sunglasses. She plucked them from where they hung on the collar of her shirt and tucked them behind her ears, resting comfortably on her nose. Jack gave her a thumbs-up then returned to his weed whipping. He expertly trimmed around the small barn, hacking off the weeds without damaging the building. He hadn't let her touch the machine since she accidentally shredded the siding at their parents' house.

Desperate to make Jack proud, Callie turned back around and got to work. The levers moved easily with the gentlest touch. The machine glided forward. The mower-made breeze cooled her skin as she sped around the park. Acres of overgrown grass shrank in front of her as she zipped about. Finally, something she couldn't mess up. She'd be done in no time.

Even with the breeze, however, the late-morning sun cooked her skin. By the time she'd finished half of the lawn, sweat soaked her shirt. Her lips were cracking. Not until her tongue felt fuzzy did Callie admit the truth—she was dehydrated, and her water bottle was in the truck. Even more than her desire to finish quickly was her desire to stay out of the emergency room. No need for another trip due to heat exhaustion. She needed to get her water.

Pulling the right handle toward her rib cage while pushing the left handle away from her, Callie turned the mower to the right. After a quick spin around, she pressed both handles forward and enjoyed the ride toward the truck.

As she moved along, Callie admired the effects of her work. The thought of mowing for Jack had originally depressed her, but now she realized it was the one thing she could do without needing his constant supervision. That alone transformed the once tedious task into a literal carefree ride in the park. Her straight, even rows looked great.

THUD.

Callie jerked forward, losing her grip on the handles and sliding off the seat. She jammed her knee onto the deck, stopping her forward motion just before she slid into the back of Jack's truck.

Jack's truck. Fear clogged Callie's throat. Her face was a foot away from the rear end of her brother's baby. How had she not seen the monster? Heat stroke and the emergency room were a better option than having to tell Jack she'd dented his truck.

Callie jumped up and looked, expecting to see Jack running to the rescue. She couldn't see him anywhere. Good. He might have missed the bump.

Dropping back onto the seat, tension seized every muscle in Callie's body. She grabbed the controls and moved the mower back. Letting it idle, she hopped off to inspect the damage. She'd plowed right into the back passenger tire. Between the protruding hubcap and excessive rubber, however, the mower hadn't touched the truck.

Not a single scratch.

"Oh, thank God." The tension melted, and Callie pushed herself up on wobbly legs. She scanned the area again, looking for a panicked Jack. Still nothing.

Callie collapsed onto the mower's seat and smiled. She hadn't failed Jack. Everything was going to be okay.

Her arms shook as she slowly maneuvered around the back end of the truck. She could get her water bottle and get back to work. No harm done.

When she pulled around the tailgate, she saw him. Callie's innards wrapped around themselves. Jack walked toward her, but he didn't look angry. He was just motioning and talking. She drove toward him to see what he wanted.

That's when she spotted the garbage bag on the ground. It must have rolled off the pile when she plowed into the tire. Oh, well. Jack didn't need to know how it ended up on the ground. She'd toss the bag back up after she finished with the grass. Until then, she'd just push it out of her way.

As she moved toward Jack, he moved faster toward her. Then he dropped the weed whacker and started running. Oh no—was something wrong? Callie hit the throttle and sped toward him.

Then she noticed the garbage bag. It didn't roll. It wavered and shook, then a corner disappeared under the side of the deck—

WHOOSH!

PLEW!

"Callie!"

Jack's voice cut through the protective ear muffs as a million bits of garbage exploded into the air.

The world stopped moving as Callie turned off the engine. What had she done? Jack stood three feet away staring at his legs. Confetti and goo clung to his skin and hair before dropping onto the ground. She swiveled around, her gut wrenching as she took in the sight. Finely chopped pieces of trash surrounded her. They covered the grass, the parking lot ... and Jack's truck. Her throat constricted. Tiny rainbow flecks covered the tires and truck bed.

When she turned toward Jack, he was looking at his truck.

Callie jumped off the mower and yanked off the ear protection. "I'm sorry, I'm sorry, I'm sorry," she said, rushing to his side. "I bumped the rear tire and must have knocked off the bag. I thought I would just move it out of the way. I didn't realize —"

Jack held up a hand. His chest heaved as he examined the mess, but his face didn't flinch. How mad was he? Fighting the urge to cry, she tried again. "I'm really, really sorry. I didn't know it would—"

Jack took one step toward her.

She pressed her lips together.

"You're fired."

CHAPTER 25

Ryan didn't know Callie could sit silently for so long. After the forty-minute car ride to church and the hour-long service, she'd barely uttered a dozen sentences. Aside from asking him to drop her off at Mae's house after church, she'd been quiet. Even as people filed out of the sanctuary around her, she sat quietly in her chair, scribbling away in a small notebook she'd pulled out of her purse. He considered leaving her there, but she had his pen.

"Callie." He nudged her shoulder again. "People are leaving."

She glanced up, then returned to her writing. Shiny strands of wavy hair slipped off her shoulder and hid her flawless face. Maybe the pen wasn't the only reason he hadn't moved. Ryan leaned back in his chair, content to watch and wait.

Callie made a few more notations before finally closing the note pad. Handing back his pen, she smiled. "Thanks for letting me use that. I had so much going through my head that I just couldn't concentrate. I should be good now that I've got it all on paper."

Ryan smiled back. He hoped that method worked for her. No amount of note-taking would help him concentrate around Callie. Another reason to move out. Soon.

"I'm hungry." Callie popped to her feet. "Do you want to get lunch someplace? I don't even remember if I had breakfast, I was so distracted. I could probably pack away a whole pizza."

Apparently, the quiet spell had ended. "Are you in the mood for pizza or just tossing out ideas?"

"Ideas. That might be too greasy. What are our options?" She picked up her Bible and tucked it into her purse, but she kept the notebook in her hand. After the next family passed their row, Callie stepped into the flow of traffic. Her dark skirt snagged on the edge of the chair as she walked away.

She didn't seem to notice the snag or the way it pulled the fabric close to her hips. Ryan did. He noticed everything now, like the way she applied her Chapstick and moisturized her hands, and how her eyes sparkled when she wore blue but darkened when she wore red.

Shaking some sense back into his brain, he followed her out of the sanctuary, careful to watch his footsteps and nothing else. Once in the foyer, he searched the crowd for Jack.

They usually sat by each other at church. Not today, though. Jack was just getting in the shower when it was time to leave. Ryan scanned the crowd until he saw a head of wild-man hair. He didn't have to see the face to recognize Jack. Since he didn't want to break his promise, Ryan figured the best idea would be to invite Jack to lunch too.

Ryan cupped Callie's elbow. As she turned toward him, he picked up a light apple scent. Her cheeks matched her pink shirt. She looked young, fresh. He added pink shirts and apples to his mental checklist before returning to the present. "I found Jack," he said. "I'll go see what his plans are."

She smiled. "I'll be here."

Ryan nodded and rushed away. He didn't take long to weave through the church members, but he had good motivation to get to Jack then hurry back. When he finally caught up with his friend, Ryan had to take a moment to figure out what he was seeing. Jack—talking to a woman.

Ryan walked up to the couple, slapping his friend on the back. "Hi. I'm Ryan."

The tall, slim brunette offered her hand. "Kathleen." Almost as tall as Ryan, she looked him in the eye. "It's nice to meet you."

"You too. I don't mean to interrupt, but I need to talk to Jack for a minute."

"Not a problem." Kathleen touched Jack's arm with a tanned hand. "It was nice to meet you Jack. Maybe I'll see you again next week." As she walked away, Ryan couldn't stop himself from comparing her athletic gait with Callie's more feminine steps. No doubt Kathleen was attractive but not his type.

Ryan looked at Jack. "Who's Kathleen?"

Jack shrugged. "I got out of the house late and we walked in together. Church had already started, so we didn't talk much."

"You sat with her?"

He shrugged again.

Never a dull moment with Jack, but Ryan didn't have time to chat about it. "Callie wants to get lunch. Do you want to come?"

"Sure."

They turned around and Ryan bumped into Stacey. Callie stood behind her.

Both women smiled. They couldn't look more different, yet something in the way they stood together sent up a warning flag.

Jack cleared his throat. "You know, I think I'm going to pass. There was a mess at the compactor station yesterday. I should go back and make sure everything is okay."

Stacey's eyes widened. "You don't even have time for lunch?"

"I'll get something on the road. You guys have fun." Jack looked at Stacey, then, like a rabbit running through traffic, he bolted.

Ryan considered running after him, but he didn't mind some extra time with Callie, especially since Jack officially knew it wasn't a real date. It would be a nice afternoon, just the two of them.

Stacey sighed. "I guess it's just the three of us."

And now he understood the warning flag.

Callie clapped her hands. "Then, let's go. I didn't eat breakfast. I'm starving."

The women headed out first. When Ryan stepped outside, he noticed another young woman had delayed Jack's hasty departure. Ryan recognized Jack's wide-legged, hand-on-the-neck, I-don't-want-to-be-here stance. Ryan chuckled. By the time he had his sunglasses on, he stood next to Jack.

"Sorry to interrupt," he said, grabbing Jack's shoulder, "but I need to steal him for a minute."

Jack nodded at the woman. "Bye." Then Ryan spun him away. They marched straight to Jack's truck. "Thank you."

"No problem. You sure you don't want to grab lunch?"

"I'm not ready yet."

Not ready yet? They stopped beside the freshly washed pickup. Jack blew out a quick breath. "Thanks again. And don't forget our agreement."

"This is hardly a date."

"Remember that. Have you found a place to live yet?

Ryan shook his head. "It's not easy to find an affordable place to rent in Traverse City for the summer. I'm putting my stuff in storage right now. If all else fails, I'll find a bedroom to rent someplace."

Jack cocked an eyebrow. "You'd do all that just for a date with my sister?"

"At least I'm doing something." Ryan scanned the parking lot. Stacey and Callie glowed in the sunlight, chatting and laughing like old friends. "Do you want us to get you anything?"

"I'm good." Jack opened the truck door and grabbed his ball cap that barely fit over his crazy hair. "I appreciate what you're doing."

"Don't mention it."

Jack climbed into the truck. "I won't."

Ryan met the girls on the sidewalk.

"I don't understand him," Stacey said, watching Jack's truck drive by.

Ryan looked down at her and smiled. "He's a good guy with a good heart. Beyond that, I don't get him either."

"At least I'm not alone."

"Hardly." Callie shifted the purse on her shoulder. "Where do you guys want to eat? There are a few places we can walk to."

"I have coupons for the cafe around the corner," said Stacey.

Ryan nodded. "Sounds good."

Callie started walking, her heels clapping on the cement. "Then let's go."

Stacey's stomach growled again. The line to get a table had been short, but she seriously doubted whether or not she'd ever see her food. Ryan offered her the last breadstick.

"Thanks. I should start bringing snacks to church."

The trio sat in a small booth near the windows of the crowded cafe. The sun warmed the table, but the air inside kept them cool. Callie had set a good pace, getting them into the restaurant before the crowd surged in behind them. Between the unending talking and the clanking of dishes, Stacey had to lean across the table to stay in the conversation.

She sat across from Callie and Ryan, trying not to stare. Callie had sworn that she wanted to rekindle some old romance, but Stacey couldn't ignore what she saw for herself. Callie and Ryan looked natural together. Comfortable. Definitely attracted. Ryan's face practically lit up like a Christmas tree when he slid into the seat beside Callie.

The beautiful brunette clutched her stomach and groaned. "I'm about to gnaw off my own arm. I should have grabbed a bagel or something this morning."

Stacey tore off part of her breadstick and gave it to Callie. "You really shouldn't skip breakfast. It's the most important meal of the day." Ryan chuckled. "What?"

He leaned into Cal. "She lives by that motto. She doesn't often miss a meal."

Callie rolled her eyes. "Don't say it like that. You make me sound like a compulsive overeater." She linked her fingers together before leaning forward to lock eyes with Stacey. "I like breakfast food. That's all. I'd have French toast and eggs every day if I could. And maybe pancakes. And biscuits with gravy. With lots of bacon."

"You have time to make that every day?"

"I make time, but today I was a little distracted."

Stacey looked at Ryan. She could see how he might be distracting.

He shook his head and held his hands up in surrender. "It wasn't me."

Callie nodded. "He's totally innocent, I swear."

Stacey's stomach growled again. "What could be so important that a person forgets to eat?"

"Excellent question," said Ryan. He crossed his arms and swiveled toward Callie. "What's going on?"

The bright sunlight hid it well, but Stacey thought she saw Callie blushing. It struck her as odd, since Callie didn't seem to be the type of person who blushed, especially about something like breakfast. If it made her that uncomfortable, Stacey didn't want to be pushy. "You don't have to tell us. It's not really any of our business. Let's just forget about it and talk about something else. How was your date with Kyle?"

All of the color in Callie's cheeks drained away. "Interestingly enough, that's not really much of a subject change." She grabbed her ice water and took a long drink.

Guilt clobbered Stacey's heart. "I'm sorry." She knew by the heat in her neck that this time her skin had reddened. "I didn't mean to put you on the spot. I'll stop talking now."

Callie shook her head. "It's okay. It's not like I haven't talked with both of you about Kyle before. The thing is, it's not going the way I'd planned, and then Jack fired me—"

Stacey gasped. "He fired you?"

Ryan's hand covered Callie's. "Wow. I'm sorry, Cal."

Stacey's eyes flickered to Ryan's face. Though he said the words, the corner of his mouth twitched, as if he couldn't decide whether or not to smile or frown. She didn't understand his confusion. An irrational Jack was nothing to smile about.

"What happened?" she asked.

Callie's shoulders sagged. "I sort of ... ran over a garbage bag with the lawn mower."

Ryan cocked an eyebrow. "You, sort of, ran it over, or you did run it over?"

Stacey tried to picture the scene, imagine Jack's reaction. The more she thought about it, the more she wanted to smile. Stacey looked down at her lap, fighting back the giggles.

Then Ryan snorted.

She looked up. He hid his face behind a glass of water, but his shoulders shook as he tried to drink. Callie elbowed him, and water splashed everywhere.

Callie smiled though. "How was I supposed to know his mower would suck it in like that? I used to push things around with my parents' mower all the time. His super Hoover sucked it up like a piece of lint. It shot pieces of garbage all over the grass, on the back of his truck, and on his legs."

A picture of the scene popped into Stacey's mind. Callie on a lawn mower. Jack's neck vein bulging as he tried to keep his temper. A giggle popped out of her mouth. Ryan laughed out loud. By the time their food arrived, all three of them were in tears.

"Well, Squirt, at least you went out with a bang." Ryan tweaked her nose.

Callie punched his shoulder. "Don't call me that."

"Maybe you should say grace."

She did, but Stacey didn't pay much attention. Even with her eyes closed, she pictured their faces and tender interactions. She wanted that type of relationship with Jack, but she wanted to be more than just friends. Of course, Stacey had her suspicions that Callie and Ryan would probably be more than friendly if it weren't for Kyle. Kyle had to be pretty amazing for Callie to pass up Ryan for him.

The prayer ended, and Stacey decided to find out. "So, do you want to talk about your date with Kyle?"

Ryan's posture stiffened.

Stacey bit into her turkey sandwich.

Callie shrugged. "I don't think I'm doing this right." She tore into her own lunch, mumbling around the food. "But I don't know what I'm doing wrong."

Ryan set down his hoagie and looked at her. "You can't do it wrong. You ask him out. He says yes or no. What did he say?"

"He said yes the first time, but this last time, two of his coworkers joined us." Callie shook her head. "The one girl is beautiful, and she and Kyle are really … chummy. And the longer the dinner went, the more I realized that he wasn't treating me any differently than her. We're just … chums."

Stacey tossed a chip in her mouth. "Did you tell him it was a real date?"

Callie responded by filling her mouth with food.

Frustration bubbled up in Stacey's chest. Dropping her food, she crossed her arms. "Seriously? Men don't get subtle. You can't drop hints. You have to tell him what you mean." She thought about Jack and Home Depot. "Even that's no guarantee that he'll know how to respond. If you really want to reconnect with Kyle, then you need to tell him."

If Stacey hadn't been sitting directly across from Callie she might not have noticed, but Callie stopped chewing for a nanosecond and glanced at Ryan. The tiniest of movements, but Stacey saw. Picking up her sandwich, she rolled her eyes. "And I thought Jack was the one with issues."

CHAPTER 26

Sweat rolled down Callie's back as she pulled another weed from Mae's garden. The late-day sun beat down as fiercely as it had after church. Tiny pebbles poked into her knees. In spite of the irritations, she kept pulling. With each tug, she released a little more frustration.

Mae set a glass of ice water in the dirt as she walked by. "You don't have to do this. We could just sit here and talk."

"I might as well make myself useful to someone this summer." Callie scooped the dirt out from around a gargantuan hairy stem. Using her fingers as an auger, she burrowed toward the roots, trying to loosen the soil. "Besides, this flower bed has got to be making you crazy."

"It is. Charlie tries to help out, but he's busy enough with work and the girls." The old wooden swing groaned. Then Mae groaned. "I am so ready to have this kid."

Callie twisted the weed in her hand, wrapping it around her fingers and adjusting her grip. She propped one foot forward, then leaned back and pulled. Her hand slipped, so she wrapped both hands around the stem. She leaned, pushed, twisted, pulled. The rough surface scratched across her palms. Her foot sank into the dirt, pulling, pulling, pulling—

THWAK!

Callie crashed on her rear, trophy in hand.

Mae whistled, piercing the air. "Bravo! I thought I was going to have to call a tree service for that one. Thank you."

Tossing the long-rooted weed in the wheelbarrow, Callie sprayed her legs and feet with dirt. Most of it fell off when she stood, but a layer of fine dust stuck to her damp legs.

She grabbed her ice water and joined Mae on the swing. They settled into a rhythmic motion, the wood and chains protesting their weight. Callie sipped. Mae sighed. The shade of the giant oak tree cooled her skin more than the barely noticeable breeze created by their rocking. Callie closed her eyes, savoring every crick and creak that didn't come with a chatty tourist.

"How was church today?"

But there was always Mae. "Good. I think."

"What was the message?"

"Something about forgiveness and mercy. I don't remember the entire thing. Are you sure Charlie doesn't mind taking me home? I can call Jack and see if he'll come pick me up—or even get a cab."

"No way. I'm giving him money and making him take the girls. You mention ice cream on the ride home, and I should get at least ninety minutes to myself."

Callie laughed as she reached over to rub her friend's belly. "Is everything okay? Are you two getting enough rest?"

"We're fine." Mae's head dropped onto the back of the swing. "I'm going to have this baby tomorrow. I have to. It's getting hotter. I'm getting crankier. My feet are so big that I'm wearing Charlie's flip flops. I need this little guy to come home. Soon."

"Sticking with a boy then?"

"I just know it's a boy ... I think."

Callie chuckled. "What if he decides to hang out for a few more days?"

"We're ready either way. My mom is planning to take the girls, Charlie's boss is great and is going to let him take time off whenever I deliver, and I'm ready to scratch my ankles again." She slapped Callie's knee, stinging the hot skin. "Enough about me. Why weren't you paying attention at church?"

"I was reevaluating why I'm here."

"Uh-huh. And what did you find out?"

Callie wiggled her fingers into the tight front pocket of her shorts and retrieved the now damp piece of paper. "I was looking back at what happened, trying to figure out where I went wrong. How I can get back on track." The page flopped around as she unfolded it. "Here's the original plan."

- Move in with Jack
- Work for Jack
- Contact Kyle
- Reconnect with Kyle

"That was the entire summer plan, and I failed."

"You didn't fail. You *did* do all of this. There's nothing wrong with your list. You just finished the items faster than you thought you would."

That theory did weird things to Callie's chest. That couldn't really be true. "Then what am I supposed to do for the rest of the summer?" Her chest clenched again. Maybe a little liquid would help things loosen up. She sipped her water.

"Do whatever you want." Mae huffed. "This list doesn't say anything about spending the whole summer with Jack or dating Kyle. Those were your expectations." She dropped the soggy paper on Callie's lap. "Sometimes we're wrong."

The tightness returned. "If I was wrong about these, how do I know I wasn't wrong about everything else?"

"Just because you interpreted part of God's plan incorrectly doesn't mean the *whole* thing was wrong. Your plan didn't go the way you expected, but it still worked."

"Technically." Callie jammed the stupid paper back into her pocket and gave the swing a good push. Ryan's face flashed through her mind. "And what about Ryan?"

The swing stopped, but Callie and her glass flew forward, crashing to the ground next to Mae's foot. She looked over her shoulder to find her pregnant friend leaning forward and grinning.

"What about Ryan?" Mae wiggled her eyebrows.

Lunch. The night by the fire. Ice cream. Difficulties breathing. "I don't know." Callie sat in the grass so they could see each other. "He's as wonderful as he's always been, but he's moving—"

"What? Where?"

She shrugged. "Somewhere in town. I don't know why he's moving, but it looks like he'll be out soon." Then she wouldn't have to see him every day. Maybe she'd be able to forget about their lunches and focus on work … and figuring out what she did wrong. "Ryan was never part of the plan anyway."

"He wasn't a reason for you to move here, but he could still be part of God's plan." Mae's eyes twinkled. "You have the whole summer to see what happens." She patted Callie's filthy knee, smearing the sweat and dirt. "You don't have to know all of the details. Just go as God leads. He'll take care of the rest."

"I don't know." Two months of spontaneity? "That never works out well for me. Remember the night I went for a spur-of-the-moment bike ride and broke my leg?"

"Yeah. You spent the whole summer practicing the violin and won a scholarship to that music camp."

"Okay, fine. That might have worked out, but what about the box of red hair tint that we decided to buy? My hair turned purple."

"Oh, that one." Mae leaned back and started rocking.

"I failed the audition for the youth orchestra because of their dress code."

"I remember. You didn't play the violin that whole summer."

The memory pricked at Callie's heart. "I was so upset I could barely look at it."

"Yep." Mae nodded, still rocking. "Instead, you bought a used a guitar and taught yourself to play."

Had it been that same summer?

Mae chuckled. "See. It doesn't always turn out bad."

Callie dropped her chin to her knees. Frustration slipped into her already emotionally overloaded blood stream. "I hate when you use logic."

"Someone has to keep you sane."

"I'm as far from sane as I am from Hong Kong." And the frustrations just kept mounting. "Do you really think I might be here because of Ryan?"

"Calista!" Mae popped up like a jack-in-the-box. "You're missing the point. Why you're here doesn't matter. God will tell you what you need to know *when* you need to know it. Stop looking at your so-called failures and just enjoy yourself."

"Enjoy yourself." The unknown future. A summer of uncertainty. At the very worst—two months of chaos. At the very best, well, maybe she'd get stranded somewhere and find a lottery ticket on the side of the road. She pushed herself off the hard ground as she considered the possibilities. More debris clung to her legs and palms. Definitely a dirty summer.

Mae raised her arms and twisted her midsection, groaning like an eighty-six-year-old arthritic woman. When she finally finished her calisthenics, she looped her arm through Callie's and led them toward the house.

"You can do this, Cal. Relax and take each day as it comes. One at a time."

"You make it sound like a twelve-step program."

She laughed. "With you, the program might take twenty-four steps."

Halfway to the house, Mae stopped. She released Callie's arm and pressed her hand to the small of her back. Her eyes widened. "You might have to work through the steps pretty quickly. Tomorrow might really be the day."

CHAPTER 27

Callie tossed another rag into her bucket and closed the closet door. As she stepped out of the bathroom, Jack nearly plowed her over.

"Do you need anything else? I'm going fishing today, and I'm turning off my phone. You're on your own." He stopped beside her and looked into the bucket of supplies. "You're going to clean again? Mondays and Tuesdays are your day off."

"Technically, every day is my day off now. Remember? I figured I'd at least earn my keep."

Jack shook his head. His shaggy hair bounced around his stubborn head. "Don't start. You know this is the best option for both of us. I'm going to Duck Lake. I'll be late."

"I'll be here."

He reached over and yanked on Callie's ponytail.

She swatted his hand. "Grow up."

He laughed.

"Are you really not going to let me work for you anymore?" she asked. "I don't want to be a burden."

Jack groaned. Ignoring her, he marched toward the kitchen.

Callie followed. "I was sort of planning on that money."

He stopped on the dining room steps. "Do you need money?"

"Not yet, but I might."

"Why, what happened?"

"Nothing yet, but you know what's going on with the schools. There are budget cuts everywhere, and I'm a music teacher."

Jack's jaw twitched. "Are they firing you?"

"Not that I know of, but I want to have a healthy savings, just in case."

He nodded and started walking again. "Let me think about it."

"Can we talk about it later?"

"I'm technically back to work Wednesday. Let me think about it until then." He opened the fridge and grabbed everything off the top shelf. She couldn't imagine why he needed the half and half, but he obviously wasn't in the mood to talk about it. Jack returned to the fridge for mustard, ketchup, and a jar of capers. Callie was obviously distracting him. Instead of contributing to his madness, she went outside to find his fishing cooler.

On the way to the garage, she walked past her car, then Jack's, then the empty spot where Ryan's car had been. Callie couldn't identify the sudden tension that seized her chest the first time she saw Ryan moving his things. Now she cringed at his missing car.

Even though she didn't have proof, Callie had a gut feeling that Ryan was moving out because of her, though she couldn't imagine why. Jack would never confirm it, but she sensed she was the reason. Maybe Ryan was trying to be a gentleman and give her space to spend time with her brother. Not that she had asked for time with Jack ... or needed it. And if that was the case, why wouldn't anyone talk to her about it?

It didn't make sense for Ryan to move out because of her. She was only staying for a few more weeks. Really, she should be the one moving out, especially since she wasn't working with Jack anymore. She just had to find a place she could afford with no summer income.

Inside the garage, she quickly found the cooler and headed back to the house. By the time she returned to the kitchen, Callie hadn't come up with a single good option that would let her stay in Traverse City rent-free without displacing Ryan. She had the rest of the day to figure out something though.

"Thanks." Jack relieved Callie of the cooler. He removed the lid and leaned it against the counter. Using both hands, he swept an armload of food into the abused Igloo.

Callie pulled a couple of ice packs out of the freezer tossed them on top. "You promise that we'll talk when you come back?"

"I promise." He pressed on the lid. Something popped.

"Can we also talk about why Ryan's suddenly moving out?"

"You'll have to ask him. I'll see you tonight." He didn't look at her when he picked up the cooler or when he put on his hat or when he passed her on the way out the door.

She followed him onto the deck and across the lawn. What had just happened? "Are we good?" she asked.

Jack stopped. He looked back at her and winked. "We're always good, Squirt. I'll see you later."

The charred wood glared at Callie. Crossing her arms, she inspected the chair again. Blackened paint covered the front legs of Jack's Adirondack. Only one leg needed serious attention, but she doubted Jack had the right color paint for a perfect match, and a trip to town would take too much time. She wanted to surprise Jack. The sooner she finished, the better.

Her phone twittered. Curiosity tugged at her, but the chairs held her full attention. She didn't know how long they would need, and they were her top priority. Reaching into her pocket, she silenced the ring tone. Time to get started.

Callie entered her brother's lair. Floor-to-ceiling shelves covered the entire back wall of the garage, and assorted cans of paint and chemicals bulged off of each one. The closer Callie stepped, the more the wall overwhelmed her. So many options.

Picking a shelf, she grabbed the first can she could reach. Not even half full. Perfect. She could eliminate all of the small cans and anything less than half full. There was no way she was going to run out of paint.

Nearly an hour later, after lots of can-shaking, she lined up her options on the workbench. Stains were out of the question—they would require too many coats. White, pink, and pale green paint. She couldn't imagine Jack sitting on any of those, so she put them back on the shelf. Periwinkle. Why did he have a can of periwinkle paint? She'd ask him about that later. Until then, that color went back on the shelf. After discarding a few more questionable cans, Callie had five masculine options left. Her heart palpitated when she imagined picking a color Jack hated. Snagging the phone from her pocket, she called Ryan.

"Good morning." She could hear his smile, which calmed her nerves. "What's up?"

"I'm in the garage. I need a hand."

"I get off work at five, but I can probably skip lunch and make it back earlier."

Callie's innards fluttered. Working with Ryan would be nice, but that might not give her enough time to finish before Jack got home, and she had to think about Jack. And his chairs. And how she almost burned them up. "Thanks for the offer, but I really just have a question. I'm repainting Jack's chairs, and I don't know what color to use. I have tan, brown, gray, slate blue, and something that looks like rust."

Silence. Something scurried across the roof.

"Ryan?"

He cleared his throat. "Are you sure you want to paint them? They're in rough shape as it is."

"The chairs are in great shape. They just need a fresh coat of paint. I might as well do it, since I charred the one."

"Cal—"

"I'm going to do it. Jack has paint stripper in the garage someplace, so I can't possibly gouge myself again. I can handle paint. I just need to know what color to use."

Ryan sighed. "Why don't you wait for me to come help you? Please?"

Something in Callie's gut clenched, killing off any remaining flutters. "I'm not a child, Ryan. I didn't call for help. I called for color suggestions, but I'll figure it out myself. Bye."

She'd just stuffed the phone back in her pocket when it dinged. A quick glance told her the text was from Ryan. Her jaw tightened. *BLUE.* Callie's stomach relaxed. Setting the blue paint aside, she returned the rejects back to their shelves.

She took half an hour to decipher the paint stripper from the paint thinner from the other assorted chemicals, but after she found that, it only took a few minutes to round up the rest of her supplies and step outside.

By the time Callie reached the chairs, the late morning sun was baking the air. She dropped her things and tightened her ponytail. The forecast called for an unseasonably hot day, but Callie was determined. She didn't want to disappoint Jack again. If she could at least remove the burned paint before he got home, he'd know that she wasn't a complete tragedy. She could fix her own messes.

Callie picked up the small metal can of paint stripper and found the directions. Well ventilated ... clean rag ... away from flames, high heat ... protective clothing. She skimmed the back panel until she found what she wanted.

Apply liberally... check progress after 10 to 15 minutes by scraping a small area with a paint scraper. Oh, well. If the paint is softened all the way down to bare wood, the stripper is done. If not, put more stripper on the scraped area and wait five more minutes.

"I can do that," she told the can, then pulled on a pair of Jack's rubbery work gloves. She twisted off the cap and doused a rag with chemicals.

Fumes seared in her nostrils and burned her eyes. Callie tipped her head away, but she didn't stop. Tomorrow Jack's chairs would look like new.

She wasn't just fixing a burn, she was preserving a part of his past. That thought soothed her aching sinuses.

A breeze stirred, blowing away the chemical stench, but also carrying away the clouds. The sun baked Callie's skin. Her hand trembled and dripped as she swiped a thick coat of stripper over the arm of the chair. Sweat rolled down her forehead.

Silence.

The chair didn't collapse. Nothing exploded. She wasn't bleeding.

Callie laughed. An unknown weight lifted from her shoulders. The first successful swipe eased her heart and mind. With a bit more confidence she covered the supporting pieces, the legs, the back. The sun cooked her. Sweat dripped. She kept swiping.

As she coated the last piece of wood with paint stripper, Callie sighed. Jack and Ryan were wrong to doubt her. In ten to fifteen minutes she'd prove them wrong. She'd also have to figure out what to do with the paint after she scraped it off.

In the garage, she found a metal pail, a plastic bucket, empty paint cans, old take-out containers. Maybe she should make one more quick call to Ryan, just to make sure she picked the best one.

Callie peeled off the sweaty, sticky gloves and grabbed her phone. It started ringing in her hand. She didn't recognize the Alma number, but she answered anyway "Hello?"

"Callie, finally! I've been trying to reach you. We're getting laid off."

CHAPTER 28

Callie stared at the demon apparatus in her hand, the one destroying her life and her career. She could *not* lose her job. "Who is this?" she asked.

"Jan."

The middle school music teacher, and the person Callie kept forgetting to call back. "What are you talking about?"

"The school board. They have to make cuts."

Callie's heart dropped to the ground, right next to her disgusting gloves. Layoffs had been happening all over the state for the past few years, which was why she'd always worked during the summer. Suddenly, she didn't care about working with Jack. Her job—her *real* job—was on the line.

"Are you still there?"

Callie shook her head. "I'm sorry, yeah. I'm here. You just caught me at a bad time." She took a deep breath, preparing herself for the worse. "What's going on?"

"The state budget came back, and the school board has to make cuts."

"They always have to make cuts, and they're never as bad as we think it's going to be." This couldn't be happening. "They'll present a worst-case scenario, then we'll go back to school with sandpaper-brand toilet paper to save money."

"I know they've done that before, but this time it's serious. You haven't responded to your work emails, so I thought I'd call. I know you're out of town and didn't know how much you've heard."

"About what?"

"Nothing's set in stone yet, so ..."

"Jan, *you* called me. What's going on?"

Silence.

Budget cuts. Phone call from Jan. The worst summer of her life. "I'm fired, aren't I?" Callie braced herself, squeezing Jack's work bench until a splinter pierced her skin.

Chocolate. Now.

She ran into the house and straight into her bedroom. The bag of M&Ms pulled her into their gravitational field. Grabbing them from her desk, she dropped to the floor. Crunchy candy coating crackled in her mouth. Creamy, sweet Valium.

Her muscles relaxed. Breathing came easier, and Callie realized Jan was talking. "Wait, stop. I missed that. What were you saying?"

"They're talking about redistributing the workload because the junior high bands are so small." Jan took a deep breath. "They want to blend the seventh and eighth grade bands and cut the fifth and sixth grade bands."

"What about the strings class? And woodwinds?"

"Cut."

One band, two teachers. The chocolate curdled in Callie's throat. "What about high school music? What are they doing with Ken?"

"He would take over all band classes."

"All of them? He already teaches jazz and concert band, plus music appreciation classes."

Jan sighed.

M&Ms dropped to the floor.

"They want him to pick up junior high band too."

"So, you and I are fired."

"Not exactly."

A tear pushed past Callie's lashes. "We're vying for the same job."

"That's what it looks like."

The weight of the reality pressed Callie lower against the wall. "Except you've been with the district for two years longer than me." Her voice cracked. "You've got seniority."

"I'm so sorry, Callie."

"It's not your fault." Callie wiped a tear off her cheek. "I know how the union works."

"But I don't want you to think that I called to rub it in. I'm not entirely safe either, so I've spent the last few weeks looking at all of my options."

"Your options?" Callie sat up. "Like what?"

"I've sent out some résumés, just in case."

"You'd leave?"

"I don't know if I'll find anything, but I'm going to look. Things have been getting worse every year. I'm sick of always wondering what I'll be doing next year. If I can find a better job in another state, it might be time to move on. And if I move—"

"My job is more secure." The birds started singing.

"I haven't found anything yet," Jan said, "and I might not be able to find anything, but I wanted you to know. I didn't want you to get a call from someone on the board without giving you a heads-up."

Somehow, Callie's heart managed to rip apart and rejoice at the same time. "I don't know if I should wish you good luck or not."

"Don't worry about it. Nothing's set yet, so there's always the chance that things could change again." Something shifted on the line, and Jan's voice muffled. When it cleared she said, "I should get going. I hope I didn't ruin your day. I just thought you should know."

"Thank you. You haven't ruined anything." Callie poured the M&Ms right into her mouth. "Thanks for the heads-up," she mumbled.

"I'll call you if I hear anything else."

"Okay."

"And Callie?"

"Yeah?"

"I know you want to stay in Alma, but it might not be a bad idea for you to start looking around too. Just in case."

They exchanged a few quick pleasantries, but handful after handful of crunchy candy stole Callie's concentration. After she finally hung up the phone, her body collapsed under the stress, tipping to the side and sliding down the wall until her shoulder sank into the disgusting blue carpet. Laying there motionless, heavy with the weight of unemployment, she stared at the wall trying to figure out how she felt, but too many emotions raced through her heart.

She could lose another job. Even if she kept her position, she'd have to revise her entire curriculum. And she'd only keep her job if Jan left. Callie wanted to cry, laugh, yell, and possibly even quit teaching entirely.

She might lose her second job in a month. Jack might let her do the housework for a while—cooking, cleaning, more cooking. She'd have to talk with him when he got back. She could dust, clean the furniture.

Callie popped up.

The chairs!

She checked the time on her phone. Oh, no. Thirty minutes. An extra fifteen minutes wouldn't be that bad, would it? She had sort of read the warning label. Ventilation. Flames. High heat.

Callie flew out of the blue room, spraying M&Ms across the carpet and into the living room. Her heart raced. She considered following it right off the peninsula. A truck door slammed. Maybe it was just another tourist.

"Calista Marie!"

Maybe not.

CHAPTER 29

A giant, black booger clung to Jack's gloved hand.

Guilt stabbed Callie's heart as she examined the streaks of goopy paint stripper covering the once green chairs. She picked up a dead branch and poked the wood. It stuck to the gooey mess. Bits of bark clung to the chair as she scraped at the destroyed furniture. She yanked the stick away before looking at Jack. "I thought you were fishing today."

His eye twitched. "The township called. They need some paperwork for a meeting tonight. I thought I'd run home really quick, get them off my back, then go back out." He pointed at the chairs. "Obviously I can't. What did you do?"

"I, I ..." She looked at the chairs, then her brother, then the chairs. Her arms dropped to her side. "I don't know what to say."

"Try an explanation." Jack ripped the glove off of his hand and threw it in the grass. "I told you we'd talk when I got back." He pointed a rough finger at her face. "All you had to do was sit back and relax. You didn't have to do anything. Why can't you just—"

"I wanted to do something nice for you." Callie straightened her spine, bracing herself for the worst, but he clamped his mouth closed, breathing deeply through his nose. She tried to make eye contact, but he squeezed his eyes shut, pressing his lips together so hard they disappeared into a thin, white line. She could have handled yelling, but this? She didn't even know what it meant.

A muscle in his cheek twitched.

Shame joined her guilt. He had to know that she wasn't purposefully trying to ruin them. "I'm sorry. I got this phone call, and I didn't think it would take so long. I was doing everything right, but I wasn't sure what to do with the waste, so I was looking for a bucket, then I decided to call Ryan for help, but then Jan called. There was no way I could know how long the call would take and Jan totally distracted me, then I forgot about the chairs, and I didn't think, I mean, the directions ... I never thought the sun ..." Those stupid tears clogged her eyes again. She sniffed. "I'm so sorry."

Jack's eyes opened into slits. "What were you thinking? Why were you even doing this?"

"I wanted to repaint them. To make them look nice for you."

"So, you used paint stripper? Do you have any idea how dangerous those chemicals are?" He stepped toward her. "Look at what the chemical did to the chair. This is toxic. You could have burned yourself. A nice-looking chair isn't worth another trip to the hospital."

Callie stepped back. "You mean you're not mad about the chairs?"

"No, but you shouldn't be working with these chemicals."

With a blink of her eyes, her shame melted away and anger burned in her chest. "Are you serious?" She moved forward until they stood toe to toe and eye to chin. "I am *not* a child, Jackson. I may not be very skilled with your tools, but I am *always* careful. I wouldn't have tried this if I didn't think I could do it. I may be a little accident prone, but I'm not an idiot. I'm sorry I ruined your chairs, but I'm not sorry that I tried to do something nice for you!"

"You don't have to do anything nice for me! I've been trying to tell you that since you called and asked if you could stay with me. Why can't you just relax and stop adding to your problems?"

Every word out of Jack's mouth fueled the fire that raged inside. The sweltering sun had nothing on her anger. "Is that what I'm doing here? Creating problems?" She jabbed a finger into his shoulder. "Then why don't you kick me out?"

"Because I know you're supposed to be here. I'm just not convinced that you're supposed to be working for me." Jack poked her in the shoulder. "I don't understand why you won't let this go." Poke. "I don't need your help." Poke. "Just enjoy your summer vacation like a normal person." Poke, poke.

Callie smacked his hand away. "That's not part of the plan!"

Jack's eyes nearly popped out. He stumbled backward, shaking his head. "Are you kidding me? This is all because one of your 'plans?'" She could have forgiven his snarky tone, but the finger quotes pushed her over the edge.

The ruined chairs taunted her from behind Jack. Jan's voice echoed in her ears. Her students' faces jumped up to greet her. She could almost feel their little hands in hers. Sorrow clogged her throat. "It's not just about the plan." Tears erupted from her eyes, rolling down her cheeks.

Regret. Fear. It wasn't just anger that clawed at her heart, tearing her soul to shreds. Jack was right. She destroyed everything she touched. Her love life. Her jobs.

A glob of stripper and paint splattered on the grass.

Now she was ruining Jack's life too. One chair at a time.

First the yelling, now the tears. Jack's feet refused to move him away from the hysteria. Even if he could move, he didn't have a clue what to do. She was the one who'd globbed up his chairs, and she was mad at him? If she'd stop crying long enough, he could keep lecturing her. Instead, she stood there making more racket than his chain saw.

"Cal," he said, proud of his good start. The next line kept tripping him up. He cleared his throat and forced the words out. "Do you want to talk about it?"

"No!" The seagulls scattered. He dug a rag out of his back pocket and handed it to her. She'd wiped grease all over her face before he noticed. Probably best not to mention it.

He waited for her to calm down, but the sobbing continued. Grabbing the bottom of his shirt, Jack mopped the sweat off his face. "Do you at least want to go inside? Get out of the sun?"

"Everything's falling apart." She kept crying. "And now …" She looked at the chair. Her face scrunched up tight, like she'd just bitten into a lemon. Jack had never heard a sound like that before, but chances were good that she'd scared away the rest of the wildlife, maybe even some of the tourists.

He scratched his head. "I don't really know what else to do. It's just a chair, Cal. Do you think you might be overreacting?" The rag hit him right on the chest, and before Jack could comment on her ridiculous actions, Callie ran into the house. At least she took one of his suggestions.

The door slammed shut.

Sort of. Jack grabbed his phone and dialed.

"Hello?"

The most beautiful sound he'd ever heard. "Stacey, I need help."

"Jack? What's wrong?"

"It's Callie, and I don't know what's wrong."

"Where are you? Is she hurt?" Her voice got higher. "Do you need me to meet you someplace?"

"I don't think so." Jack scratched his head again, looking between the clumpy chair and the front door. "I don't know what happened. I was telling her how dangerous paint stripper is and why she should just enjoy her vacation, then she started crying and ran into the house."

The door flew open.

"Wait, she's coming back outside."

Jack stood in the yard watching. His sister ran down the steps, over the gravel, and to her car. Tears had cut through the grease marks, streaking her face and piercing at his heart. "Oh, man. She's still crying."

The little car peeled out of the driveway, flinging pebbles everywhere.

"And now she's gone."

Stacey sighed. "Jack, did you really just call me because your sister is crying?"

"Yeah."

"And how old are you?"

"What does that have to do with anything?"

Stacey laughed. That didn't make sense to him. "I think you're old enough to figure out how to handle your sister," she said. "Why don't you just ask her what's wrong?"

"I did, and now she's gone."

"Tell me exactly what happened."

Jack recapped the situation, from seeing the chair, talking to Callie about safety, urging her to relax, her unexpected tears. None of it made sense to him. "What do you think?"

"I don't know what to tell you." Not good. "I don't know Callie that well. Does she usually cry?"

"Not like that."

"Like what?"

"Like a dying elk."

Stacey coughed. A lot.

"You okay?"

"I'm fine," she said, but something sounded funny.

Jack was pretty sure she was laughing at him. "This isn't helping."

"I'm sorry." She cleared her throat. "I'm okay now."

"So, what do I do?"

"You need to talk to her, but you should probably give her some time to calm down. You need to find out what happened so you can apologize and move on."

"Apologize?" Jack looked at the chair again. Heat waves radiated up from the wood. The stench of chemical fumes crept toward him. "I'm not really sure that I'm the one who did anything wrong."

"I'm not saying that you did, but you were the one yelling at Callie when she started crying."

"I wasn't yelling!"

"Really?"

Jack mentally replayed the conversation. "Maybe."

"So, it was either something you said or the way that you said it that made her cry."

"How?"

"That doesn't matter. Somehow you played a part in upsetting your sister. It might not have anything to do with you, but you were there. You're the one who sent her over the edge."

Jack kicked at the ground, connecting with one of Callie's gloves and launching it through the air. It splattered against the chair, sticking to the goop. Great. Now he needed a new pair of gloves. "This is why I hate talking to my sister. I don't understand her, especially when she gets so emotional."

"Do you love her?"

His jaw dropped. "Of course I love her!" He'd done everything he could to keep her safe and relaxed since she got there.

"Then it doesn't matter *why* she gets emotional. You don't need to figure that out. You just need to be her big brother and support her."

"But if I can figure out why, maybe I can help her."

Stacey blew into the phone. "Jack, do you want my advice or not? Because you called me, but you keep arguing with everything I say."

"If I didn't want your help, I wouldn't have called." He kicked the second glove at the chair on purpose. "Just tell me what to do."

"I told you. Talk to her, but don't try to fix her. Just ask her what's wrong, then listen. Don't offer any advice unless she asks for it."

"But that doesn't—"

"Jack!"

He snapped his jaw shut. When had beautiful little Stacey learned to channel his mother?

"This is the advice I'm giving you. Take it or leave it, but I'm not going to argue with you about it anymore. I have to get back to work."

"Then why did you answer the phone?"

She hesitated. "Because I saw that it was you."

Nothing about the way she said that reminded Jack of his mom. Those were the nicest words he'd heard all day. "Thank you."

"You're welcome, but I really have to go now."

Jack nodded but suddenly didn't want to hang up. He tried to think of something to keep Stacey on the line, but he didn't want to keep her from her work. "Can we talk again later?"

Apparently, the question surprised Stacey as much as it surprised him. She didn't say anything.

"Stacey?"

"I, I'd like that."

He smiled. "I'll call you."

"Okay." She squeaked. "Bye."

Jack clipped the phone back onto his belt. Strolling to his chairs, he pulled the gloves off as he listened to the birds sing. No, it wasn't the birds. He was whistling. The fishing trip was ruined, but suddenly the day had potential.

Callie had obviously overreacted, but maybe he had too. Sure, the paint stripper was toxic, but she wasn't going to eat it. In fact, she had the chairs outside, gloves on the ground, and a trowel nearby. It looked like she had everything under control.

And he could save the chairs. Another thick application of stripper and he'd be able to clean off the wood, but not in this heat. Using the ruined gloves, he picked up the goopy chairs and hauled them into the shade.

The chairs could wait, though. Right now, he needed to call his sister.

CHAPTER 30

Ryan pulled into the driveway and parked next to Stacey's subcompact death trap. Next to Jack's behemoth truck, hers looked like an abused clown car. Ryan climbed out of his Jeep and wondered where Callie had gone. Maybe she and Stacey were out together.

He grabbed the laptop bag out of the Jeep, ignoring the photo-happy tourists, and walked straight to the house. As he stepped inside, he almost tripped on a tiny pair of sandals. Then he heard the talking—high-pitched and chatty. Not Callie's rich, musical voice. He looked at the shoes again. Too small to be Callie's. "Jack?"

"Yeah?"

"Stacey?"

"Hi, Ryan."

Warning bells. Not the kind that made him fear for his life but the kind that made his head spin. Something very strange was happening. He left his bag and keys on the counter before heading up to the living room. Jack sat on one end of the couch. Stacey sat in the middle.

Ryan blinked. He wouldn't have been more surprised to find the Russian ballet practicing in the house. Everything looked the same, but the two people on the couch—together—confused him. Jack stared at him. Stacey smiled. The fan overhead hummed, stirring the air and Ryan's confusion.

He searched for the right words, but all he came up with was, "Hey."

"Jack was having a crisis," Stacey said. "I came out to help."

Ryan looked back at Jack. "You okay?"

His friend shrugged.

"Why aren't you fishing? And where's Callie?" Had she finished the chairs?

Jack shrugged again.

Ryan sighed and turned to Stacey.

She sat a little straighter. "Jack got called back for a meeting. We don't know where Callie went."

So much for clarification. "What am I missing here?"

"Jack and Callie had a fight."

"We didn't have a fight." Jack punched his fingers through his hair. "She freaked out and ran off."

Stacey leaned over and touched Jack's hand. He didn't even flinch. "They had a fight. Callie left a few hours ago."

Ryan dropped into the empty recliner. "You know her. She'll come back. She just needs to cool off." Which often involved a call to him.

Jack shook his head. Stacey shifted, scooting a little closer to him.

Since they weren't offering answers, Ryan kept digging. "What made this such a crisis?"

Jack groaned. "She was crying."

"She's cried before." Though not often. "What's the big deal?"

"It was the *way* she was crying."

"The way? There's more than one way to cry?"

Stacey nodded. "She sounded like a dying elk."

"A what?"

"It was awful." Jack dropped his head back and closed his eyes. "And then she started yelling. And then she left."

None of it made any sense. Ryan had witnessed plenty of confrontations between the Stevens siblings, and nothing had ever inspired Jack to seek female reinforcements. "Has anyone called Callie?"

Jack nodded. "She's not answering."

Not surprising. "She'll call when she's ready."

"I know."

Yet, he'd still asked Stacey to come over, and she was scooting closer to Jack. He didn't even lean away. Their comfortable sitting situation suggested the invitation had more to do with Stacey's presence than it did with Callie's absence.

In all the years Ryan had known her, however, he'd never heard Callie break down to the point that she sounded like a dying animal. If the sound upset Jack so much that he called in back-up, then Callie would definitely need a friend. It wouldn't be a date, so Ryan could help. If he could find her.

Ignoring the weirdness on the couch, Ryan stood. "I'll see you later."

Ignoring the chirping, Callie relaxed into the driver's seat and let the wind whip through the open windows. Her hair danced around her head, tickling her face and neck. Cars zipped by. She steered around another tight curve, leaning into it as if she could coax the car along the road. The two-lane roads up and down Leelanau Peninsula let her forget about her life and just focus on the pavement in front of her.

The phone rang again. Callie didn't even pick it up this time. First Jack, then Ryan. Neither one seemed to pick up on the fact that she didn't want to talk. At least she'd gotten ten minutes of peace between the last two calls.

Though she hadn't driven this route in years, she could practically navigate the roads blindfolded. She'd spent more than a few hours on the peninsula during high school. Cruising the lanes calmed her nerves. At some point she'd return to the real world, but not now. Too many people, too many problems. She wanted to be worry-free for a little while longer.

CHIRP! CHIRP!

Come on.

Callie swerved onto the shoulder, buzzing by a mailbox that swayed in her tailwind. Throwing the car into park, she mentally prepared a verbal thrashing for the caller. Lecture ready, she grabbed the phone. The words stalled in her throat and her anger dissipated when she saw Mae's number. "Mae, what's up?"

"Callie, thank you! I need a ride to the hospital. Now! Can you come get me?"

With a flick of her wrist and a spin of the wheel, Callie backed up her car and pulled out into traffic. She floored the gas pedal, launching the car and throwing herself back against the seat.

"Where's Charlie?" She swerved around cars and suddenly wanted to thank Jack for all those years he tortured her with NASCAR.

Mae whined. "He just got to Gaylord. It'll take him almost two hours to get back here."

"Your mom?"

"She took the girls to a movie. I told her I thought it would be fine if she kept her phone on, but she's not picking up."

"Why did everyone leave you alone?" A horn blared as Callie's late-nineties Cavalier whizzed past a shiny red Mustang.

"I just wanted some time alone. I didn't think it would be such a big de-e-e-e-a-l-l-l-l."

Callie tried to push the pedal through the floor.

Mae panted on the other end of the line. "This is happening too fast. The girls took hours. I thought I could handle a couple of hours by myself." She hissed out the last word. "What if something's wrong?"

"I'm hurrying, but I'm near Leland. It'll take me at least fifteen minutes to get to there."

"Oka-a-a-a-a-a-a-a-y."

Panic propelled Callie down the road and around ridiculously calm tourists. She white-knuckled the steering wheel, willing traffic to clear.

"Is that you?" Mae asked.

"Is what me?"

"Someone's here."

The phone banged on something hard while Callie veered around a stationary SUV. Mae squealed. Doors banged. Footsteps. Callie's heart thundered.

"Cal?"

"Ryan?" His familiar baritone soothed her harried nerves.

"I just put Mae in the Jeep. We've got her bag, and we're going straight to the hospital. She wants you to call Charlie while she calls her doctor."

"Yeah, of course." Relief flooded Callie's heart, spilling out through her eyes and down her cheeks. The road blurred in front of her. "Thank you so much. I'll meet you there."

Callie hung up. She'd never been so excited to hear Ryan's voice. And as much as she wanted to get to the hospital to help Mae, the thought of seeing Ryan tickled her heart.

Flashing red lights grabbed her attention.

Apparently, she'd be seeing him later than she'd hoped.

The steel elevator doors whooshed open. Ryan stood in the middle of the long hallway, just a few feet from the doors. When he smiled at Callie, unemployment and a hundred-dollar speeding ticket didn't seem quite so bad.

He met her halfway. "Mae's waiting for you." Even in the over-bleached, glowing white walls of the hospital, Ryan's earthy scent cut through to her senses.

"How is she?"

"Adamant that you call Charlie."

"Done. He'll be here in less than an hour. Other than that, how is she?"

"I got her here in good time." Ryan cupped Callie's elbow in his hand as he led her down the hallway. "Other than that, I, uh ..."

"You left her alone in the room, didn't you?"

"Hey, there are doctors and nurses in there. No one needs me getting in the way." They stopped in front of a door. "This is where I get off. I'll just wait out here for Charlie."

Not until she turned to face him did Callie realize how pale Ryan had become. Grabbing him around the waist, she hugged him close, letting her relief and gratitude surround him. "I'm so glad you were there."

His arms wrapped around her, and Callie felt his chin rest against her head. "Me too, but now it's your turn."

Gratitude forgotten, Callie spun around and shot through the door into Mae's birthing suite. She had visited her friend in the cozy room after each of the girls' births, but this time the room felt cold and lonely. She rushed to her friend's side. "How are you?"

Tears clung to Mae's eyelashes. "This is happening so fast. It wasn't like this with the girls. I need Cha-r-r-r-r-g-h-h."

Fear coursed through Callie's body. Mae's face contorted while her hands strangled the bedding. An older lady in scrubs watched a monitor as it beeped and flickered. When Mae finally started to relax, the nurse patted her hand.

"There don't seem to be any complications, you're just moving along quickly. Dr. Miller called to say he's on his way, but Dr. Craig is going to come and check on you, just in case."

Mae nodded, but Callie could see the panic on her friend's face. Not sure what to do, she picked up Mae's hand before forcing a smile at the nurse. "Her husband will be here soon. How long do you think it'll be before she has the baby?" Visions of fluid and cords and blood swirled in Callie's mind. Mae squeezed her hand. "What?"

Her friend chuckled. "You look sick."

Callie tried to ignore the nurse peeking beneath Mae's sheet. No matter what came out from under there, she'd stay with Mae until Charlie arrived. "I'll be fine. You're having a baby. Let's focus on that."

Mae pulled Callie close, wrapping her in a mama-bear grip. "I'm so glad you're here."

Bring on the messy. Anything for Mae.

"You're at nine centimeters, Mrs. Krieger. Dr. Craig will be here soon. If I were you, I'd get ready to start pushing." The nurse smiled. "You're doing just fine."

"But Charlie's not here." Mae barely forced out the words. "He's always here."

Callie held Mae's hand tight. "He'll be here any minute now."

She nodded into another contraction. Callie didn't need anyone to tell her what was happening. She felt the force in every bone in her hand. She'd barely recovered before Mae let loose with another groan. Adrenaline surged through Callie's veins as she tried to keep up with Mae and the nurses and the now present doctor.

Monitors beeping. Groaning. People racing. Weird utensils and bodily noises. Callie ignored as much as she could, turning her back on the chaos and focusing on the scared, sweaty face of her friend. Nothing mattered beyond Mae.

Another contraction. Another groan. The door swooshed open again.

"Charlie!" Mae practically jumped out of the bed when her husband ran into the room.

"Baby, I'm sorry." He rushed past Callie and kissed his wife. Mae's face contorted as she moaned. Charlie cradled his wife beside him, whispering in her ear and kissing the damp hair at her temples. The nurse returned, and Callie took a step toward the door. When the contraction stopped, Mae rested her head on her husband's shoulder. The nurse offered encouraging words. And Callie slipped out to the hallway.

Relieved that Mae and Charlie were together, Callie wanted to put as much space between her and the delivery room as possible. A quick scan of the hall and she spotted the waiting room sign. Moments later, she stepped into the comfy room. Plush burgundy carpet, big tan couches, and Ryan.

Her breath stopped in her throat. "You're still here?"

He stood, his long legs unfolding as he pushed himself off the low couch. "I thought I'd wait with you."

She moved toward him as if being pulled in by a tractor beam. When she was within nose-shot of him, she inhaled his rich scent. Ryan opened his arms and wrapped her in comfort. She melted into him, listening to his heartbeat and letting his strength become hers.

Thump-thump. Thump-thump.

Callie relaxed. Something inside her tingled.

"Are you going to get that?"

"What?" She pulled away, looking up into Ryan's eyes. He'd stayed at the hospital … for her. More tingling.

"Cal." He pulled the purse off her arm. "Your phone is vibrating."

"Oh!" That's right. The nurse had mentioned something about turning it off or turning it down. Callie popped open her bag and fished around, trying to concentrate with Ryan so near. Her hand finally closed around the device, and she smiled. Then she looked at it.

"Kyle."

CHAPTER 31

Callie stared at the phone as Ryan's arm slid away from her, exposing her to the chilly hospital air. She wanted to step back into his embrace, back into his warmth, but the phone rang again.

It couldn't be a coincidence that Kyle was calling. This was her plan, yet a big chunk of her heart wanted to ignore the call. Sit with Ryan.

The phone vibrated again. She shook her head—stick with the plan. She answered the phone. "Hi, Kyle."

"Hey, Jack left me a message—said he was looking for you."

Not quite what she had hoped for. "I've been found. Thanks for checking in."

"How's Mae?"

"How did you know I was with Mae?"

"I made a couple of calls myself."

Callie's heart did a funny dance. "Oh, she's fine. She's in labor."

"I heard. Are you all still at the hospital?"

"Yeah. How do you know all of this?" she whispered.

Kyle laughed. "Jack told me. He talked with Ryan. I pumped him for information until he told me where you were."

"Well, I'm surprised my brother remembered so much. He's not usually one for details."

"I remember. I also seem to remember that you never did well with, uh … bodily fluids. How are you holding up?"

Kyle's concern warmed Callie from the inside out. "I'm okay. Ryan's still here, and Charlie finally got here, so they let me out of the delivery room."

"Would you like some more company?"

The comfortable warmth flared into an uncomfortable burn. "You're coming to the hospital?" She looked at Ryan. "Now?"

"I'm already here. I'll be inside in a few minutes."

Callie watched Ryan as he stood in front of the couch holding her purse. He smiled at her, but something wasn't right. The smile didn't feel the same. Lately, the curve of his mouth shook the ground under her feet. Not today.

"Sounds good," she said, watching one man, speaking to another, and trying to figure out whom to blame for her heart issues.

Kyle might have said goodbye. She didn't remember. Ryan was walking toward her, holding out her purse. When he passed it to her, their hands completely missed each other. Crisp, filtered air passed between them, free of his warmth or scent.

"Kyle's on his way up?" Ryan asked.

"Jack told him we were here."

Ryan nodded. He smiled, crossed his arms. Stiff, formal. "That's good news for you, right?"

"Sure. It's great to know he still cares. And that he remembers how much I hate hospitals." And that he's probably in the elevator, so it definitely wasn't the right time to ask Ryan for another hug.

Someone knocked on the glass. Callie turned. Casual and confident, Kyle strode into the room, his smile somehow lighting up the already bright room. This was the man she had left behind, and within seconds she remembered why he was part of the plan.

"Hey, there." He stopped beside Callie and pulled her in for a quick hug. He released her and offered a hand to Ryan. "How's it going?"

Ryan shook it. "Just waiting for a baby."

Kyle refocused on Callie. "You seem to be holding up pretty well."

She shrugged. "I got out of there before I had to see any bodily fluids. Charlie's with Mae now, so I'm off the hook."

Kyle grinned at her. She smiled back, then looked at Ryan. He was already looking at her.

As a digital voice paged someone, the trio stood there in the middle of the waiting room, looking at each other. Confident Kyle. Serious Ryan. Totally confused Callie. Heat rushed to her cheeks. What happened to the cold indifference of the hospital air?

"So …" she said, but her heart issues seemed to affect her concentration too.

Ryan cleared his throat. "How's work?"

And with that, he took over. Motioning to the furniture, he sat in an overstuffed chair. Kyle dropped onto the couch with a *thwump*. When he smiled up at Callie, her knees melted, and she sank to the cushion beside him.

Ryan guided the conversation, bringing Kyle back into their circle after three years away. The men talked work, trucks, and traffic as if no time had passed. She should have been put at ease, but the conversation grated on Callie's frazzled nerves. Situated between the two men, the alternating heart palpitations and rolling stomach nearly sent her to the nearest nurse's station.

Kyle's hand landed on hers, and Callie jumped. The guys laughed. "You okay?"

"Fine. Just daydreaming. What were you saying?"

"I asked how it's going with Jack, working with him at the lighthouse?"

Anger, frustration, and disappointment swam together, vying for top billing in her story. "It's not going well."

"I thought you guys would work well together."

"We do. We get the work done, then Jack takes me to the hospital."

"What?" Kyle's eyebrows buried themselves in his hairline.

Ryan laughed. "It's not that bad."

Not by itself, but combined with everything else the summer was enough to make her swear off planning forever. Almost.

"It's a boy!"

Callie heard Charlie before she saw him charge into the waiting room, tears streaking his face. "It's a boy! He's perfect, and Mae's amazing." Callie jumped up, and Charlie grabbed her shoulders, pulling her into a crushing hug. "Thank you for getting her here. Thank you so much for taking care of her."

Callie tried to respond, but she needed air to speak. Then, as quickly as he'd grabbed her, Charlie let her go. "I'm glad I could—"

"I have to get back in there. Mae wanted me to come tell you, but," his voice cracked, "I really want to be with my wife and son right now."

Love for Charlie bubbled up in Callie's heart as she looked at the ecstatic man who cherished her best friend. "Tell her I love her."

Kyle's hand appeared beside Callie before she realized he was standing beside her. "Congratulations," he said, shaking Charlie's hand.

The proud daddy pumped Kyle's arm like he was hoping to get water. "Thanks." He looked past Kyle and nodded at Ryan. "Thank you so much. I need to go." The skinny bearded man ran out of the room.

A boy. Mae had been right.

Charlie burst back in, looking right at Callie. "Oh, and don't go anywhere! Mae wants to introduce you to him, but it'll be a little while yet. I'll come get you."

Callie opened her mouth to speak, but Charlie was already down the hall.

A boy.

Emotion clogged Callie's throat. Tears blurred her eyes. Mae's mom was missing. Charlie had shown up late, but now he was here. Mae was safe, and they had their son. Nothing went as planned, yet it all worked out. What a perfect day.

"Are you okay?" A warm hand landed on her shoulder, and Callie looked up into Kyle's concerned eyes. He scanned her face before focusing again on her eyes. "Do you need anything?"

She shook her head. "I'm just really happy for Mae. I can't believe I got to be here for her." So had Ryan. Callie peeked at him behind Kyle, still sitting in the chair, stoic. When he saw her, he smiled. Joy radiated from his face.

Callie didn't try to stop the happy tears that rolled down her perma-grinning cheeks. "We helped deliver a baby ... sort of. If it hadn't been for you, Mae might have had that kid in my car."

Ryan laughed as he pushed himself up. "And if it hadn't been for you, I might have had to wait with Mae until Charlie got here." He pulled his keys out of his pocket, then clapped Kyle on the shoulder. "This is more excitement than I was expecting tonight." He reached back into his pocket and pulled out a rumpled napkin, offering it to Callie.

She wiped her face as Ryan stepped away. Then reality hit her. "You're leaving?"

He looked over his shoulder, his gaze flickering to Kyle before resting on her. "I just wanted to make sure Mae was okay. She has you and Charlie now. I'll see you later. Kyle, nice to see you again."

Ryan turned his back on her and walked away again. When he stepped out into the hallway, something inside Callie clenched. "Wait. I'll walk you out."

When she looked up at Kyle, he nodded. "That's okay, I'll wait here."

She squeezed his arm, then hustled after Ryan. As soon as her shoes smacked on the shiny linoleum, he started moving. "I meant to ask you this earlier, but we keep getting interrupted," she said. "What were you doing at Mae's?"

"Looking for you."

Callie's feet faltered, but Ryan kept walking. "Why?"

He shrugged. "Jack was worried. I wanted to help."

"Oh." Her heart deflated. "So that's how Jack knew we were at the hospital. You told him."

"I figured he'd want to know."

"He doesn't care when Mae has her baby."

"No, but Jack cares about you." They stopped in front of the elevator. Ryan pushed the down button.

"And you care about Jack."

"I do."

"Well, thanks for looking out for him."

"I was looking out for you too."

Oh, heart palpitations. "You were?"

"Of course." Ryan glanced at her. "How are you doing?"

With Kyle in the waiting room? With Ryan standing beside her? "I don't know how I'm doing, but I'm glad you're here."

A nurse walked up beside them and smiled, then turned to wait for the elevator. A young man with a squeaky food cart walked behind them. The scent of warm bread surrounded them.

"Me too," he said. "I'm glad Kyle came. I want you to be happy."

Finally, the double doors slid open. Ryan and the nurse stepped inside. They each gave Callie the same polite smile. Did Ryan really look at her the same way a stranger did? The weight of the realization trapped Callie in her spot long after the elevator doors closed.

Somehow, she convinced her feet to start moving again. One step at a time she moved down the hall, the image of Ryan's polite smile swimming in her head.

When her feet touched carpet, Callie looked up. Kyle stood in the middle of the room, his hands deep in his pockets, shoulders relaxed, watching a baseball game on the television. When he looked at her, a little bit of the pain eased out of Callie's heart.

Mae's life might work without a plan, but it only brought confusion and heartache to Callie. She never should have doubted herself. She never should have doubted the plan. If she had just stayed focused, she wouldn't have considered other options, wouldn't have opened her heart, wouldn't care whether or not Ryan walked away.

The room wavered in front of her.

Kyle cocked his head. "You're crying."

She swiped at the tears. "I'm an aunt again." The thought of Mae with her newborn son covered Callie's wounded heart like a salve. "Come on. Let's go meet Junior."

CHAPTER 32

Callie sat on her piano bench staring at the barely-visible piano. She'd left the hospital less than an hour ago, after some serious baby snuggling, and taken the scenic route home. She couldn't go inside, though. Ryan was inside, and she wasn't ready to see him. She didn't understand what had happened at the hospital, so she didn't know how to process it. What she did know was that she needed some serious time with her piano.

The sun had finally set, and she didn't feel like turning on the garage light. Sitting in the dark suited her. Only the fading glow from the lighthouse porch light offered any illumination. But she didn't need light. Once she placed her hands on the keys, her fingers moved automatically.

This time, however, they didn't play a familiar song. They roamed the keys, pressing out chords and runs that blended and harmonized in a way she'd never heard before. Dissonant and ever-changing, her hands played the song that her heart poured out. No time signature. No tempo. Just music.

When was the last time she'd sat down and just played? Not a hymn or a classic or a wedding march but the music she heard in her head and felt in her blood? When had she given up music to only play someone else's songs?

Callie let her fingers move higher, forgetting the bass line to tinkle out a fairy-esque dance. She locked her fingers into place, punching out chord progressions in a quick staccato song. Then she relaxed, and her fingers traveled across the full range of the keyboard—quickly, slowly, softly, loudly.

She played and played and played until something settled on the inside of her. Calm. Comfort. Peace. Callie lifted her fingers from the keys while her foot pressed the piano's pedal, sustaining the final sounds.

"Cal?"

She jumped, slamming her knee into the piano as her heart tried to burst from her chest. Spinning around, she recognized Ryan's silhouette against the dim light. She pressed a trembling hand to her heart. "What are you doing out here?"

"I was going to ask you the same thing. It's almost eleven thirty. Is everything okay with Mae?"

"Mae's fine. I just needed to play for a while."

Ryan leaned against the open garage door. "What song was that?"

Callie shook her head. "Nothing. I just started playing."

"You wrote that?"

"Not really. I mean, I made it up as I played, but I doubt I could play that exact song ever again."

"The music was amazing." He chuckled. "It sounded like you."

"What does that mean?"

He moved away from the wall far enough that Callie could see his smile. "There were so many different parts, but one of the most beautiful things I think I've ever heard." His smile faltered until it disappeared completely. Ryan stuffed his hands into his pockets. "I'm just glad I got to hear you play it. I'll leave you alone now. I just wanted to make sure you were okay."

He disappeared as quickly as he'd appeared, taking all of Callie's peace with him. One of the most beautiful things he'd ever heard reminded him of her? So much for the calming influence of her piano.

Callie eventually came in, but Ryan tried not to notice that he heard her bedroom door close after midnight. He also tried to avoid her the next morning, and the morning after. Not an easy thing to do in a cramped lighthouse, so he worked longer hours, spent a lot of time on the trails, and volunteered to do the grocery shopping. Between his padded schedule and what he assumed were her date nights with Kyle, everyone was happy.

He reminded himself of that as he ran through the woods one afternoon, his feet pounding against the mulch. As he rounded a corner, he grunted. Another family up ahead. They always crowded the trails, stretching across the whole width of the path as if no one else could possibly need to get by.

"Coming through!"

Mom and Dad turned, then corralled their kids to one side.

"Thanks."

The littlest girl looked at him with huge, terrified eyes. Ryan couldn't blame her. Sweat saturated his clothes and hair. Dirt clung to the sweat. He tried to smile, but his legs burned. She pressed closer to her mom, so he stopped trying.

A few long strides, and he passed them—ready to stop scaring small children and let his body rest. Just another hundred yards until he cleared the trees, then he'd be able to see the lighthouse. With any luck there would only be his and Jack's trucks in the driveway. Callie had been getting ready to go out when he finished his first jog. Ryan doubted he could survive a third trip around the hiking trails.

When he finally cleared the forest, Ryan popped out on the southwest lawn of the lighthouse park. He was far enough away that he couldn't hear or see anything going on inside, but he was close enough to notice Callie's car was gone.

Good. She was out having fun with Kyle. That's what she wanted. To waste her summer chasing a guy that she'd already broken up with once. And all Ryan wanted was for Callie to be happy. Perfect.

He slowed his pace. His legs screamed, ready to stop. Ryan sucked in lungs full of fresh air. His chest heaved, every muscle straining for oxygen and relief. He pictured Callie on her dinner date with Kyle, and his chest strained some more.

Dragging his feet across the lawn, Ryan focused on his breathing, deliberately forcing his lungs to slow down. He stopped occasionally, stretching his overworked muscles. He hadn't run this much since high school, and that was fifteen years ago. Back in those days, he could barely move after a long run. He might need a wheelchair tomorrow.

His leaden legs got him back to the house, begrudgingly trudging up the stairs and inside. The calendar caught his attention. Tomorrow was Saturday. Everyone would be home. Better think of something else to do. His twitching quadriceps couldn't take another day on the trails.

Ryan considered his options as he downed some water. His feet and back ached. Maybe he'd just stay in his room, stuck on his bed. Or he could help Jack. "Jack!"

"Yeah?"

Ryan followed the voice into the living room. Jack lay on the couch with a *Sports Illustrated*. Sweat still rolling down his back, Ryan dropped to the floor. He spotted a pair of Callie's shoes under the coffee table. Not helping.

"What are you doing this weekend?" he asked, rolling away from the sandals.

"Nothing."

"That's lame. Let's do something."

"Fine. I'm watching the game tomorrow. You can buy the pizza."

Ryan snorted, staring at the ceiling. So much for that option. The couch creaked and groaned. A few quiet thumps, then Jack appeared, standing over him.

"What's up with you? You stink."

"I've been running. You always stink."

"You hate running."

"I hate running competitively. It's a good way to clear my head."

Jack narrowed his eyes. "So is fishing and that hurts less. How's the move going? I thought you'd be out of here by now."

Ryan pushed himself up and out of his friend's irritating gaze. "I'm still working on it, but I don't think there's any reason to hurry now."

"Why?"

Jack could be so dense. "Never mind." Ryan got up, his muscles already tight and stiff. "I'm still planning on moving, but we can forget the earlier conversation." As he lifted his arms, rotating his shoulders, he groaned involuntarily.

Jack snorted. "You're giving up pretty quick."

"I'm not giving up."

"Then what are you doing?"

"I'm letting Callie play things out." Ryan dropped his arms, unclenching fists that he hadn't noticed until just then. Must keep stretching.

"You're a chicken."

Every muscle tightened.

Jack didn't wait for a reply before heading down to the kitchen.

Ryan ran after him. "What's that supposed to mean?"

"It means you're a chicken."

Jack nearly smacked Ryan with the refrigerator door as he whipped it open.

"This isn't any of your business."

WHAM!

The door slammed, knocking napkins off the top. Ryan braced himself, not really sure what Jack planned to do.

"You made it my business when you asked if you could date my sister," he said. "It's my business because you're both living in my house. And it's my business because you're my friend and she's my sister, you're both acting like idiots, and it's making me crazy!"

"First, I'm a chicken, now, I'm an idiot?"

A muscle twitched along Jack's jaw, then on his forehead. If Jack didn't swing first, Ryan was seriously considering it.

"I just can't believe you." Jack ripped the hat off his head and threw it on the table. "You were willing to move out of here just to ask her on a date. Now you're not even going to try. Ask her!"

"It's not that simple."

"Yes, it is."

"It's not. Things are working out for Callie now—"

"So?" Jack pulled two chairs out from the table and banged them on the floor. He dropped into one and kicked the other at Ryan.

Annoyance gripped his patience. "I'll stand."

"Of course, you will. You know what your problem is? You try so hard to be this gentleman that you've turned yourself into a sissy."

Not annoyance. Anger. "I'm trying to give Callie some space." Ryan stepped forward.

Jack leaned toward him. "You're hiding behind your 'manners.' Does she even know how you feel?"

"Of course not. You told me I couldn't tell her until I moved out."

He jumped to his feet. "I said you couldn't date her, but she's never going to forget Kyle and her stupid plan if you don't give her a reason to. You know her as well as I do. She needs a reason for everything."

"How was I supposed to know that?"

Jack just shook his head and walked away.

Good. Ryan didn't want to talk about this, especially with Jack. The screen door squeaked open, then banged shut. Ryan hadn't moved an inch before he heard it again. Jack stormed toward him, stopping toe to toe with him. His entire face seemed to twitch.

"I can't believe you. You've been waiting for this for years. You need to man up and talk to Callie."

"You aren't making any sense. I thought you wanted me out of here."

"I want you to do the right thing." Jack poked Ryan in the chest. "You always do this. You go halfway, then stop. I'm sick of watching my best friend walk away from everything, and I'm not going to let you do it to my sister."

Ryan smacked away Jack's finger. "You've never cared who I date. Let it go." He tried to walk away, but a vice closed around his biceps, holding him back, then spinning him around.

Jack glared at Ryan, his face contorted and twitching, but for the first time Ryan didn't think he'd get punched. In fact, for a second there, he worried that Jack might hug him.

"This isn't just about who you date, and it's not just about Callie, even though I've seen the two of you, and I'd level anyone else who led her on the way you do."

Ryan pulled himself free. "Then what is this about?"

"My best friend always running after things, then quitting when it gets hard. If you think this can work, if you *really* think this is what God wants for you, then you need to man up and tell Callie. You could have been out of here that first night, but you're using it as an excuse, just in case you change your mind. You never fail because you never try, and that"—poke—"makes you a chicken."

Chicken. Idiot. Quitter. Ryan tried to control his anger, but his stupid friend's stupid words replayed again and again.

Jack's face relaxed, but his body stood rigid. "You're not being a gentleman when you lie to her."

Chicken. Idiot. Quitter. Liar. Rage rolled through Ryan's veins. "I don't need you to give me dating tips. At least I didn't use your sister as an excuse to spend some time with Stacey."

"Stacey and I talked. She knows where I stand."

"She does?"

"Yeah. She pretty much beat it out of me. Callie won't do that to you because of her plan, so it's on you."

Jack was right. Ryan knew it, but he couldn't accept Jack's words. Not now. "I'm going to grab a shower, then I'm going to leave. I need some space from you and Callie, both. I'll be out of the house by Friday."

CHAPTER 33

Callie closed her eyes.

Clip-clop. Clip-clop.

Another stallion walked past her bench on the way to the practice ring. The horse-crazy phase had skipped her as a kid. But when the annual horse show moved to Traverse City during high school, she fell in love with the grace and strength, the dust and hay. She and Kyle spent their first summer together attending the horse show.

"I thought we were meeting at noon."

Callie's eyes popped open. She spun around, searching the crowd but not needing to see Kyle to hear the smile in his voice. A small group passed by as she spotted him. Sandals, jean shorts, a crisp striped button down, and that amazing smile.

She waved. "I thought I'd come a little early before too many people show up."

"You were early the first time we met here." Kyle sat beside her. "We could have just planned on meeting earlier."

"I didn't want to impose. Besides, I kind of like seeing everything before the crowds." She leaned into him. "What are you doing here?"

He shrugged. "I had a hunch you might be here."

Her stomach fluttered. "Really?"

"And I had to stop at the office this morning. I didn't feel like waiting around at work." Kyle glanced at her, but his eyes drifted past her.

Callie looked over her shoulder. The resort tower sliced through the trees, its black tinted windows piercing the blue sky. "I wish I had to work. I've tried to get Jack to let me help him, but I'm still unemployed."

"How's that working out for you?"

"Pretty well, actually." She turned back to Kyle. "Charlie was supposed to have this week off work, but someone got hurt at the job site, and they called him in. I've spent most of the week with Mae and the kids."

"So, being fired didn't turn out as bad as you thought."

She shrugged. "I guess not."

"You don't sound convinced."

"I'm more worried about the fall."

"Fall? Won't you be back in school by then?"

"Maybe. I don't suppose you know if any schools in the area need a music teacher?"

"Are you moving back?"

"I'm thinking about it." No one needed to know about Alma's school budget problems ... yet. If Jan's prediction came true, however, Callie would have to double her efforts to start working with Jack again. "It would definitely be nice to pick up some extra money this summer." Just in case. "I can't convince Jack, though."

Kyle suddenly perked up, his eyes twinkling. "Maybe you don't have to. You remember Rachel from the other night?"

The hair model. Callie pinned her smile back on. "Sure."

"Her sister is getting married in a couple of weeks. I guess the piano player broke her hand or something, because Rachel spent all morning calling around looking for a replacement."

The pins popped out. "You were working with Rachel this morning?"

"We were supposed to work, but she's so upset about the wedding that we didn't get much done. I don't know why I didn't think to call you before. Are you busy two weeks from today? They're desperate."

She hadn't played at a wedding in a while, but a lot of brides used the same music. Unless Rachel's sister had an affinity for reggae or ska, Callie could probably do the job, especially if it paid. "I don't suppose you know what music they're using?"

Kyle laughed. "All I know for sure is there's a Wizard of Oz theme, but I don't know if that has anything to do with the music."

Playing might be worth it just to see what a Wizard of Oz themed wedding looked like. "I'm available, as long as it's not some crazy music. I should be able to handle anything else. Give her my number and have her call me. I'll take a look."

"Another successful day." Kyle leaned into her. "Summer might not be so bad after all."

Another horse clomped by. Kyle said something, but the elegant gait of the giant animal captured Callie's attention. The body gleaming, the muscles rippling through its shoulders and legs, the sun reflecting off shiny chestnut hair and a black, braided tail.

"I just lost to a horse."

The horse shook its head, shaking Callie out of her trance. "Lost what to a horse?"

Kyle stood, pulling her with him. "Come on. I might as well take you to the ring. Then you don't have to pretend like you're paying attention. Everyone will expect you to ignore me."

"I wasn't ignoring you."

"Sure, you weren't."

She wasn't. She couldn't have been, not when she was finally with him, right where she wanted to be. That would be rude.

He led them away from the practice ring and toward the main show ring. The crowd was bigger, but still not so large that they couldn't find a couple of seats together on the bleachers. They sat near the top, close to each other but far enough away from anyone else that Callie considered the time as being alone with Kyle. The sun hadn't done much to warm the aluminum seats, but Kyle's nearness made the hard, cool metal more tolerable.

The show started. A horse entered the ring, the rider guiding it skillfully, leading it to jumps and around obstacles. The animal seemed to pause mid-air, clearing impossible-looking hurdles with elegance and strength. Polite golf claps responded. One horse pranced out of the ring, another entered, over and over again. The majesty of the performances awed her.

Something poked her in the ribs, scaring the breath out of her lungs.

Kyle laughed. "You've officially abandoned me for the horses."

Again? "I'm sorry, I didn't mean to ignore you." She shouldn't really forget he was there so easily. This was her afternoon with Kyle. She needed to focus. "What were you saying?"

He laughed again, loud and hearty. "You're cute when you're flustered."

"Good to know." Maybe. She liked being cute but hated the flustered feeling.

"I said I'm going to go get something to drink. Do you want anything?"

"Sure." Callie popped up, bouncing the bleachers beneath her. "I could use some water." He stood close. Not that he had much of an option. The seats had filled up since she got distracted. How long ago was that?

"I'll go. You stay and enjoy the show."

Callie tucked her hand around Kyle's arm. "I'll go and enjoy your company." And salvage the date.

They headed down the bleachers together, dodging people and their bags. By the time they finally landed on solid ground, thirst clawed at Callie's throat.

"Thanks for pulling me out of my daze. I didn't realize we've been here so long."

"Anytime. You always get sucked into things. Remember that time we went with Ryan and Jack to that music festival in Gaylord?"

Callie groaned. "Jack spent the whole afternoon in the security tent."

"Because you had his ID in your purse."

"I couldn't help it. That singer was dynamic."

"They paged you. Six times." Kyle chuckled. "I'll never forget the look on Ryan's face when we finally found you."

Neither would Callie. Equal parts relief and anger, she hadn't known whether or not Ryan planned on hugging or spanking her. That wasn't an expression she saw very often. Come to think of it ... "You know, I don't think I've talked with Ryan since the night at the hospital."

"Seriously?" Kyle steered them around a small crowd and toward the food vendor. "Don't you live together?"

Heat consumed Callie's face. "Don't say it like that, it sounds awful."

"You know what I mean." He poked her ribs, just like Jack would.

"Yes, we both live with Jack, but we keep missing each other. Not that I've been around much."

"Still, it's been five days. That's a little weird."

They stopped at the back of the short line, and Kyle pulled his arm away to dig the wallet out of his back pocket. Callie reached into her purse for her wallet, and he didn't stop her. That niggled at her.

"So, how was work?" she asked. "Why did you have to stop in this morning?"

"Rachel is taking a couple of days off next week to help her sister with something for the wedding. We're putting in a few extra hours here and there to make up the time."

Extra hours with Rachel. She'd probably been coifed and polished, not wearing flip-flops and a T-shirt. And she had to smell better than the occasional waft of barnyard that filled the large field.

Callie ran her fingers through her hair as they ordered and paid for their waters. She didn't feel like scaling the bleachers again, so she led them down the row of vendor boutiques. Kyle didn't ask why, he just followed. More niggling.

They wandered past tents full of leather goods, western wear, and people offering riding lessons. Callie browsed but kept moving. Something about their conversation on the bleachers unsettled her, but she hadn't really paid attention. Add that to the new niggles, and the day didn't feel right.

"You know, Cal, I'm really glad you called."

Excitement and joy soothed her nerves. "You are?" She looked over at him. He ambled along beside her, one hand in his pocket, the other holding his water. Not exactly cool and confident, more relaxed. Comfortable. Jack-like. "I'm glad you called back. I've definitely been having fun hanging out with you."

"Me too. Rachel's been really busy the past few weeks with her sister. It's been good to have someone to talk to again."

The gnawing sensation latched onto her heart and chewed right through it. Rachel again. Was it possible? Callie swallowed. "So, how long have you and Rachel been dating?"

Kyle shrugged. "Technically, we aren't allowed. As long as we're on this project together, we have to keep things professional."

Callie would've preferred getting kicked in the head by a horse.

They reached the end of the vendor tents, landing next to another practice ring. A horse pranced by, kicking up the dirt and everything on top of it. The stench nearly choked her. She willed her heart back together as she leaned against the railing. Kyle stood beside her.

"How much longer do you have until the project is over?"

"A couple of weeks." Kyle leaned into Callie. "I hope the wedding thing works out with you. That will give us all a chance to hang out some more."

Callie stared straight ahead, trying to catch a breath of fresh air. The staring was easier than the breathing, which would have been difficult with or without the horsey aroma.

The horse in the ring stumbled but, unlike Callie's plan, it straightened up and kept on going. "You're Rachel's date to the wedding, aren't you?"

"Yeah. It's after our deadline, so she asked." His hand smacked her shoulder. "I'd like to have a friend there. Rachel's in the wedding, so I'll be alone for most of the night."

A friend.

Pounding hooves thundered in her ears. The remnants of her heart struggled to keep beating. A friend. "Of course." Her last bit of hope for the summer disappeared.

People clapped in the distance. A fly buzzed around Callie's head. Kyle leaned forward, his eyes scanning her face. When their gazes locked, his eyebrows shot up, eyes wide. So much for hiding her emotions. Something gave her away.

"Callie." Her name caught on the wind, blowing away with her hope. "You didn't think ..." Kyle wiped the sweat from his forehead. "I mean ... I didn't mean to lead you on. I just thought we were, at least I didn't imagine ... oh, man."

Kyle turned away, and for a split second she thought he might run. "Of course not." She grabbed his arm, leaning into him without having to face him. "I know we're over. I mean, I broke up with you, remember?" Forced laughter. "I guess I just wasn't expecting there to be anyone else, not that there shouldn't be, right? You're an amazing guy, and Rachel seems ... special."

His hand covered hers. "I'm sorry, I didn't know."

"There's nothing to know. Really, it's okay. I just wasn't expecting it, that's all."

Not expecting it at all.

CHAPTER 34

The sun blinded Callie as she struggled to stay on the road. After Kyle left, she'd waited for the tears to subside before getting onto the highway. But now she couldn't find her sunglasses, and the sun threatened to run her off the road. Half blind and frustrated, she pulled into a parking lot to look for her glasses.

She never ceased being amazed at how she could lose items in a purse. The glasses couldn't have gotten up and walked away. The bag was only so big. She continued to dig until her hand bumped her phone.

Mae. Callie needed to talk to Mae. She'd been right all along. Callie should have talked to Kyle right away. She should have told him the first time she saw him. She should have told him the truth at the horse show, regardless of Rachel. Maybe he would change his mind if he knew.

But he did know. He'd figured her out and it hadn't changed anything. Would it have really mattered if she'd confessed first?

Callie dialed Mae's number and waited, struggling against the heartache that threatened to push up more tears. The disappointment. The confusion.

"Hi, Callie."

"Charlie, how are you?"

"Perfect. I can't thank you enough for everything you've done for us this week."

A light balm soothed her heart. "I've never been able to help such a tiny baby before. It was my pleasure."

"Chip thanks you too."

"Chip?"

"Two Charlies is confusing, and Mae refuses to let me call him Chuck. I don't want him to be a Junior."

"So why Chip?"

"He's a chip off the ol' block."

He certainly was—Callie had burped him. "How's Mae?"

"Sleeping."

Of course she was.

"Should I have her call you?"

And ignore her family because of Callie's failure? "No, that's okay. I was just calling to check in."

"We're good, thanks to you."

As Charlie hung up, Callie could hear the girls chatting and laughing in the background. Hopefully, he'd get them quieted down. Mae needed her sleep. Any mother of three needed a good nap. What she didn't need was a constantly failing best friend who couldn't keep her life together.

Callie dropped her phone back in her purse.

Something cracked.

Looking down, she found her sunglasses ... under her phone.

Wonderful. Kyle had a date with the beauty queen. Mae had a family to care for. Callie would rather have her teeth pulled than talk to Jack about this mess.

Ryan?

Her heart might have flipped if it hadn't already been chewed up and spit out.

She could talk to Ryan. He understood her. She trusted him. He would give her good counsel.

Ignoring the sun and her tears, Callie thrust her car into gear and headed home.

Gone.

Callie read the note again. *Here are the keys. Ryan.*

She looked at the key ring—definitely keys to the lighthouse. She knew Ryan was planning to move out, but that was it? No goodbye. No forwarding address. Just *here are the keys*?

She opened her phone and dialed before she had a chance to talk herself out of it. Ryan's voicemail picked up.

"It's Callie. I, uh—" She swallowed a sob. "—just wanted to let you know I got your note and the keys. I'll make sure Jack gets them. I guess I didn't realize, didn't know you were leaving so soon. It was kind of a surprise, but, well—" Emotions clouded her brain. "I should probably just go."

Her phone hit the counter as another tear escaped. Callie looked around the tiny kitchen, the walls closing in on her, snuffing out all hope. No job. No Kyle. No Mae. No Ryan. Every realization squeezed a little more oxygen out of the room.

Then why was she here? What did God expect from her? None of it made sense. She needed to play something fierce. Something challenging. Chopin's *Opus 66*, or Liszt's *La Campanella*.

But she couldn't. The last time she'd played, Ryan had been there. He'd called her beautiful, or he'd called her music beautiful. She still wasn't sure what he'd meant, and she didn't want to be thinking about him while she played. The piano was supposed to be her escape. Now what?

A drive. She could get away from everyone. Clear her head.

Callie flipped over Ryan's note and grabbed a pen.

Went for a drive. Need some time alone. Back later. Callie

That should eliminate some of the confusion from last time. So should this—she tossed her phone on the counter. She didn't need the distraction.

An hour later, Callie turned off the pavement and onto a narrow seasonal road. Dust kicked up behind her car as she carefully maneuvered through the shrubs and trees. If she stayed on the road, she'd eventually hit Empire, but then she'd have to deal with people again. A few yards ahead of her the sun snuck through the trees. As she crept closer, Callie recognized the clearing.

She pulled off of the dirt road and parked in the shade of a tall tree. From the back seat, she grabbed her water bottle and a blanket before heading through the trees across the road. She trudged ten minutes through the underbrush before she heard a squawking seagull. The familiar caw interrupted the crunching leaves and twigs.

Callie stopped and listened. Another caw. A gentle rush, then a lull. Rush and lull. Callie raced ahead, pushing past branches that scratched her arms and snagged her clothes. Rush. Lull. She hurried. Sun streamed into the forest, bouncing off the deep blue shore.

Lake Michigan.

Callie stepped out of the trees and into the breeze. In and out, the waves came and retreated. No people. No phones. Just Callie and the water … and a life to figure out.

She moved toward the shore, helpless to resist its beckoning. The beach grass thinned as she approached the water. Soon her sandals sank into the ground. The only other footprints belonged to the birds. Perfect.

Spying a relatively dry patch of beach, Callie spread her blanket on the ground, squinting against the late afternoon sun. As she settled herself on the blanket, she decided to review her summer.

But the sun warmed her skin, and the water whispered its lullaby. She had plenty of time later to figure out what she'd done wrong. It's not like she had to go to work. Or on a date. Or over to Mae's. Callie lay back and closed her eyes. All of the tears had drained her energy. She just needed a little nap before facing her mess of a life. It would still be a disaster when she woke up.

Her life was pitch black, except for the stars.

Callie blinked. The stars twinkled, but nothing else moved. She sat up, scanning the beach. The lake called to her, but the darkness had swallowed the water. Looking up again, she searched for the moon. Nothing. Just thousands of tiny stars.

Fear crept in. She didn't have a flashlight. She was just going to take a quick nap, but it had to be after ten for the sky to be so dark. She had to get home before Jack freaked out. He'd want to take her car away after this.

Callie grabbed the blanket and stumbled toward the trees, tripping in the sand. Two more steps and she tripped again. Brushing off her knees, she stood back up. Her sandal snagged on something.

Panic replaced the fear.

No use. She couldn't see her hand in front of her face. There was no way she'd find her car through the woods. She'd pretty much followed the sound of the waves to find the beach. Her car wouldn't make any noise. Plus, she'd passed some poison ivy on the way in. The last thing she wanted was another doctor's appointment.

Callie tried to focus her eyes on anything, but all she could see were shadows and even darker shadows. A chill ran down her spine but not just from the cooling night air. Every few years, the cops found a body in the woods. Another person lost, starving, or bleeding to death. There was usually alcohol or other extenuating circumstances, but Callie didn't want to push her luck.

Suddenly she wanted to be back in the suffocating lighthouse kitchen. Out here she had tons of space but no place to go. Did she really need this now?

She looked up, watching the stars, looking for God. "Okay, you've got my attention. I've got no way to get home, no way to call anyone, and one bottle of water. What am I supposed to do? I make a plan—it falls apart.

I come out here without a plan—it's a disaster, so what do you want from me?"

Nothing.

Figures.

Not a cloud in the sky, so she didn't have to worry about rain, but cold might be a problem. Callie picked up her blanket and headed back to the beach, unwilling to risk the woods. The sun would come up eventually.

Callie shuffled back to the shore and dropped onto the blanket. She didn't want to think about how the summer could possibly get any worse— she wasn't ready to attend anyone's funeral. Nothing she did seemed to matter, though. Nothing worked. Where did that leave her?

Any plans for the next few weeks were bound to fail, but she didn't think her heart could take this kind of spontaneous stress on a regular basis. All she wanted was to do God's will, so why did he keep making it so hard for her to figure it out?

"God?"

Still nothing. No birds. No waves. Not even the hint of a breeze.

"That's it?"

Silence.

Callie waited. Her mind reeled, but the world stayed calm. Emotional chaos. Physical tranquility. If it would stop being so nice out she might be able to concentrate on her problems.

CAW!

Callie jumped but didn't see anything. Maybe she should have been more specific. "Can't you just tell me what to do?"

A bug buzzed by.

"That's it?" She laid down and looked straight up into the sky. Eventually, she'd see something.

Despite her problems, the view really was amazing. Millions of stars crowding the black canvas from hundreds of light years away. One star escaped, burning across the sky. God's creation never ceased to amaze her. He put the entire world into motion, hanging each star above her. She truly didn't take enough time to admire the beauty. She was usually too busy pumping God for information.

Callie closed her eyes and let the quiet consume her. Her pulse relaxed as her heart calmed. She thought about her job. Her pulse kicked up. Forget the work—think about God. Peace.

Kyle's face drifted into her thoughts. Her muscles tensed. Okay, back to God.

What about Ryan? Butterflies.

Only when she focused on God did the bone-deep peace settle inside her. Only God kept her calm, safe. He'd given her total peace about the move to Traverse City, but this was the first time since arriving that she'd felt it again. Why?

Callie stroked her fingers across the cool sand as she replayed the last few weeks. She hadn't really talked to God since she moved in. She'd been piecing things together on her own, letting logic and reason guide her steps. She also suspected the very same logic and reason were giving her ulcers.

The more she focused her thoughts on God, the less her plan seemed to matter. Despite the solitude, the darkness, and the cooling air, peace wrapped her in warmth and contentment. If she could stay focused on God, she could survive the summer.

Callie yawned. She just needed to survive the night.

CHAPTER 35

Jack hit his alarm clock, but the beeping continued. Stupid machine. He fumbled for the cord, yanking it from the wall.

BEEP! BEEP! BEEP!

How was Callie sleeping through this? Chatty tourists he could ignore, but that beeping! Jack looked at his clock. It was dark, but the noise continued. He tapped his cell phone. Five thirty in the morning. Not his best time of day. If he wanted to sleep until a reasonable hour, he had to silence that noise.

Rolling out of bed, he sluffed down the stairs, following the sound into Callie's room. Weird. He turned off the obnoxious clock and looked at the bed. Still made. Even at five thirty, he knew that wasn't right. He scanned the room—no purse. His pulse spiked.

Wide awake, Jack ran out to the kitchen. Callie's phone sat on the counter, right where he'd seen it last night. As far as he could tell, nothing had moved. He nearly ripped the doors off the hinges as he charged outside, scanning the parking lots.

No car.

Jack was back inside and upstairs in seconds. He grabbed his phone and dialed Ryan's number while grabbing clothes off the floor.

Ryan yawned. "Jack, do you know what time it is?"

"Callie didn't come home last night."

"What?"

Jack tripped into his clothes as he ran back down the stairs. "She left me a note last night, said she needed to take a drive. She's not back, and she left her cell phone here."

"You think something happened?"

"She took the time to leave a note. If she wasn't planning on coming home, she would have said something."

"What do you want me to do?"

"Drive by Mae's house. See if Callie's car is there. Then meet me at the Burger King by the peninsula." He scribbled several notes to his sister and taped them up around the house before running outside and climbing into his truck. "Call me if you find her."

Jack jumped out of his truck the second he saw Ryan's Jeep. It was already after six, and Jack's patience was running low. He wanted to be out there looking, but he knew he needed help. Ryan, the idiot, may have bailed on his plan to ask Callie out, but he couldn't possibly be over her that quickly. Judging by the way Ryan sped into the parking lot, skidding to a stop, Jack was right.

"She's not at Mae's," Ryan said, as he ran toward Jack.

"I called Kyle. He didn't pick up."

Ryan's jaw clenched. "You think she might have stayed out all night with him?"

"No, but she mentioned something about seeing him yesterday. I thought he might know where she went."

Ryan nodded, but his face never relaxed. "Now what?"

"We go look for her. Where did she go the last time?"

"She said she went up to Northport. Think she'd go back?"

"I have no idea, but if she went up the Leelanau peninsula once, she might go there again. I'll head up the east side, you take the west." Jack opened his truck door. "And don't forget to check the parks and trails. You know how she likes to drive those."

"What if she heads home while we're out looking for her?"

"I left her cell at the lighthouse. If she beats us there, there's a note to call me." One taped to the door, one on the refrigerator, the TV, and the bedroom and bathroom doors. She was bound to see one of them. Ryan headed back toward his Jeep, his shoulders tense and jaw still clenched. The idiot. Who got up before dawn to search for a woman he wouldn't even ask out? "Ryan."

His friend turned back.

"She's either worth the hassle or she's not."

Far too many uncomfortable minutes passed as the two men stood there staring at each other over the hood of Jack's truck. Maybe he should've kept his mouth shut. The last thing he needed was more friend trouble on top of sister drama.

But then Ryan nodded. "Point taken."

Callie pulled the blanket tighter around her shoulders as she trudged over the dew-covered ground. Once again, she thanked God that it hadn't gotten very cold, but the dampness chilled her. She bumped another sapling, dumping more dew on her head. Sand clung to her body, getting into every crease and wrinkle.

She had to get home. Jack would be furious. She hadn't planned on disappearing again. He'd definitely ask her to leave now. She couldn't mess up any bigger than—

A ray of sunlight cut through the trees, blinding Callie and halting her footsteps as well as her pity party.

Right. No more whining. Focus on God.

She stepped out of the warm sunshine and back into the cool shade. Her car should be just over the next hill.

Her sandals slipped on the wet leaves, but she pushed herself up. Any second now. Over the crest and onto the road, Callie saw the clearing ahead and ran.

"No, no, no!" Her shoes flung up dirt as she raced toward her parking spot. She saw tire tracks, but where was the car? Maybe it was the wrong clearing. She spun around, looking for an alternative. That's when she saw the NO TRESPASSING sign tacked to the tree. Below it, a hand-written note.

This is private property—NO trespassing, NO overnight parking! Your car has been towed by W.E. Towers.

Seriously? Callie looked down the road. Not another car in sight. Of course not. That's why she liked this road. No one to bother her.

Pity rose up in her chest, but she quickly squelched the urge. "Fine, I'll walk." Stuffing the note in her pocket, she headed toward the main road. "It's a great day for a walk."

Another clap of thunder sounded in the distance.

Ryan wanted to hit the gas, but the line of cars ahead of him crawled across the pavement. He'd been able to keep the anxiety away until the first raindrops fell, but that was over an hour ago, before he'd caked his Jeep in layers of mud from miles of seasonal roads. He cranked up the wipers. A car zipped by, splashing more water onto the windshield.

His phone rang. Ryan's gut clenched as he grabbed it.

"Did you find her?"

"No. The storm is slowing me down."

"Same here."

"I'm about halfway back down the peninsula. I didn't pass any wrecks on the way up." Taillights glared ahead of Ryan. He hit the brakes. "Looks like I better get off the phone, so I don't cause one."

"Call me later."

Ryan kept his eyes on the cars ahead of him. One at a time they veered to the left. Occasionally traffic stopped, then picked up again. At this pace it would take him hours to get back down the peninsula. A lot could happen to Callie in that time, God protect her.

He'd already wondered what it would be like to find her. Ryan considered scolding her, hugging her, trying to joke with her. The gentleman in him told him to take her back to Jack and Kyle, but that thought made his head ache. Kyle wasn't the one searching for Callie. Ryan wouldn't want him here anyway.

Jack was right. Time to let the chips fall. Find Callie and tell her—the car ahead of him pulled over—if he ever found her.

The car pulled over far enough that Ryan could finally see what was happening. Someone was walking in the rain, wrapped in a blanket. A red blanket. An Alma Schools blanket. Apparently, a car had stopped to help.

Adrenaline shot through Ryan's veins. He swerved right, rumbling onto the shoulder behind the sedan. The drenched pedestrian nodded. She reached for the back-door handle. Ryan jumped out of the Jeep.

"Callie!"

Thunder rumbled. Rain drummed against the concrete. She opened the door.

"Callie!" Water soaked his clothes as he ran toward her. "Cal!" She turned around. He ran faster. The driver got out of his car, and Ryan waved. "It's okay, I've got her!"

Callie walked toward him, smiling. Beautiful. "What are you doing here?" She stepped up to him, laughing. "How did you find me?"

Instead of answering, he dragged her to the back of the Jeep and opened the tailgate to provide some cover. They faced each other, water dripping around them, seeping into his clothes. He tried to wipe the moisture from her cheek, but it didn't help. It didn't matter. She just kept smiling at him.

She was safe, happy. Every word Ryan had rehearsed vaporized. Words didn't matter. Only Callie mattered. He pulled her into his arms and kissed her.

Callie hesitated, then wrapped her arms around him, sliding up his arms, over his shoulders as he kissed her again and again and again. He needed to stop. He needed to tell her how he felt, that she needed to forget her plan, forget about Kyle.

Ryan told her everything with another kiss. Soft willing lips kissed him back. Her arms held him close. He squeezed her closer, picking her up as she clung to him. She leaned back, but his lips followed hers, needing to tell her everything.

A horn honked, and Ryan put Callie back on solid ground and pulled back, just enough to look at her. Eyes closed, her lips parted. He didn't resist the urge to taste her again. When she pulled away, her eyes fluttered open. Ryan didn't know what to say, so he took her wet blanket, tossed it in the Jeep, and grabbed his own emergency blanket for her.

Callie reached for the blanket. He wanted her reaching for him, so he held it, smiling. She raised her eyebrows as he wrapped the plaid cloth around her shoulders, pulling her close, wrapping his arms around her back.

She leaned into him, resting her head against his chest. "You kissed me."

"You kissed me back." He wanted to see if she would again.

"Why did you kiss me?"

His heart swelled. "I couldn't help myself."

Callie leaned back and looked at him. Her forehead creased, brows together.

"I know this isn't your plan, and you probably need some time to think about it—"

She bounced up and pressed her lips to his.

Every synapse in Ryan's brain misfired. His hands found her face, cradling her cool cheeks as their warm breath mingled. Her lips sought his, drawing him into her.

Nothing mattered except the woman kissing him. He buried his hands in her hair, needing her closer, wanting her to know what he couldn't say, deepening the kiss.

Callie was in his arms, kissing him because she wanted to.

They finally came up for air, but Ryan didn't let go. He pulled Callie right back against him, the blanket around her already soaked through. He had to say something, had to tell her what he felt. She'd want an explanation, something to plan around. Had he planned something to say? He tried to think back to the drive, but her breath tickled his neck. Say something!

She kissed his jaw.

Anything. "I love you."

Callie jumped out of his arms like she'd been struck by lightning. Eyes like saucers stared back at him. Something like terror flashed across her face. "You what?"

"I didn't mean to tell you like this, but it's true."

She nodded but didn't move. "That would explain the kissing."

Ryan stepped toward her, testing the water. "Why else would I kiss you?"

She shrugged. "You were happy to see me, got caught up in the moment."

"Is that why you kissed me?" Another step closer. "You're just happy to see me?"

Callie shook her head.

"Then why?"

Another shrug.

Not good enough. Ryan closed the gap, pulling her back into his arms. Callie gasped but he held tight. "Talk to me, Cal." He leaned down to look her square in the eyes and saw them—tears. His throat closed around his breath. "What's wrong?"

"Nothing. Nothing's wrong." The little liar sobbed.

"Except you're crying."

"I know." Her face scrunched up as her shoulders started shaking. Ryan tried to wipe away the tears, but that seemed to make her cry even harder. What had he done?

His phone rang, blessed relief. Holding Callie with one hand, Ryan answered with the other.

"Any luck?" Jack's voice barked.

"I found her. She's safe."

"Thank God. Oh, thank God." Ryan heard the tension melt out of Jack's voice. "Do you need me? Should I meet you someplace?"

"We're fine."

Callie hiccupped.

"And you were right. She's worth it. You're on your own for dinner tonight."

"I don't want to know anything. Call me later."

As Ryan hung up, Callie pulled away, furiously wiping at her puffy eyes. "Are you asking me out?"

Finally. He smiled. "Yes."

"So, you kissed me, told me you love me, and now you want to go out? Aren't you working backward?"

"Yes, but I'm not letting you off the hook. Why did you kiss me back?" She blinked. Tears pooled in her eyes again. Regret? Ryan's chest tightened. He'd been so focused on talking to Callie that he hadn't fully considered the consequences. His head spun as he figured it out. "You were just reacting, right?" He stepped back. "Just happy to see me."

"No!" She pulled the blanket closer. "No. It's just ... I just ..."

He should have known better. Callie had a plan for a reason, and her plan didn't include him. He had to get her home, drop her off with Jack, then go. He'd played his cards, and he lost. "It's okay. That was presumptuous of me, I'm sorry. Let's go."

"No!"

Ryan sighed. He couldn't stand this much longer. "Cal—"

"I love you too."

CHAPTER 36

Callie's heart tried to bust through her ribs. She'd said it, but he'd said it too. He loved her. After all of these years, Ryan loved *her*. Ryan stared at her, unmoving, while tears of joy spilled down her face. She tried to explain, but love overwhelmed her, choking off the words as she tried to speak.

"I..." Sniff. "You..." Sob. "I, I..." Ryan's face contorted. Pull it together! "I do. I really, really do. I love you."

His arms surrounded her, pulling her into his love. "Then why the tears?" His lips brushed against her ear.

Shivers. "Because nothing worked out. It didn't. Everything's gone wrong since I got here, but ..." Overwhelming peace enveloped her, and Callie sighed. "God's plan worked out in spite of me."

"And that makes you sad?"

"No." Callie tightened her hold on him, burrowing into Ryan's strength and soggy warmth. "I just can't believe it."

Ryan nuzzled her ear. "So, these are happy tears?"

"Oh, yes. My entire plan failed, but I'm so happy."

"You don't mind that Kyle's not here?" Ryan whispered, brushing a kiss below her ear.

Warm tingles shot down her spine. "Who?"

"Good answer." His lips tickled her jaw. "Am I just a good substitute?"

Callie tilted her head to give him access to her cheek. His lips followed. Her knees wobbled. If only Ryan knew. "You're not a substitute. You're the standard."

"The standard?" He pulled back, taking his warmth with him.

She nodded. "I think I've loved you forever."

Ryan blinked.

"It was a silly schoolgirl crush, but then you grew up into this amazing man, and I've compared every guy I've ever known to you. I just never imagined ... I mean, you're Jack's best friend. You've seen my Barbie pajamas.

"And then I lost my job, and Kyle's dating someone else, my car got towed so I got stuck in a thunderstorm, and now the man I've judged every other man by suddenly loves me. It's just—" Emotion clogged her throat. "I can't believe how God took this disaster and"—hiccup—"and after this disaster, He gave me the deepest desire of my heart, even though I never had the guts to ask for it."

More tears mingled with the rain on her cheeks, but Callie never took her eyes off Ryan. He beamed. At least it looked like beaming, but it was hard to see anything through the tears.

"I'm the deepest desire of your heart?"

"Yes."

His lips took hers, claiming them. The flood stopped, and Callie kissed him back, clinging to her dream. Melting beneath his soft, treasured kisses.

HONK!

They jumped, but neither of them stepped away. She loved him, and he loved her. Callie couldn't control the joy that blossomed on her face. "You really love me?

Strong hands framed her face. "I really do. I'm sorry I didn't tell you sooner."

"I'm not."

"But you could have made a different plan."

"Yes, but then I wouldn't have ended up stranded on a beach with no one to talk to except God."

Ryan cocked an eyebrow. "So, even when your plan fails you still won't admit you might have been wrong?" He swooped in for another kiss. "I love your optimism."

"It's not optimism, it's the truth. I wouldn't say that my plan necessarily failed."

"You just admitted that it did."

"Not exactly." She pushed up on her toes, looking Ryan straight in the eyes. "It didn't work out the way I thought it would, but I came up here to make a change, to commit myself to a man I could love." Leaning forward, she teased his lips with hers. "I just didn't realize it would be you."

Ryan closed the distance for another kiss. "You can make lousy plans anytime, as long as you end up with me."

Callie started to protest, but Ryan smothered her words again. Nothing had ever felt so wonderful, so right. As he held her, cherished her, Callie's heart swelled with love for him, but also for the God who let her fail in her plan to help her recognize his.

Ryan was right. Callie didn't care if another plan ever worked out as long as they all ended like this.

EPILOGUE

Callie leaned against the fence and watched a bride glide down the park steps, her hand on a temporary handrail Jack had installed at the lighthouse's public beach. A few dozen guests shifted on white plastic folding chairs. The bay breeze cooled the intense August heat but couldn't help with the humidity. The bride didn't seem to notice the weather. She glowed, smiling at her groom as her sundress danced around her ankles.

"What's so exciting?"

Ryan's voice warmed Callie's cheeks while excited chills ran down her spine. She peeked over her shoulder to watch him walk across the yard. Casual. Handsome.

Hers.

He walked up beside her, slipping an arm around her waist. "I missed you this week." A kiss landed on her cheek.

"I missed you too. You were busy."

"But now the conference is over, so I can focus on more enjoyable things." Another kiss. Tingles. "Who are we spying on?"

"We're not spying. If you decide to get married on a public beach, you better be prepared for some uninvited guests. Besides, I wanted to see how this turned out. I've been to a lot of weddings this summer."

"After playing at Rachel's sister's wedding, I realized I know a ton of people in the industry. This bride called Jack in panic about the chairs, and I knew some people. Jack was so happy to let me handle the call that he's letting me help with two more weddings here this month."

"Does that pay well?"

Callie laughed. "They tipped him fifty bucks. He gave it to me."

"Not bad. If you could plan ten weddings a week, it'd be a good part-time job. Speaking of which," Ryan turned toward her, guiding her into his arms. "What did you find out about your job?"

Sadness settled in Callie's chest. "Jan's taking it." A flicker of panic tickled her conscience, but she reminded herself of God's provisions. "I've haven't had any luck finding another job in Michigan, so I'm going to stay with Jack, at least through Christmas."

Ryan's face split into the biggest smile she'd ever seen. "That's awful."

"Yeah, I thought you might feel that way." Despite the uncertainty of being unemployed, her knees melted at the look in Ryan's eyes.

"What's the plan now?"

Peace flowed through Callie's veins. "I don't know. I picked up another piano gig because of Rachel's wedding, and I've gotten a couple of calls about lessons. I can give lessons and substitute teach until I know the next step."

"I love hearing you talk like that." As if to prove it, Ryan leaned down and kissed her. Her heart jumped just like it had the first time.

When he pulled away, Callie followed, trapping his lips again. In his arms with his lips covering hers, the heat and the humidity—even the tourists—didn't bother her. Maybe it was the wedding behind them. Maybe it was the thought of four more months in Traverse City. Maybe it was just Ryan, but Callie leaned closer, happy to absorb all of the love and warmth he offered.

Laughter.

She leaned back and looked at the wedding. The minister continued to talk as the guests and wedding party chuckled. Love and laughter. Everything Callie wanted. Ryan tickled her side. Everything she already had. She grabbed his hand. "Let's get you out of this sun. I'm roasting. You must be dying in those clothes."

"Anything for you." His fingers laced with hers as he pulled her under the tree beside the hammock. He didn't release her, and she didn't complain. "I need to talk to you about something."

"Shoot."

"Not now. How about having dinner with me tonight?"

Callie stepped back and looked at him. Those clear blue eyes twinkled. She narrowed her gaze. "What's going on?"

"Have dinner with me and I'll tell you."

His left hand moved up her arm, but Callie shook free of his distracting touch. "If I've learned anything this summer, it's to trust God, but a close second is to not put off those things that need to be said." She crossed her arms over her chest. "We can talk about it now."

Ryan cocked his head. His eyebrows arched. "You really want to do this?"

"Yes." She nodded for emphasis. "With my luck, I'll slip on a banana peel and end up in the emergency room instead of at the restaurant. Out with it."

"Okay." He stuffed his hands in his pockets. "I have an idea about where you can go next year."

"To teach?" Not exactly what she'd been expecting, but potentially helpful.

"No, not to teach. I have an idea about where you could live."

Callie dropped her arms. "That's it?" Apparently, some things *could* wait to be said. She tried not to look too disappointed, but the spark left Ryan's eyes. She wasn't hiding her feelings very well.

Ryan scrubbed a hand across his face. "This isn't exactly how I'd planned this."

"Sometimes planning doesn't always work out, you know. Things happen, and—"

"Hi, Callie!"

Stacey's voice cheered up the atmosphere. Callie peeked around the tree, waving at Stacey as she bounced across the lawn. Jack trudged along beside her. Interesting.

Stacey rushed up to them. "Are we interrupting?"

Callie shook her head. "Not really."

"Yes." Ryan gave her a squeeze.

She elbowed him in the ribs. "Don't be rude. Jack, weren't you going to town today?"

"I went."

"Then he called me." Stacey beamed.

Ridiculous. Stacey was more excited about a call from Jack than Callie would be about a winning lottery ticket. When Stacey looked up at Jack, he smiled at her. Not just a friendly smile. Jack looked … smitten. *Eew.*

"Are you two …" Callie waved a finger between them.

"Going out to dinner? Yes." Stacey practically floated off the lawn.

Double eew. Callie summoned enough excitement to push up a smile. She could be happy for Jack, but poor Stacey. She had to eat dinner with him. "You know, Ryan and I were just planning our own date. Maybe we could double?"

"No." Jack and Ryan answered together.

"What is wrong with you?" Callie looked up at the strange, rude man beside her. "It's just dinner."

"Yes, but we have plans."

"We can change them. Come on." She turned on the charm, giving him her sweetest smile. "You've finally won me over to your side. Let's change plans."

Ryan sighed. "We need to have that talk."

"You two talk, I need to change." Jack grabbed Stacey's hand and pulled her toward the house.

So weird.

Ryan leaned into her sightline. "Callie?"

She pushed him out of the way, her eyes fixed on the happy couple. "It's like seeing something out of *Ripley's Believe It or Not*." No wonder Jack never wanted to hear about her issues with men. Seeing your sibling with a significant other did strange things to your insides. Callie couldn't quite figure out the simultaneous urges to protect and vomit.

"Calista." Ryan whispered in her ear. "Focus."

Tingly. "Okay." She looked back into his handsome face.

"How long do you need to get ready for dinner?"

"I just need to change."

"Great." Ryan dropped a kiss on her cheek.

"I can change right after we have that talk."

His hands dropped to his sides.

"I'm serious." Callie stepped back. "No more waiting for the perfect moment. What is it?"

Hands on his hips, Ryan shook his head, but smiled. "Fine. We'll do it your new way and forget the plan. Will you marry me?"

"What?" She must have heatstroke. She was hallucinating, hearing things.

Ryan stepped toward her, smiling. He grabbed her left hand, raised it to his lips. Electricity shot through her arm. He opened a small white box. Where had *that* come from?

"Calista Marie Stevens, I love you, and I very much want to spend the rest of my life with you."

A perfect, round solitaire in the hands of her perfect, wonderful man. The diamond sparkled, even in the shade. She should say something. "You want to marry me?"

"Yes, I do."

Not the plan. She picked up the box, inspecting the ring from every angle. So not the plan.

"Cal?"

"It's beautiful."

"Do you want to keep it?"

Forever. Especially because Ryan came with the ring.

People cheered. They really cheered. No, wait. Callie looked over her shoulder as the groom kissed the bride. The audience applauded, encouraging the groom, who dipped his new wife. How appropriate.

Callie couldn't stop her smile. When she looked at Ryan, his ocean-blue eyes captured hers. Pushing up on her tiptoes, she leaned into him, pressing her lips to his. "I never thought anything like this could happen without a plan," she whispered against his lips. "I'm so glad I was wrong."

"I love you."

Heat and shivers and butterflies, all while Callie pushed back the tears. "I love you too."

"So you'll marry me?"

"Yes, yes, y—"

Ryan cut off her words, kissing her again and again.

No job, no home, but perfect. Callie smiled against Ryan's mouth.

He leaned back just far enough to look into her eyes. "You're happy?"

"Absolutely. And now I get to plan *my* wedding."

—The Beginning—

ABOUT THE AUTHOR

Karin Beery grew up along the Lake Michigan shoreline, the product of a rural community. She earned a Bachelor of Arts degree in English from Hillsdale College before getting a "real" job in the hospitality industry.

Though she'd been writing stories since high school, not until her husband's cancer diagnosis did she turn her hobby into something more. Eleven years, more than five hundred fifty articles, and four manuscripts later, she received her first book publishing contract.

Today, Karin is a fulltime writer and editor. She is active with the Christian Editor Network, serving as the Christian Editor Connection Coordinator, and teaching several classes through the PEN Institute. She also teaches writing and editing classes at local and national conferences. She works from Northern Michigan where she lives with her two cats, two dogs, and amazing husband—who is cancer-free! She loves to talk about books and writing, so please don't hesitate to say hi!

Made in the USA
Columbia, SC
09 September 2019